Novels by Stephen Blackmoore
available from DAW Books:

CITY OF THE LOST
DEAD THINGS
BROKEN SOULS
HUNGRY GHOSTS

HUNGRY GHOSTS

STEPHEN BLACKMOORE

DAW BOOKS, INC.
DONALD A. WOLLHEIM, FOUNDER
375 Hudson Street, New York, NY 10014

ELIZABETH R. WOLLHEIM
SHEILA E. GILBERT
PUBLISHERS
www.dawbooks.com

First Printing, February 2017
1 2 3 4 5 6 7 8 9

ACKNOWLEDGMENTS

Sometimes books are easier to write than thank you notes. Who do I thank? Everybody? Do I have that many pages to name them all? Will I disappoint someone because I missed them? Will they even care? Will they even notice?

The point is that a lot of people helped me with *Hungry Ghosts* and though I would like to thank them all, I don't have nearly enough space here. They answered questions, vetted details, helped me with my deplorable Spanish. But they also helped me get through a rough year that saw this book torn down and rewritten from the ground up.

Thank you to my readers and their infinite patience. I hope this book is worth the wait.

My wife, Kari, for putting up with me while I hammered out draft after draft, tore everything down and started over. Thank you for helping me maintain something resembling sanity. I love you.

Angus and Emma, the two best dogs a guy could hope to have. Even if they do think every mailman and pizza delivery guy is a murderer.

Friends both authorly and not, whose support helped

immeasurably. Chuck Wendig, Richard Kadrey, K.C. Alexander, Kevin Hearne, Jaye Wells, Jaclyn Taylor, Delilah Dawson, Lilith Saintcrow, Kat Richardson, Brian McClellan, Kristin Sullivan, and so, so many more.

My agent, Al Guthrie, the Scottish Ninja, whose kindness and stoic demeanor hides a truly dark soul. Respect.

My editor Betsy Wollheim, Josh Starr, and the outstanding staff at DAW. Thanks for helping make this the best book it could be.

R. Andrew Chesnut, PhD, Santa Muerte scholar and all around stand-up guy. His book *Devoted to Death* is the best scholarly examination of Santa Muerte and her followers out there, and I highly recommend it. It takes an honest and unflinching view of the movement, both good and bad. Anything I got wrong about Santa Muerte or her followers, and there are oh so many things, are all me.

And finally, a shout-out to the Bony Lady, herself. La Flaca, la Dama Poderosa, Señora de las Sombras. I have taken liberties, and I hope she doesn't mind too much.

Chapter 1

Sharpie magic is the best magic.

I stand on the side of the road, cool fall breeze blowing through the scrub brush. Half a dozen trucks pull out of a gated, hillside compound in the moonlight, kicking up dust and gravel. The men in the truck beds wear ballistic vests, skull-printed face masks, wicked looking guns clutched tight in their hands.

I wave as they go by, but they have no idea I'm here. I've got a "Hi My Name Is" sticker on my chest with the words "NO ESTOY AQUÍ" written in Sharpie and pumped with enough magic to keep me hidden from them. I didn't need to write it in Spanish, the magic doesn't work that way, but I've been speaking almost nothing but for the last two months, and it helps me focus.

They're on their way down to a warehouse on the outskirts of Tepehuanes, Mexico, just down the road. It holds several thousand kilos of heroin in varying degrees of processing. It's currently on fire.

I set the fire.

I don't care about the heroin or the Sinaloa Cartel men entrusted with operating and guarding it. I just need them out of the compound. With them gone there should be about half a dozen men left inside. Plus the one I came to talk to.

The estate of Manuel Bustillo is fairly modest by narco standards. He's not terribly important in the Sinaloa Cartel. Middleman stuff. Processes heroin, cocaine, meth. I hear he used to handle a lot of pot coming up from the south, but with medical marijuana in the U.S. getting so popular and so much weed being grown inside the states, the cartels have had a hard time moving product. Things are tough all over.

I'm not here because Bustillo is a Sinaloa man, or because he's a murderer, thug and all around bad guy. I've hung out with worse people. Lately, I've been wondering if I might be worse people.

I don't much care about Bustillo at all, actually. I'm here because he's a stepping stone. A link in a chain. I'm looking for someone, and he's going to help me find her.

I got his name from a guy in Hermosillo a couple weeks back. And I got that guy's name from somebody in Ensenada, whose name I got in Tijuana. I found out about the Tijuana guy from somebody in San Diego, who I tracked down from a guy whose arms I broke in an alley behind a strip bar in Los Angeles.

It's been a busy few months.

Bustillo's house sits on ten acres of hilltop Durango real estate looking down on rocks and scrub brush. It's surrounded by an electrified fence and a ten-foot-high, brick wall. Spanish Colonial. Terra cotta tile, fake adobe.

I sling my messenger bag over my shoulder, pick up my Benelli M4 twelve-gauge, and stroll unseen through the gate before the two men watching it shut it up tighter than a nun's butthole.

The men in the courtyard have no idea I'm here, but once the gunfire starts—and boy howdy is there gonna be gunfire—the Sharpie magic's going to be pretty useless. Them not seeing me depends on them believing they can't see me. It's hard to ignore a guy firing at you with a shotgun at the best of times.

I find a convenient spot out of the way and take a seat. The men walk the courtyard nervously fingering the triggers on their guns. A while later I check my pocket watch, an antique, railroad grade, 1911 Sangamo Special. Aside from being a nasty piece of magic that can twist time into ugly knots if you use it right, it's a really good watch.

It's been half an hour. That should give Bustillo's men enough time to get down to the warehouse and out of my hair. I slide the watch into my coat pocket and pick up the Benelli.

"If it helps," I say, though I know the spell keeps them from hearing me, "this isn't personal." I unload a couple of shells into the backs of their knees and they drop, screaming. If they get to a hospital soon they might not die. But if they do, well, them's the breaks.

The front door to the main house is this massive oak monstrosity that looks like it was pulled from a cathedral. Religious carvings all over it. Lots of Virgin of Guadalupe stuff. Considering who I'm looking to find from Bustillo the irony is almost too much to bear.

I dig a couple more shells out of the messenger bag slung across my shoulder and load them into the shotgun. For backup I've got a variety of magical charms and a World War II era Browning Hi-Power, an ugly Nazi pistol with decades of evil energy baked into its frame. I can tap into that with my own magic and really fuck a guy up.

I've been watching Bustillo's place for the last couple of weeks trying to figure out how to get close to him. He's not the sort of person you just make an appointment with. Or someone who's likely to tell you what you want to know.

I've kept a low profile, stayed hidden. It wasn't until I saw a shipment to the warehouse come in on a couple of semis that I got the idea to set the place on fire.

I won't have a lot of time before they get back, but it should be enough. At some point they're just going to write the whole place off as a loss. Tepehuanes doesn't exactly have a robust firefighting force. The warehouse is the most modern building in the whole town.

I give it less than an hour before they come gunning for me. They should already be getting frantic phone calls to come back. I need to get in, get my answers from Bustillo, and then get the hell out before thirty guys with AKs come busting in on the party.

I put the barrel of the Benelli against the door lock and pull the trigger, blowing a hole the size of a cantaloupe out of the wood. Sure, I could have just tried the handle, but where's the fun in that? I wouldn't get the satisfying shriek as buckshot tears into the poor bastard on the other side of the door. I step out of the way and let the inevitable rain of bullets punch through the wood in return.

The guy I shot through the door stares at me as I kick it open, the Sharpie spell too weak to hide me from him, anymore. The door was thick enough to stop a lot of the shot, but more than enough went through to make this a really bad day for him.

He points his gun at me in shaking hands. A crappy, little TEC-9—I didn't think they made those anymore—and pulls the trigger on an empty chamber. I hit him in the head with the butt of the shotgun and he goes down like a drunk prom date.

There are a lot of ghosts here at the compound. Echoes in the courtyard, mindless recordings of people's last moments. Every one of them an execution. Bullet to the head kind of stuff. All in nearly the same spot. They blend into each other like fractals, jerking this way and that as phantom bullets enter their heads over and over again. A few Haunts, too. Again, murders. Ghosts trapped in the house until their essence drains away to whatever afterlife they're destined for.

And then there are the Wanderers, self-aware spirits borne of trauma and tragedy, but not locked to any particular location, they travel from place to place doing, well, whatever they do. Watching mostly, being hungry and looking for some shreds of life to feed on.

That's the thing about ghosts. There's not much going on in the land of the dead. Most can't even see the living, just like most of the living can't see them.

But they can sure as hell see me. I show up to them like a neon sign that says GOOD EATS. They want life. Any life. Lucky for all of us they're on that side of the veil. So when I attract their attention they follow me around like hungry wolves after caribou.

Yay for necromancy, huh?

Counting the murdered in Mexico's drug war is tough. Anywhere from fifty-thousand to over a hundred in the last five years alone. Not all of them leave ghosts. Not all of those ghosts become Wanderers.

But holy fuck are there a lot of them. I picked up a handful in El Zona Norte, Tijuana's red light district. Murdered prostitutes and student protesters, low level cartel bagmen caught in a cross-fire, police officers, tourists, locals in the wrong place at the wrong time. In each city I've picked up more. Some of them I even killed myself. They've been trying to keep up as best they can. They're not fast and I have a car, but they're tenacious little bastards.

There are at least forty standing behind me, following me around as I shoot the place up. I've been seeing ghosts my entire life, so an audience of the dead is nothing new. But standing room only can get a little nerve wracking. I could push them away, but there are so many dead around more would just take their place.

The foyer is terra cotta red tile covered in rugs, wrought iron chandeliers. Real old school Spanish style. I hear two sets of running feet coming down the hallway. At this point, the Sharpie magic's useless. I've made too much noise and the magic can only do so much. I take up a position on the edge of the doorway and wait.

Two men with AK-47s run into the foyer, see the guy on the floor. One of them's stupid and runs for him, the other one's smart and turns to check the rest of the room. I put buckshot in his chest before he can fill me full of .30 caliber rounds and another into the back of his buddy's knee. I kick the guns away from the one who's still alive, even though I'm pretty sure he won't be conscious long.

If I hadn't made so much noise the sticker on my chest would have let me come in here and walk right on by everybody. Could have caught Bustillo in his bathroom or something. Or I could have used one of the perks of my particular magical knack and popped over to the ghost's side, walked past Bustillo's guards and popped back. It's not fun, it's not safe, but sometimes it's damn convenient.

Aside from the fact that the ghost's side of the world

will leech out my life if I stay too long, they'll try to eat me. With all of the dead here and the ones that have been following me it would be like jumping into a shark tank wearing a suit made out of meat.

But the truth is that I wanted to do this loud and I wanted to do it messy. Word's been spreading the last couple of months of "The Gringo With No Eyes". Some scary motherfucker with eyeballs black as midnight asking questions, causing problems when he doesn't like the answers. I get to be the boogeyman. My newfound reputation has made this trip a lot easier.

Plus I have anger issues.

It's a big house, lots of hallways going off the foyer, a staircase leading to the upper floor. Finding Bustillo could take time I don't have. I dig a charm, a small hematite pyramid carved with runes and hanging from a string, out of my messenger bag. I let it dangle from the string and in a few seconds the charm rises, pointing down the left hallway, then veering sharply to the right. I pocket the charm, load a couple more shells into the Benelli and head down the hall.

Twenty feet and a right hand turn leads me to a pair of open double doors. Like the front door, these are heavy oak. Bustillo, a slight man with a balding head and a mustache you could sweep streets with, sits behind a desk in the room, a fat, little submachine gun on the desk in easy reach. Next to that is a bottle of tequila and two shot glasses. Both of his hands are in plain view.

Either Bustillo is very stupid or this is a trap. I don't think he's stupid.

"Eric Carter," he says. "Come in, come in. Have a seat." His Spanish is flawless, cultured, unlike my shoddy American accent. He pours a measure of tequila into each shot glass. He gestures at the chair opposite him. "I won't shoot if you won't."

"Fair enough," I say and step slowly into the room. I've been keeping a low profile in Tepehuanes while I've been scoping out Bustillo's estate, using Sharpie magic to hide from the locals or make them think I'm something I'm not. I've never used my name. The fact that he knows it is troubling.

"Inspired move," he says. "Burning my warehouse. I was wondering how you were going to get my men to leave the estate. You put in so much effort, it would be rude of me not to play along."

I'm not sensing any active spells, and I'm not seeing anything on the walls, floor or ceiling that might be a magical trap. Of course he could have a claymore sitting under the chair to shoot up, but that seems a bit drastic, even when dealing with me.

I sit, placing the Benelli onto the desk, my hand on the pistol grip, finger hovering over the trigger.

"You were expecting me," I say.

"I was. Been waiting for weeks. Had I known you would show such caution I would have made myself a more tempting target."

"This isn't how this usually goes," I say. "There's a lot more screaming involved. Broken fingers, that kinda thing."

"Oh, I heard plenty of screaming. The men you shot were stealing from me, so you have my thanks. We have all the time we need. The others won't be back for a while. They think the heroin is important."

"And you don't?"

"Only as a tool. Like money is a tool. Or a gun is a tool. Or magic is a tool."

"You're a mage."

"A minor talent at best. Not someone with nearly your standing. Tell me, why do they call you the Gringo With No Eyes? I have heard rumors, but I don't know if they're true. Is it the sunglasses?"

"No," I say and take them off. The whites and iris of my eyes are gone, replaced with pitch black orbs. I tend to wear sunglasses a lot so as not to scare the straights. It's an unfortunate side effect of a bad decision I made a while back. Kind of like chlamydia.

He cocks an eyebrow, curiosity on his face. "I see."

"So why'd you send your men away, Mister Minor Talent? You're either awfully certain that I won't just kneecap you and make you tell me what I want to know, or you're monumentally stupid."

"Hopefully the former. I know where the one you're looking for is. And I'm happy to tell you."

Everyone else I've talked to has had a little more in-formation—talk to this guy, that guy knows something, maybe see this other guy—but they've all just been links in a chain. Breadcrumbs leading me further and further down the trail.

Bustillo is just one more of them. He might think he's important, they all think they're important, and him be-ing a mage is just going to reinforce that. But he's only as useful as what he knows and what he can give me.

I think he's going to be surprised when he figures that out.

"You're a mage. You know what I'm here for. You are just full of surprises. And here I thought I was going to have to torture you, or . . ."

I pull a small, obsidian knife from my inner coat pocket. The handle is simple wood and leather, the blade only a few inches long. It's wicked sharp and I've been through three custom sheaths already. I place it on the table. Manuel stares at it, looking nervous.

"Perhaps it is time for a drink," he says and lifts his shot glass, his hand shaking a little.

"Perhaps it is." I'm not worried about poison, my body is crawling with tattoos infused with spells for protection. I have at least three against poison. I think. Maybe four? I've lost track over the years.

I take my hand off the shotgun, but hold on to the knife. It's the more dangerous of the two. We down our shots. If it's poisoned it's worth it. It's damn good tequila.

"I see you've heard of the knife," I say. "Mictlantecuhtli's blade. The Aztec king of the dead made this for Xipe-Totec, the Flayed God, to carve the skins of his enemies and absorb them into himself. A few quick cuts, toss the skin over the shoulders and everything a person is, everything they know, goes to the one who uses it. You're not gonna make me use it, are you, Manuel?"

"No," he says, eyes firmly on the blade.

"I'm glad to hear that. I don't know what nest of vipers are bouncing around inside your head, but believe me I don't want you in mine. Now you seem awfully eager to be having this conversation. Why is that?"

"Señora de las Sombras told me to," he says. Lady of the Shadows. Also known as La Flaca, Señora Negra, La Madrina.

"I'm not looking for Santa Muerte," I say. Which is true. I know exactly where she is.

A while back I got backed into a corner, and to get out of it I made a deal with an Aztec death goddess. She used to go by the name Mictecacihuatl, Queen of Mictlan, the Aztec land of the dead. In more recent years she's transformed, recreating herself as Santa Muerte, Saint Death.

Her movement, religion, cult, whatever you want to call it, has spread to over two million devotees throughout Mexico and the United States and across the world, getting bigger every day. She's seen as the Narco Saint, a protector of killers and thugs, but she's so much more than that. She's a protector of the innocent, an instrument of vengeance, and, oddly enough, a love sorceress.

And she's my wife.

That was the deal I made. Marry my power to hers. Necromancy and a death goddess. I got the pitch black eyes and a ring covered in calaveras on my hand. She got me. I'm her champion, her consort. Neither of which is a job I'm particularly thrilled with. She's got some other plan in mind for me but I don't know what it is.

I had a friend, Darius, who told me it was a bad idea. I should have listened to him. He's had some experience with her, though I don't know what kind. He had the sort of perspective you're not gonna get from most people.

Darius is special. He's a Djinn. Hundreds of years old if he's a day. He came over to California five hundred years ago with Cabrillo, and his bottle got lost in Los Angeles. Now he uses it as a pocket universe and lets people in from time to time so he doesn't get bored.

Once I took the deal with Santa Muerte, he and I were on the outs. Should have listened to him. Wouldn't be in this mess if I had.

The thing Santa Muerte didn't tell me was that she already had a husband. Mictlantecuhtli, King of Mictlan. Darius told me he was dead. Turns out not quite. Dead gods are more complicated than I thought. It was more like sleeping. Sitting in a tomb in Mictlan, a statue locked in jade.

And by a fucked up piece of cosmic logic—Mictlantecuhtli is the King of Mictlan, but the King of Mictlan is married to Mictecacihuatl and since I'm married to Mictecacihuatl I'm the King of Mictlan—he and I are trading places. I'm getting access to his power. But I'm also slowly becoming jade, the stone replacing my flesh like petrified wood. He's slowly becoming ... whatever it is Aztec death gods count as flesh. I don't really know.

The last time I saw him I was just beginning to change and he was still stuck in his tomb in Mictlan. Now a good forty percent of my body is green stone, flexible, movable, but stone nonetheless.

"Her avatar, then," Bustillo says. "Tabitha Cheung."

"Ah," I say. "Now her, she's the one I'm looking for."

Chapter 2

Because my situation with Santa Muerte and Mictlante-cuhtli wasn't weird enough, I met a girl, Tabitha Cheung. Worked at a friend's bar in Koreatown in Los Angeles. We hooked up a couple of times. She helped me out of a jam.

And then I found out that she'd actually been killed a while back and the only thing keeping her upright was that Santa Muerte had stuck a piece of her soul inside her, turning a mid-twenties Korean waitress from Fullerton into her will made flesh.

When I figured it out and confronted her, Tabitha showed me her true colors. She told me that she's Santa Muerte, but she also told me she's a combination of the two of them, blurring together until she can't tell where one ends and the other begins.

That means it's possible there's some of Tabitha still in there. I have a lot riding on that.

She walked out and I let her. I've wondered since if that was maybe not the best decision I could have made, and boy howdy have I made some bad decisions. Killing her would have just killed Tabitha's body and whatever was left of her inside it. It wouldn't have touched Santa Muerte. And I wouldn't have the opportunity that I have now.

I tried to keep track of her, but she went to ground. It's taken me months to pick up the trail of men and women she's seen or talked to. Santa Muerte herself has trouble talking to people in person. Most can't see her. So she appears to them in their dreams.

But with Tabitha, Santa Muerte gains a physical presence. She can actually see her followers, show them proof of who she represents. Whether operating through an avatar limits her power at all, I have no idea, but I'm not sure how much that matters.

It's not surprising that Santa Muerte knows I'm down here, and if she knows it, then it's a good bet Tabitha knows. I've made a point of making as much noise as I can to get her attention. I want her to know I'm coming for her. I want her to think she's got the upper hand. I want her to get lazy. It might be a stupid move, but it's not likely I could surprise her, anyway, so I'd rather work with what I've got.

But if she's set this guy up with a message for me then it's not just that she knows I'm in Mexico looking for her. She knows that eventually I'd have come here for him to give it to me. I've been herded in this direction from the start.

"You should know she wants very much to see you again," Bustillo says. "She knew you would be coming here not long after her visit."

"How long ago was that?"

"A month ago? Little more?"

"What'd you guys talk about? Best ways to dispose of troublesome Federales? The ins and outs of the heroin trade?"

"Tithes, mostly. Sacrifices to Santa Muerte. Spreading

her word among the faithful. Señora is powerful, and she has many devotees, but she needs more."

This is pretty much what I've heard from everyone else. Santa Muerte's looking to consolidate her power, grow her flock. Every day she gets more followers. Among the narcos, sure. But also, oddly enough, among Mexican and U.S. law enforcement, not to mention the millions of men and women who are caught in that crossfire, or the ones who simply see her as an alternative they can understand.

They follow her for different reasons, but a lot of them do it because they think she'll help when the saints they grew up with and the god they follow won't.

Santa Muerte will not judge you, will not tell you what you are doing is right or wrong. She will help you with vengeance, she will help you with your rocky relationship, she will help you when the chips are down and there's nowhere else to go.

Unless she doesn't. She can be fickle. She is Death, after all.

"All right. So where is her avatar now?" I ask.

"Tepito."

Of course she is. Tepito is a barrio in Mexico City that has one of the highest concentrations of Santa Muerte devotees in the world. There are others, Tultitlán north of the city, Ciudad Juárez just on the other side of El Paso. But Tepito is where her base is. Where the people who need her most live.

Tepito's a slum, a massive, blocks wide, open-air bazaar. You can find food, drugs, electronics, guns, phones, computers, anything you can think of. As long as you're okay with questionably sourced goods and illegal trade, you're golden.

"You know where in Tepito?" I know of the place, heard a lot about it, but I've never been there myself.

He spreads his hands and shrugs. "She didn't say. Can you answer something for me?" Bustillo says.

"Possibly."

"You want to kill her," he says. "Why?"

"Santa Muerte, or her avatar?"

"Both."

"Santa Muerte murdered my sister. Her avatar, well, she's got a piece of her in her head. They're pretty much the same person. You've been a devotee of hers long?"

"Many years. Even before I knew it. There is an honesty to her I find refreshing."

I can't help but laugh. "Honesty. Right."

"I have heard some of what she did to you. But tell me. Did she lie, or did she merely keep the truth from you?"

This is actually a question I've been struggling with. She's never flat out lied to me as far as I can tell. When we first met she offered to tell me who killed my sister, Lucy. I didn't take her up on that offer, the price was too high. So instead she offered me a cryptic clue that wasn't, technically speaking, incorrect. If I'd taken her up on her offer right then and there, would she have told me the truth? I think she might have.

"No, she hasn't lied to me. That's not why I'm going to kill her."

"Of course not. But she is a product of her time. She has not fully grown into this modern world. It is regrettable that your sister died, but Señora only knew one way to get your attention. You cannot expect her to be anything but true to her own nature, even as she tries to change it."

"Yeah, and I can't blame a bear for trying to eat me,

either, but I can put a bullet in its brain so it doesn't."
Something he just said catches my attention. "Wait, what do you mean about trying to change her nature?"

"She hasn't lied, but she has deceived. That's new to her. Foreign. She tries to accommodate this new world, but doesn't know how. Her ways are not—"

"Sane?"

"I was going to say subtle. She may only know death, but she is not the instrument of it. To enlist you in her cause she used the only tools she understood. So, as I said, she has an honesty that I find refreshing. She's simply death. There's nothing more honest than that."

He has a point. Death is the great equalizer. It'll lay you low whether you're the richest motherfucker in the world or the lowliest peasant.

"Well, aren't I lucky."

"She needs you for something," Bustillo says. He pours out more tequila for us. "Do you know what?"

"No. And I don't care." Not anymore. For a while it was driving me crazy. Second guessing her. Trying to figure out her game. But then I realized, it didn't matter. Because whatever it is, I'm not going to let it happen. I'm going to kill her. I'm going to kill her husband. I'm going to kill her avatar. I'm going to kill anyone who gets in my way.

"You don't? It seems you've been given a gift. Why not accept it?"

I've heard this one before. Everybody seems to think it's like a fucking Christmas present.

"I know this game. This is where I say, 'I don't want it,' and you say, 'But the power! The opportunity!' And I say, 'You don't get it,' because you don't. It's not a gift. It's my sister's murder. It's my friend's death. It's me trapped in jade. It's a debt I haven't paid back, yet. And now I think we're done here."

"Yes," he says. "I am very sorry."

He says it less as someone offering condolences and more as someone who is apologizing for something he's done. Or, more likely, something he's about to do. I don't give him the chance.

I grab the shotgun and pull the trigger. It goes off in my hand with a thunderous blast that should vaporize Bustillo's chest, but he's fast. I feel a flare of magic as he lets off a spell he already had primed, and the desk, a thick, oak monstrosity that has to weigh a few hundred pounds, flips up blocking him and forcing my shot to go into the ceiling.

Minor talent, my ass. With as much power as he's got I can see why his ass is so chapped that he's not the one with Santa Muerte.

Buckshot tears through the edge of the desk, and I barely keep from being flattened as it comes crashing down toward me. I kick backward, rolling out of the way and to my feet.

So far Bustillo is the first mage I've run into on this trip. It was really just a matter of time and I'm actually a little surprised it's taken this long. Most of the people whose heads I've busted have been your run-of-the-mill narco thugs. Tough bastards, dangerous, but normal. Normal I can eat for breakfast.

I unload the Benelli at him. Five rounds, but I'm not really expecting anything to connect. He's already on the move and any mage worth the title is going to have defensive spells ready to go at a moment's notice. Bustillo works for Sinaloa, which is about as cutthroat a cartel as they come. They're not known for coming at you in a fair fight. He's going to have something extra special up his sleeve for just such occasions.

Sure enough the buckshot scatters as it gets close, splitting into two streams of pellets and peppering the wall on either side of him with holes. I drop the shotgun, it's useless, anyway, and scoop up the obsidian blade from where it's embedded itself into the floor. As I grab the knife, Bustillo gets hold of his submachine gun and stitches a line of bullets across the room.

I drop behind the desk. Like Bustillo I have defensive spells, too. Apparently, they're not as good as his are. Even with the magic in my tattoos redirecting most of the rounds I get tagged by a bullet in my shoulder. Normally, that would be a problem.

But normal left the building a long time back. The bullet that gets through my protections mushrooms on contact and stops dead. The jade crawling through my body has gone up to my shoulders and down most of both arms. I can't scratch it, can't break it. And it's really good at stopping bullets. A small bright spot in an otherwise fucked situation.

I pull the Browning. I don't think I'm going to get close enough to him for the knife to be very effective. Even the Browning isn't going to do much good. It'll make big holes, but unless I can do something about his magical defenses it's not going to do a whole lot.

"So was I right?" I say. "You think I'm an idiot for rejecting Santa Muerte's 'gift'? I'm thinking you see yourself as a much more worthy recipient of it, yeah?"

For somebody who's just one more stepping stone to getting what I want, Bustillo's turning out to be a big pain in my ass.

Bustillo says nothing, but I can hear footsteps nearby.

I can feel him drawing power from the local pool of magic. It's slow, a trickle. He's hoping I won't notice. That gives me an idea.

Mages get their power from within and without. We have our own reserves, and we can tap into the ambient magic that infuses a place. Different places have more or less power. Some places are better for certain types of spells than others. And each place has a flavor, a scent to its magic given by its people, its history.

New York tastes like hot metal and granite, San Francisco like hammered brass and filigree. Los Angeles is a twisty mess of cultures and flavors that changes from block to block. The magic here in Durango is wild, violent. Hot and sweet. A product of its history.

"Because, you know, I've heard that before. Folks who figure if they can kill me they can take my place as Santa Muerte's favorite. Better yet, if they can get hold of Mictlantecuhtli's blade, they can take my skin, take my place as Santa Muerte's pet. That's why you were really waiting for me, isn't it? Wanted some uninterrupted quality time to take my skin?"

When mages draw power from the pool, they're doing it because their own power isn't sufficient to do what they want. That's a plus and a minus. On the one hand, yay, more power.

On the other hand, we're all drawing from the same, constantly replenishing pool around us. But it doesn't replenish quickly and there's only so much of it at a time. Right now, Bustillo is using a drinking straw to suck on a lake. And as long as the power is there, he can keep pulling it in, building it up. Use it for whatever big spell he thinks will take me down.

"You know, a guy tried to do that to me a while ago,"

I say. "Carve me up like a chicken and wear me like a suit. I stuck a bomb in his eyeball and blew his head up. The hell of it is, that didn't kill him."

"You don't deserve it," he says.

"Damn right I don't deserve it. Nobody fucking deserves it. I'm in the middle of a cosmic threesome I didn't want to have and I'm the one getting fucked."

"So give it to me," he says. "You want to get rid of it. I want to take it."

"Dude, you have no idea what you're asking," I say. "Believe me when I tell you, if I could give it to you, I'd wrap it up in a bow and hand it to you. You think this is going to put you at the right hand of God. It won't. It would just put you under her thumb."

Since becoming tied to Santa Muerte my abilities have amplified. Spells I couldn't do without days of preparation and hours of ritual I can pop off with a thought. I've always been able to draw a lot of power, but now I can pull it in like a firehose.

I've also got access to Mictlantecuhtli's power, so casting is easier, but it comes with one hell of a big string attached. Every time I tap into it more of me turns to jade. Casting spells has become a delicate balance of making sure any energy I'm using is mine and mine alone. I touch his power and another chunk of my body turns green. So far it's mostly hidden under my clothes, but it's spreading.

So I've been really careful about what magic I'm using and how big a spell I'm casting. Casting something powerful just fucks me more. But pulling in power from the local pool? Well, that's just charging up the batteries. Doesn't mean I have to use it on a spell.

And that's what I do. I open the taps and power floods

into me. Not because I need it, not because I particularly want it.

But sucking it all in keeps it away from Bustillo. The pool drains like it's burst a pipe. I can feel him grasping for it, desperately trying to hang onto whatever bits he can grab hold of. But it's mine. I've got it all.

Magical cock-block.

My defensive spells are inked into my skin, not an unusual thing for a lot of mages, but the sheer volume of my tattoos is. I make the illustrated man look like a yoga mom with a tramp stamp. I've stored power into my tats, so if I run out of my own juice, or I can't get anything from the local pool, they're still going to work. Even the jade hasn't affected them. They just look like they're etched into the stone.

They've saved my life a time or two. From the sudden flare up and darkening of magic I'm sensing from Bustillo, it looks like his spells are drawing on his own power and the pool to keep running.

He can't get anything from the pool, so he's going to draw on his own to build the spell. Only he doesn't have enough to do it.

I stand and gesture toward the desk with a spell. Nothing big, nothing showy. More importantly, nothing that takes too much juice. I can feel Mictlantecuhtli's power inside me perk up, but I shove it back down. It's tempting to use it. It *wants* to be used.

But aside from the fact that it'll just fuck me up faster it'd also be like using a flamethrower to take out a mosquito. God power is overkill. And much as I like the idea of Bustillo as a red smear across the floor, it's a bit much even for me.

I make the desk slide across the room and crash into

the wall. Bustillo and I face each other. I've got the knife in one hand, the Browning in the other pointed at his head. He holds his empty submachine gun in his shaking hands.

"You've lost, Manuel. Or do you want to try throwing the gun at me?"

He lets it slip from his fingers. Must be strange for him. I wonder if he's ever felt really afraid in his life. Like he couldn't just magic his way out of a bind.

Magic can give a guy a level of wealth and privilege that even a normal can't touch. Sure, some guy can build a massive financial empire, but I can think of half a dozen ritual spells that can make it all go away.

Magic's not about money, it's about power, it's about knowledge. We're special. Top of the food chain. The one percent of the one percent of the one percent. Lots of shit in this world just can't touch us. Lot of mages get to live in their ivory towers and no matter how much shit they walk through they don't even get so much as a stain on their shoes.

I'm betting Bustillo's like that. Probably figured out his power as a kid, honed it as best he could, maybe picked up some pointers from another mage. Bit by bit he grew until he had all the power he wanted.

Oh, sure he could be running a cartel, but why? Big pain in the ass, that. Mages who think on that scale are fucking dangerous, don't get me wrong, but unless they're playing some other angle, they tend not to be big thinkers. Why run a multi-billion, worldwide, criminal enterprise when you can spend your time prying out the secrets of the gods instead and still eat filet mignon every night?

Yeah. Bustillo's that kind of guy. I can see it in his

eyes. I've seen that fear before. I've felt that fear before. If I were a better man I'd just kill him. He knows that's where this is headed. But I'm tired and I'm pissed off and I don't much like him. So instead I feed that fear.

"I could carve you up, Manuel." I trace the air with the knife like I'm filleting a steak. "Slice your skin from your bones with Mictlantecuhtli's blade and put it on like I'm putting on a jacket. I could take you with me. Everything you are, everything you have would live on after a fashion. It's maybe not immortality, but something of you will survive in me. Would you like that?"

Bustillo, eyes wide and body quaking from fear. I've cut him off from the pool, and his own power is next to nothing now. He's used it all up. I'm still drawing power from the pool, pulling it down faster than it can fill back up. There's nothing there for him.

"Or I can shoot you. Got a round in the chamber with your name on it. Well? I asked you a question, Manuel. What'll it be? Do you want to live on? Or do you want to die?"

"Live," he says. "I want to live."

The fear has taken him and I bet if I told him to beg for it, he'd do exactly that. It's not just that he's afraid to die, though he's sure as hell that. It's that he's run up against the limits of his own power and arrogance. That's broken him more than anything else possibly could.

"Too bad," I say and pull the trigger.

Chapter 3

I pull my car, a '73 Cadillac Eldorado convertible, out from where I've hidden it half a mile away from Bustillo's compound. I got it off a whackjob necromancer who was kidnapping Voodoo Loa and stitching them into his soul. I took him down in a bar in Texas and took the Eldorado for my trouble.

I drive down the rocky hill from Bustillo's compound toward Tepehuanes, the throaty rumble of the Cadillac's V-8 echoing through the darkness. The Caddy's been un-intentionally mothballed for about a year and it feels it. Even with new pads and rotors the brakes aren't great, the engine sounds like it needs another tune-up and the rag-top is so thin you can see light through it.

I had to abandon the car on a dock in San Pedro when I took it over to the land of the dead and didn't have enough magic to bring it back. Kind of like if you do valet parking and you lose your stub.

I was being chased by a fire elemental at the time and had my ex-girlfriend and a burnt-out hobo of a mage in the car with me. It was kind of a stressful day.

The other side of the veil is pure entropy. Life drains

away, magic leeches off into the fabric of the place. So by the time I got the car from the other side and off the dock the gas in the tank was as combustible as water, the metal was starting to pit, the rag top was falling apart and the tires were about ready to turn into dust.

The only thing holding it together was some residual magic left over from wards that were inscribed into it by the previous owner. At least those kept the inside of the thing in one piece. A little work and it was, well, not good as new, but better than it was.

Normally I don't much care about cars. I need a ride, I steal one. But I've got a soft spot for the Eldorado. When everything else was going to shit the car worked even when it shouldn't have. It's built like a tank, steers like a goddamn cow, but it's saved my life a couple of times.

I only had the Cadillac a short while before I lost it on the dead side, but having it back here feels right. It's reliable, a trusted friend. I figure on this trip I can use all the friends I can get.

I pull off Bustillo's dirt road and onto Highway 23 on the south side of town. In the distance I can see the burning warehouse casting a shifting red and yellow glow into the night sky. I pass a Pemex, the bright fluorescent lights of the gas station stark against the unlit highway and see the pickup trucks with Bustillo's men, their faces blackened with soot. There are definitely fewer returning than left.

I had hoped to not see them at all when I walked out of Bustillo's place. The Caddy stands out no matter where it is, but at midnight on a darkened road in Durango after their drug warehouse burned down? Just wait until they get back to their boss's place. I want to be long gone before that happens.

I check a map I picked up in Puerto Peñasco, when I realized I didn't know where the fuck I was going, and find Mexico City. I do some quick math. It's about a twelve-hour straight shot. Even with Adderall, which I've been popping like Tic Tacs for the last month, I won't make it. I haven't slept in three days. I need a shower. I need a place to hole up and figure out my next move. Zacatecas looks like a decent place for it. Hell, they even have a Walmart.

Zacatecas is only about three hours away. I can do that easily enough. I'm still buzzing on adrenaline from my fight with Bustillo and from the Adderall I took a few hours before.

When I started trading places with Mictlantecuhtli he appeared to me and laid it all out. He's trapped in a tomb in Mictlan, resting, being alone with his thoughts. According to him he likes it that way. He doesn't want to rise again. Told me that it was all Santa Muerte's idea. Their kingdom, Mictlan, needs a king and a queen and, self-esteem and arrogance notwithstanding, I don't fit the bill.

She wants to bring Mictlantecuhtli back and I'm the sacrificial lamb. The only way out, he tells me, is to kill her. Without her I become just some run of the mill, old and boring necromancer. Mictlantecuhtli's obsidian blade is the way to do it.

Only Mictlantecuhtli put a little extra bite into the knife and made it so it wouldn't just kill people and let you take their skins, it would kill gods, too. Why? Fuck if I know. At a guess I'd say he was thinking he might need to use it on the other gods.

And then there's his wife's side of the story.

Santa Muerte didn't deny what was happening to me.

That I was slowly turning to jade, that I was going to take his place as a piece of statuary if I didn't do something about it. She knew it was going to happen when I took her deal. She tells me the same thing he tells me about Mictlan. It needs a king and a queen. Two halves to make it whole.

But, and this is where the stories diverge, she wants me to be that king. She wants me to be by her side in Mictlan. Mictlantecuhtli is old news. There's bad blood there. But in order to take his place I need to be more than just her husband. I need to break this bond Mictlantecuhtli and I have and take his place at her side. The only way to do that, she tells me, is to kill him once and for all. No sleeping in stone beneath Mictlan. He needs to be *dead* dead.

And this is where their stories reconnect, because to kill him, like her, I need to use the obsidian blade. I'm stuck between two Aztec death icons in a domestic squabble. One's telling me one thing, the other's telling me another. To complicate things they both deny that they arranged to get the blade into my hands. One of them has to be lying.

I've seen meth-head marriages that were less dysfunctional.

If Santa Muerte is telling me the truth the only way to save myself is to kill Mictlantecuhtli. If Mictlantecuhtli is telling me the truth, my only way out is to kill her. I'm being played, but I'm not sure which one is playing me.

So I'm going for Option C, which, let me tell ya, I'm a big fan of. Kill them both.

What I don't know what to do with is Tabitha. When I saw her last she showed me that she was Santa Muerte, but I've been wondering if that's true ever since. The story is that she died years ago and had a piece of Santa Muerte's soul inserted to bring her back.

If she's just an extension of Santa Muerte then she's just as responsible for killing my sister as Santa Muerte herself. She's just a limb of Santa Muerte and killing her won't be any different from pruning a tree.

But what if she's not? What if she's just Tabitha Cheung with a piece of a death goddess in her head? What if she got stuck with Santa Muerte the same way I'm stuck with Mictlantecuhtli? Some things she said have me thinking things might be more complicated. But part of me wonders if maybe I just don't want it to be simple.

Either way I need to find her. I probably need to kill her. But before I do that I want to be really goddamn sure.

———

I've got one eye on the road ahead of me, the yellow lines of the highway zipping out of the darkness, and one eye on the rearview mirror. The road stretches ahead of me, dark blue beneath a thin slice of moon. No other cars on the road. At some point Bustillo's men will discover that he's dead and either a) celebrate and choose a new leader like drunken buccaneers or, much more likely because this isn't *Pirates of the Caribbean*, b) hit the road and come gunning for me.

They saw my car pass the gas station. At least some of them will remember it. And they'll realize that there's only one road out of Tepehuanes, and it's the only one I could be on. They're a bunch of murdering thugs, not idiots.

Whether they come after me really depends on how

pissed off they are. I'm in contested territory, now. From what I understand Los Zetas and Cártel del Golfo are fighting for dominance over this particular patch of dirt. But the players in this game change depending on who's got the bigger budget, so fuck knows who's really running things. The only sure bet is it's not the government no matter how many soldiers they send down here.

This highway is a main thoroughfare for transporting marijuana and heroin up to the border. Bustillo was working for the Sinaloa Cartel. The Zetas and CDG might not take it too kindly if they find his men down here. Or they might help them shoot me. Could go either way.

Behind me I can see headlights, cars rumbling down the road. Only they don't look like those trucks I saw in the gas station. They're too big, too wide. They've got lights on the roofs. Police? No. A military convoy.

Doesn't mean it's not Bustillo's men, of course. Whether they have any particular loyalty for the man doesn't matter. They're sure as hell going to have loyalty to Sinaloa. The guy who brings in my head is looking at a promotion.

That's, well, not worst case, but close enough to. It could be one of the other cartels, or actual soldiers or police working for them. A lot of the cartels have gotten their hands on some heavy hardware, and they've managed to buy a fair number of cops and politicians.

I could gun the engine, but where the hell am I gonna go? It's a straight shot down to Zacatecas and the next turn off isn't for another fifty miles. Better to meet them here in the open, where I have more options, than have them run me off the road.

I pull over to see if they'll pass, the engine still running. The convoy's a good twelve or thirteen cars long.

Trucks, APCs, a goddamn tank. They're not cartel, they're army. Or if they are cartel, this country's more fucked up than I thought.

Behind me one of the trucks pulls over and stops. A soldier jumps out of the back with a flashlight and an assault rifle. I make sure the Browning's good to go and hide it behind the door. I scribble "CONFÍA EN MÍ" onto one of my stickers and slap it on my chest. "Trust me."

I roll down the window. The soldier's young, early twenties maybe. Crew cut hair, earnest face. Nervous. If I was him I would be, too. With the bullshit going on between Los Zetas and Cártel del Golfo out here, some random guy on an empty stretch of road in the middle of nowhere is nothing but trouble. Any stop could end with him dead. It has for some of his fellow soldiers. Their ghosts cluster in so close they might as well be hanging off him like Christmas ornaments. Dead soldiers, dead civilians. So many dead. Did he kill them? Or was he just there when it happened?

The thing that really grabs my attention is the scapular, a piece of cloth hanging on his chest from a braided cord around his neck. It's a Catholic thing. They're not big, usually have a prayer on them and they come in different colors. Red for The Passion, blue for the Immaculate Conception, black and blue for St. Michael. Lot of Catholics down here, so that's not too surprising.

But this one's enormous. Black with red edging and an embroidered image of Santa Muerte hanging from a red, black and white cord. Catholics don't flaunt their scapulars, they wear them under their clothes, keep them private. But with Señora de las Sombras, you wear that shit like it's a fucking badge.

Above it all hangs a gold crucifix. I've seen this sort of thing before. Some in L.A., but much more frequently down here. The cognitive dissonance is something that tweaks a lot of people.

The Catholic Church has been denouncing Santa Muerte for years, but she's gained a foothold in the public consciousness, anyway. Otherwise good Catholics are turning to her not because they've lost faith, not because they're denying their god, but because she's more accessible. When your god doesn't answer your prayers, why not try talking to Death?

The soldier asks me who I am, what I'm doing down here. I tell him I'm a priest coming down from the U.S. to work with poor kids in Mexico City. He pauses at that, stammers a bit. Finally just nods. He asks me about my sunglasses. It's after midnight, and there are no lights on this stretch of highway. I say I have an eye condition. He isn't sure what to say to that, either, but the Sharpie magic does its thing and he seems to buy it.

"Everything all right?" I say, my Spanish purposely stilted. Better to sound like an out of towner than a local. He might give me more crap, but it also excuses a lot of behavior.

"Yeah," he says. He glances back at the truck idling behind me, mosquitoes and dust dancing in the headlight beams. His nervousness doesn't seem focused on me anymore.

"When's the last time you gave confession, son?" I say. It's mean. And yes, I know, I'm a dick. I think that's been pretty firmly established by now. But the sudden look of fear in his eyes tells me everything I need to know.

"A long time," he says, frowning.

He's a good kid. Grew up right. Made his abuela proud when he joined the army. Only, well, it ain't so simple. Maybe he took a bribe. Maybe he looked the other way when a commanding officer did. Maybe somebody's got something over his head that he can't seem to shake.

Whatever it is, he knows he's compromised. His perch on the moral high ground is cracking beneath him, and he doesn't know what to do. Eventually he's going to have to make a choice. Keep fighting the good fight or don't.

The crime down here is savage, sudden, and a big moneymaker. Kidnappings, murders, marijuana and heroin carted up to the border. There's cash in murder, money to be had in brutality. Violence is currency.

Not to say it's like that everywhere in Mexico, but only an idiot doesn't recognize that the cartels are the real kings. Ruling through fear and intimidation. Criticize too much and end up missing your head, or with a slit throat and hanging from a bridge with half a dozen others.

The cartels are holding the nation hostage and every time the government thinks they've cut one down it regroups under a new name, a new look and the same old bullshit.

It's no surprise that this soldier's both a devotee of Santa Muerte and a Catholic. He's conflicted, but he's not stupid. Even the devout down here don't always think God can save them amidst all the violence. Santa Muerte might not be able to save you, but she doesn't promise anything, either. Prayers to her are suggestions at the best of times. Honoring her is like wearing a talisman against dying. Maybe she'll listen. Maybe she won't.

But when you draw your last breath she's the one you'll see. Everything dies eventually, and that's the only thing you can be sure of with her. It's like Bustillo said. There's nothing more honest than death.

The soldier's got that look that says he's thinking back to when it was simple. When things made sense. The cartels were bad, the police and the army were good. But there's poverty and low pay and too much violence and too many dead friends. And no matter how many times he tells himself he's doing the right thing when he has to make one of those gray area choices, he doesn't really believe it.

"Might want to see your priest, then. Lot of things weigh on a man's soul."

He nods, his entire focus shifting inward. I'm forgotten except as a cursory task he has to deal with. He wishes me luck and gets back into the truck to rejoin the convoy. I give it a few minutes before pulling out back onto the road. I don't want to be too close to them. There have been ambushes against police, occasionally soldiers. The last thing I need is to get caught in a crossfire.

The rest of the drive to Zacatecas is uneventful. No speeding headlights come my way, no chatter of AK fire. I pull into the city around four in the morning. Traffic's increased on the highway. Semi-trucks, mostly. Some commuters. The hustle and bustle of a city just waking up, getting ready to start its day.

Not everything down here is violence and drug money. It's like anywhere else in the world. Most of the people are just trying to get by. Live their lives, find love, have families. When all I see is ghosts and death it's sometimes a little hard to remember that.

I pull into Zacatecas proper and start looking for a

place to crash. Not long before I find a hotel off the high-way. Big, yellow box of a building in between two vacant lots filled with scrub brush, the only decoration a bizarre, rococo-style double-staircase leading to the lobby that looks as out of place as a wig on a pig.

I get out of the car as a hot wind picks up. It's a short burst of blast-furnace air. Like the Santa Ana winds up in L.A., but harder, dryer. Like sandpaper against my skin. Just as suddenly it's gone, replaced with a cooler breeze that makes more sense for the early hour.

I tell myself that it's just wind. But I have to wonder about that. Nothing is "just" anything these days. Maybe I'm paranoid. Enemies in the shadows I can't see. Those can sometimes be just as dangerous as the ones I can.

The wind has me on edge a lot these days. Any wind. The wind can be playful or it can be cruel. I went to a wind spirit in the desert outside Los Angeles for help finding someone not too long ago. It sees everything. It goes everywhere. It isn't just wind. It's Wind.

The Wind down here isn't the same as the one up there, but the edges blur. What one knows they all know. Their needs and desires blend together until they're in-distinguishable from each other. Anger one in Alaska, expect to feel the brunt of it in the Kalahari.

The price for the information was fire. Most winds enjoy a good blaze. In the parched, dry parts of the American Southwest fire season's like fucking Christmas. It pushes the flames along, fans them higher, spreads them across hills, down mountains, into valleys. And if people are in the way, well, what does the Wind care? It was around long before humans showed up.

But it wasn't just any fire it wanted. It was the burning down of my home. Joke's on it. I don't have one. The only place I've considered home burned down over fifteen years ago with my parents inside of it. I own a place in upstate New York, but I haven't been there in five years. I bounce around, keep moving. Home is as alien a concept for me as dry land is for a fish.

So of course I said yes. I figured I'd gotten off easy. At most some flea bag motel would catch fire. And then it pointed out to me that I was the new Aztec King of the Dead. It wanted me to burn down Mictlan.

Why, I couldn't say, but I have some guesses. Mictlan's a pretty specific thing to want to burn. That's like asking somebody to burn down Cleveland. The Wind wouldn't want it to burn unless it had a reason, and there are only a few that I can think of.

I have no idea how I'm going to accomplish this. May as well have tasked me with burning down Valhalla or Hell.

But if I don't do it, it's going to come back on me and I'm not looking forward to that fallout.

I grab my messenger bag out of the trunk and head up the ridiculous staircase into the hotel. Inside it's clean but shabby. A front desk, some leather club chairs that look like they were salvaged off the side of the road, an air-conditioner that rattles and grinds. The smell of cigarettes and Febreze is heavy in the air. A woman in a brown, bad-fitting polyester suit coat sits slumped on a stool with her head on the counter, snoring.

I ring the bell next to her head and she startles awake almost falling out of her chair.

"Whoa, hang on," I say. "All good. I'm not gonna eat ya, or anything. I just need to get a room."

"A room? Oh. Yes. A room."

There aren't many cars in the lot, so I doubt there are

a lot of people here. She probably hasn't seen anyone in hours and probably never does this time of the morning. I pass her a handful of peso notes. "Preferably near the elevator. On a floor without a lot of people on it. Better yet, no people on it."

She rubs sleep out of her eyes and counts the notes. "This is too much."

"Think of it as a tip."

Money talks no matter what country you're in. She pokes at a computer terminal behind the counter. "There's nobody on the third floor."

"That would be perfect." She codes a plastic keycard and hands it to me.

I can feel her staring at me as I cross the lobby to the elevator. I give her a big smile as the doors close.

Chapter 4

Like the lobby, the third floor is clean, but shabby. Cheap carpet, cheap light fixtures. This place is so new there are no ghosts. Nobody's died here, yet. I can feel a few Wanderers outside, and the ones that have been following me since Tijuana haven't caught up with me, yet.

I retrieve a can of red Krylon from my bag, give it a shake and spray a large, circular rune on the floor of the elevator. I press my hand to the floor and send some power into it. I do the same on the outside door, the stairwell door, a couple of spots down the hall and finish up with a few inside the stairwell itself. I paint the same one on the landing that I put on the elevator floor.

If anybody steps onto this floor through the elevator or the stairwell, I'll know about it. And if I don't like their look I have a nasty surprise waiting for them.

I find my room and unlock it with the key, but I don't go inside. I'm not going to stay in it. I just want the computer at the front desk to register my using the key. Instead I pick a room at the end of the hall across from the stairwell. I open the door with a spell that pops the lock, but shouldn't alert the system.

It might just be paranoia, but my first night in Tijuana some locals decided I looked like an easy mark and busted into my room. Started shooting up the place. It was annoying more than it was dangerous. I took them out easily enough with an electricity spell I know that's kind of like a big ass Taser. I left them lying unconscious and twitching on the floor of my room.

That would have been fine if it hadn't happened again in Hermosillo, only with half a dozen men armed with assault rifles. I think they were trying to kidnap me, or something. That didn't go so well for them, either. I shot three and gutted the rest with a straight razor. I left an extra big tip for the cleaning staff.

Ever since then I've been taking extra precautions wherever I stay. I always use runes, glyphs and wards near wherever I'm staying, but they're all low level spells to keep people from paying attention to the room. That doesn't work so well when you've already grabbed some-body's attention and they tail you to your room. So I've added some really unpleasant ones, started sneaking into different rooms, setting traps. Whatever it takes.

Inside the room I put up other wards, but these ones are less for intruders and more to keep the ghosts out. They'll show up eventually, and having the Dead watch you while you sleep isn't nearly as fun as it sounds.

I sit on the edge of the bed and take stock. I'm so goddamn tired I don't know what to do next. I need a shower. I need a shave. I need to get into some clothes that aren't spattered with Bustillo's blood.

The shower's water pressure is almost non-existent, but it's hot. I let it wash away the grime, sweat and blood. My body is shot through with jade. My chest, stomach, left thigh and down both arms to just past the elbow is a deep, sea green, dull and waxy. It crawls up my neck with thin tendrils and down my legs like varicose veins. My tattoos shimmer in the bathroom light, their colors muted in the stone.

I have one tattoo on my chest, a circular pattern with three circling crows. They move around inside their prison, shifting position. Looking too closely at them gives me a headache. In a pinch they can be released from my body, pecking and clawing at an enemy in a swarm of black feathers and razor sharp beaks. They're not real, of course. They're phantasms, constructs of magic locked away inside my chest.

Lately, they've changed. More menacing somehow, though honestly I didn't think that was possible. But now I can feel them inside my skin, angry, wanting blood, wanting to be released. That's never happened before. They've always just been another spell.

Now it feels as though they're gaining will. Is it the stone that's doing it? The change itself? I don't know. I really don't want to let them loose. Before I knew what they would do, how they operated. Now, I have no idea.

I get out of the shower and look myself over in the mirror. The last couple of months have not been kind. I've barely slept, depending on magic and Adderall to keep me going. I've been shot, stabbed, punched. Somebody took a baseball bat to my head in Hermosillo. The magic in my tattoos protected me from the brunt of it but I'm pretty sure one of my molars is loose.

Somebody else went after me with a broken bottle in Tijuana that scraped along the stone of my chest and cut a shallow furrow up the side of my neck. I had to stitch myself up with dental floss and a needle sterilized with tequila and a lighter after that one. My own damn fault for not packing a surgical kit. The scar is pink and raw. One more in a vast collection.

But things are finally starting to fall into place. I have a location on Tabitha. She told Bustillo to tell me where she was. That means she wants me to find her. She won't be moving until I get there.

One of the things I got out of this arrangement is some of Mictlantecuhtli's power. This dark, roiling thing that wells up inside me like it wants to tear through my skin. I could use that power to go straight to Mictlantecuhtli's tomb, I've done it before. Once I'm there I could just stab him with the knife. Finish this once and for all. But I probably wouldn't survive it.

Every time I tap into that power my body changes faster. Too much of it has gone to stone, already. Much more and the transition will be complete. How many times can I use it before it eats me up entirely? Two times? Three? Or worse, one? What if I get there and before I can stab the sonofabitch the transition completes?

So I'm doing this the hard way. Finding Tabitha's the first step. I don't just want her to make sure I clean up a loose end. I need her because I need a door into Mictlan.

That's really the problem. Getting there. Once I'm inside, tracking down Santa Muerte and Mictlantecuhtli can't be that hard. At least I'll know what plane of existence they're in.

The thing I'm most worried about is moving around without either of them knowing I'm there. I've got spells keeping her from tracking me out here, but in there, on their home turf, I don't know how well they'll work. I'll burn that bridge when I get to it.

For now I just need to sleep.

———

My eyes snap open when the ward on the elevator breaks. Who is it? A hotel guest who's gotten a room on this floor? Unwanted visitors with guns? I glance at the clock on the nightstand. I've been asleep about an hour.

They couldn't have waited another couple hours before they came to kill me?

I close my eyes again and reach out for the rune I painted in the elevator. I can sense six men inside. Viewing through runes is a synesthetic cross-stitch of senses that all meld into one. I can feel the men's weight, smell the gun oil on them, see the skull-printed face masks, camouflage Kevlar vests. Feel the automatic weapons at the ready.

Well, we can't have that.

I trigger the elevator rune, but I'm too late to catch them all. A column of phosphorescent flame erupts inside the elevator, hitting two of them with a furnace blast of heat. I hear screams, yelling. The blast is hot enough to cook the skin off their bones, but not hot enough to cook off the ammunition. I made that mistake once. Almost died from all the bullets in the air.

That should buy me a couple minutes as they try to save their buddies. They'll figure out pretty quickly that there's nothing left to save. I roll out of bed and throw on my clothes, slide everything but my car keys and the Benelli into my bag as quickly and quietly as I can. I don't bother to put my shoes on. No time. I step to the door, watching them through the runes.

The remaining four come down the hall, guns in shaking hands, waiting for something to move so they can shoot it. I can feel their panic, their uncertainty.

They gather around the room I'm supposed to be in. Three of them flank the door, the fourth fires a burst through it that's loud and effective for no other reason than he just used an entire magazine on it. The hollow, plywood door blows off its hinges into the room in a shower of splinters. He does a ridiculous roll into the room. What are these guys, F-Troop?

The other three follow him inside, and I take that as my cue. I slip out of the room and hit the stairwell. One of them comes out and sees me as I'm stepping through the door. He takes a shot, the bullet blowing a hole in the wall as the door closes behind me. I take the steps two at a time.

I hit the bottom floor as the two of them get into the stairwell. I trigger the rune on the landing with a thought and another column of bright, blue fire burns through them. That's four down, two to go.

That slows them down, but not by much. There's no way I can hit them with the Benelli from here, but I can do something else. I wait until I hear footsteps on the stairs. I put my hand on the metal railing and put as much power as I dare into an old stand-by, a big ass lightning spell.

The magic courses through me. I pull it back when I feel Mictlantecuhtli's power unspooling inside me. It's like being chained to a sleeping tiger. Wake it up too much and it'll eat me.

Even with that the spell's strong enough for what I need. Electricity arcs through the metal. Shrieks, the fall of bodies down the stairs, jerking from the voltage coursing through them. I don't have a good gauge on this thing, but with the power I put into it they'll either stay down for a while, or not get back up again.

Once I get to the car I'll be safer. Get on the road, get

down to Mexico City. If these are Bustillo's men, it's a pretty good bet that when they don't report in they'll just send more after me. A big place like Mexico City is a lot easier to hide in than Zacatecas. It's not like I'm planning on being there long.

I back out of the exit door at the bottom of the stairs and into the parking lot, the Benelli trained on the steps above me just in case. I turn to head to the car and stop dead.

At the gas station back in Tepehuanes I saw five pickup trucks filled with Bustillo's men in the backs. They're all here.

They stand in a semi-circle around the exit door, guns trained on me. Smart. Knew I'd cut and run, knew where I'd come out. Couple dozen guys with automatic weapons. They can pump several hundred rounds into me inside of three seconds. No matter how many protection spells I have in my tattoos, those are not good odds.

I slowly lower the Benelli to the ground, put my hands up. "Gentlemen. How's everybody doing tonight?" They don't say anything.

To make matters worse the parking lot has filled with ghosts. Some Wanderers, but seeing how closely these linger around Bustillo's men, it's more likely that they're Haunts who have bound themselves to their killers rather than to where they died. It happens sometimes, but not often. Which tells me these guys have killed a lot of people.

It also means that hopping over to the dead side as an escape route is the mother of bad ideas. The ghosts will shred me before I get three steps.

So the question comes down to, do I want to die from bullets or do I want to die from ghosts?

Chapter 5

Being eaten by ghosts sucks.

They don't take bites out of your body so much as they take bites out of your soul. The scars they leave behind aren't just physical, they're emotional and mental. Chunks torn out of the very fabric that makes you, well, you.

I've been hit by ghosts before. Hurts like you wouldn't believe. I've even fed a few people to ghosts. Took them to the other side, tossed them to the Dead like chucking trees into a woodchipper.

It's a horrifying way to go. Most of them deserved it.

The thing about being killed by ghosts is that it takes time. They're like piranha more than sharks. Death by a thousand cuts. I've had to run through a crowd of ghosts on the other side before. Some of the worst pain I've ever felt.

But I got through them. When I popped back to the living side they couldn't touch me. There aren't quite as many here, but they're more heavily clustered. I might make it through them and get to the car in relatively one piece. Provided that the spell doesn't trigger the progression of jade and I turn into a rock on the other side.

Bustillo's men look like they're not in a mood to talk with anything but their guns, so I figure it's not much of a choice. Definitely die, or probably die.

I'm about to take my chances on the ghosts when I feel a hot wind spring up around us. It grows fast. Sudden hurricane force. A wave of heat sucks the air out of my lungs, and I instinctively hit the ground and cover my head. Fiery air blasts over me. I hear screams, gunfire, the sound of torches igniting. I hazard a look and instantly regret it. My eyes singe in the hot air, but the gunmen are far worse off than I am.

Corpses lie on the ground burning. Their skin blackened and charred. There's a stink of cooked pork in the air. The ones still alive are rolling around desperately trying to put the flames out. I feel a little warm, my skin's a little red like I've spent too much time in the sun, but that's all. Nothing else is on fire. Not the building, not the ground, not even a nearby tree.

I stand and survey the carnage, orange firelight casting dancing shadows across the building. One of the gunmen, his skin crackling, one eyeball burst from the heat, crawls across the pavement, reaching for his rifle with shaking hands. I kick it out of his reach and put a round from the Benelli into him. Better to put him out of his misery than let him die in a burn ward somewhere.

"All right," I say to the air around me. I don't know where to look, which way to face. "I know you're here. What do you want?"

It's four in the morning. I'm standing in a hotel parking lot talking to the air with a bunch of burning bodies at my feet. A second later the air answers.

"We had an agreement," says a voice cracking like a

brushfire. "A compact," says another with a sound like wind through dry, desert canyons. "A deal," says a third, its hollow sound echoing in the empty lot.

The Wind's voices are different from what I remember when I spoke to it at Vasquez Rocks outside of Los Angeles. I was looking for it, then. Now, it seems, it's looking for me.

I pull shoes and socks out of my bag, and sit down to put them on. I might be dealing with an elemental of unbelievable power here, but it doesn't mean I'm going to do it in bare feet. I don't say anything until I've got my shoes tied and a shirt on.

"Why are you talking like it's in the past tense?" I say, buttoning my shirt.

"Have you reneged?" the voices say in unison. "It has been too long. The stone spreads. Soon you will not be able to keep our agreement."

"Oh, I'm sorry. I didn't realize there was a deadline."

"Deadline, yes," say the voices, and there's a hint of laughter behind it. At Vasquez Rocks the Wind was more serious, flatter in tone. Different wind spirits blend and blur together. The desires of one can become the desires of all. What is it about the Wind down here that's different? And is this where the desire to see Mictlan burn came from? Is this the source?

"The deadline will pass because you will be dead," says another voice, its S's stretching into a long hiss.

"You know, jokes aren't funny when you have to explain 'em," I say. Who knew the Wind had the sense of humor of a five-year-old? "You're really worried I won't get there in time? I didn't think I'd see the day the Wind got all panicky." It laughs, a strange, snakelike wheeze across its multiple voices that lowers until it's a single, deep, throaty sound that rolls and echoes across the parking lot.

"I do not panic," it says. The unified voice is stronger with a heaviness, a presence it didn't have before. It blends into a single voice, the three into one harmony of rumbling bass. "But I would see Mictlan burn before the end times come. I will see that place cleansed with fire and that bastard king Mictlantecuhtli and his whore of a wife blacken in flames. And you, little man, usurper to the throne, you will do this for me, or I will turn the wind upon you and flay the skin from your bones."

This is sounding awfully personal. And much more coherent. Strong, steady, pissed off. It just reinforces my suspicions. A wind spirit down here has a grudge against Mictlan, and it passed the message up the coast when I spoke to the more fragmented Wind in Vasquez Rocks.

There are only so many things that would care about Mictlan. I'm ninety-nine percent sure who this is. But I need confirmation. If I just come out and say its name, it could deny it. There's nothing saying it can't lie. Better to do something stupid and make it reveal itself.

"Which one are you?" I say. "Xipe-Totec? That crack about flayed skin fits. Huitzilopochtli? No, you're talking about wind and fire. Not blood. Tlaloc? I don't see any rain. Not Tezcatlipoca. It's morning now. You'd be too weak if you were the god of night. You're some second rate wind spirit, aren't you? One of those little godlings too weak to do its own dirty work. What, some pissed off little sprite?"

"You dare—" it says, but I cut it off.

"I dare because Mictlantecuhtli and I are connected. Which means you and I are, too. Are you one of my in-laws? What upstart little cousin of the King and Queen of Mictlan are you? You call me a usurper, but I bet you're a pretender. You're nobody important. Nobody worth considering." That last bit might have been going too far.

The wind picks up around me, and I can feel this thing's anger on it. It shifts and whips around like a snake. It wants to hurt me, but it doesn't dare. I'm its ticket for its revenge.

The wind grows in strength until it's a gale force blowing around me, pulling in trash and dirt, uprooting plants. It sucks the fires up from the corpses, taking the flames into itself, compressing them into balls of glowing flame. It coalesces in front of me in a tornado blur of burning garbage, smoldering debris.

And when it stops, that final one percent of uncertainty vanishes. It is the god of wind and the morning star. A winged snake, pulled together from waste and leftovers. Its finery ragged, its feathers made of discarded food wrappers, shredded handbills, its eyes of bottleglass. It blazes with fires pulled from dead men.

Quetzalcoatl, the feathered serpent. I wasn't sure if he was still around. So many of the old gods are gone or so faded they might as well be. And he isn't looking so great. A dying god made of rags and tatters. A burning Doritos bag flutters off one of its wings.

Quetzalcoatl's eyes flash. It lunges at me with its mouth wide, showing teeth made of screws and nails, and lets loose an unholy shriek. The sound pummels at me, almost pushing me to my knees. But I stand my ground. This is all show, trying to get the upper hand. Assert its authority.

"I am the Snake," Quetzalcoatl says. "The Feathered

Serpent and the Crow. I am the Wind that scours the desert."

I don't have a lot of experience with gods. I've worked with the Voodoo Loa, Baron Samedi, Maman Brigitte, Baron Cimetiere. But my arrangement with them has always been business. With Santa Muerte and Mictlante-cuhtli, it's been a more . . . turbulent relationship.

But if there's one thing I've learned about dealing with them, it's that you never back down.

"You're also the Duck and the Spider Monkey," I say, naming off some of Quetzalcoatl's lesser known forms. "So pardon me if I'm not exactly shaking over here."

Truth be told I am. The other Aztec gods are as close to in-laws as I've got, so I've made a point of knowing who they are and what they do. I don't know how many of them still exist, how many of those are still intact enough to remember who they are. All I have are tales, textbooks, websites. The reality of the supernatural is always a little different from the stories.

Quetzalcoatl is one of the heavies, and I've been wondering if the demands of the Wind up north came from him. The stories say he stole the bones of the dead from Mictlan and created the fifth version of humans, us. Creation myths are weird. What's truth and what's "truth" tend to blur. The important thing for gods isn't what happened, but what people believe.

Gods thrive on that. Demons, too, though they'll all kill you just as dead whether you believe in them or not. But without belief they'll wither away and die. They feed on it.

Not a lot of people these days believe the old stories, but there are enough to keep a lot of the big gods around.

Certainly enough to give Quetzalcoatl the power to kill more than two dozen men with a hurricane of fire.

Hell, I know I believe.

"You want me to burn down Mictlan," I say. "Any particular reason why?"

"My business is my own," Quetzalcoatl says. "You merely must carry out my will."

I don't mind the idea of burning Mictlan. I'm going to kill its king and queen, after all. Setting it alight just sounds like being thorough. But I would like to know why. What is it that's got him in such a snit? Jealousy? Pissed off because Santa Muerte has managed to change with the times?

I laugh at him. "Is that how you see it? No. We made a deal. I'll keep the deal. End of story. None of this 'carry out my will' shit, though. I'm not your fucking minion. You don't want to tell me why, fine. Least you can do is tell me how. Because if you were thinking to leave that up to me to figure out, man are you gonna be disappointed."

"To think Mictecacihuatl picked you as a consort," he says. He licks lips made of shredded grass and palm fronds with a tongue made of tinfoil. "And you cannot do such a simple thing."

"I'm only human."

"Indeed. Then I will give you a talisman that even your feeble mind can grasp." Quetzalcoatl vibrates, going so fast he begins to blur. He shatters in a silent explosion, pieces of trash flying only to freeze in place a few inches out. A flash of brass drops to the ground, bounces to my feet. A sound of sucking air and Quetzalcoatl snaps back into his garbage god form.

A dented and tarnished brass Zippo lighter with a mosaic of chipped turquoise on one side lies at my feet. I pick it up and turn it over in my hands. It's old, scratched, the brass worn. The mosaic has the hint of a shape, a chaotic mess of different shades of turquoise, but I'm damned if I can figure out what it is. It's seen a lifetime of use and more.

I flick the Zippo open, thumb the wheel. A spark and a flame. Yep, it's a lighter.

"Unless you're expecting Mictlan to be a lot more flammable than I think it is, you're gonna need to do better than this."

"The fires of Xiuhtecuhtli," Quetzalcoatl says. "God of the flame, the light in the darkness. Fire against the cold, and a feast in famine. He is hope where there is none. He has faded over time until that is all that is left of him. An errant spark, a flicker of his former self. Take him to Mictlan, burn it down with his divine flames."

"And this'll work?"

"The flames will set alight anything they touch. In your feeble world they will burn hot and bright, but in Mictlan once they burn they will never stop until that land is nothing but ash."

It takes me a moment to remember what Xiuhtecuhtli's shtick was. He renewed the sun once every fifty years or something. Priests would take a victim up a mountain and at the right time, carve out the poor bastard's heart and stick a fire in the empty chest. If the fire caught, yay! Happy times. Except for the guy burning on the altar, of course. And if not, the Tzitzimimeh, monsters or demons, something like that, would come down from the sky and eat everyone.

I'm betting those priests made damn sure that fire caught.

"I'll have to get me some cigars, then." I slide the lighter in my pocket.

"Do not joke. That is a proud god you hold. Do not waste his gift. Now go to Mictlan and do what you have agreed."

"Sure. I'll jump right on that." I need to get some sleep. Speaking of which, I need to find a new hotel. Dammit. Maybe I should just move on. Keep heading south.

We don't seem to have drawn any attention, yet, and I honestly don't know if anyone looked if they'd even see Quetzalcoatl, gods do weird shit like that. But they'd sure as hell see a couple dozen smoking corpses.

I pick up my bag and head toward the Cadillac. Quetzalcoatl has sucked up all the trash and dirt in the parking lot to make his form and the ground is scoured clean.

"I did not give you permission to depart," Quetzalcoatl yells, his voice booming. I answer him with my middle finger.

I open the Caddy's driver side door and toss my bag in and the shotgun onto the seat. If he wants to play games he can knock himself out. For whatever reason he wants Mictlan destroyed, he needs me to do it. And if he's just given me the remnants of a dead god to do it with, I'm thinking he doesn't have a whole lot of other options.

Police will be here eventually, and I really don't want to have to explain all the bodies. I wonder what they'll think did it. Probably a rival cartel. Burned bodies pop up with alarming frequency these days.

I pull out of the parking lot, Quetzalcoatl watching me with his coal-red eyes, his tattered wings flapping lazily. I don't know what feathered serpent body language looks like, but if I were to bet on it, I'd say he's pissed off at me.

I watch him in the rearview mirror as I get onto the street, and once the wheels touch the pavement his body crumbles, leaving nothing behind but a pile of burning trash.

Chapter 6

I gas up the car a couple hours later in Salinas de Hidalgo, exhaustion pulling me down like an anchor. I crush an Adderall onto a discarded receipt on the dashboard and snort it. It won't last as long, but it will hit me hard and fast, and that's what I need right now. I'll follow it up in an hour with another pill that should last me for the rest of the drive down to Mexico City.

I debate pulling over and sleeping, finding another hotel room. But my paranoia is kicking into high gear and I don't want to be caught like that again. Any place I stop along this road is just going to leave me exposed. And it's not like Quetzalcoatl taking out Bustillo's men solves my problems.

I've pissed off a lot of people in the last couple of months, and I know some of them are still looking for me. I've given them the slip so far, but they have long memories. Once I get to the city it'll be a lot easier to hide.

But there's more to it than just paranoia. There's the feeling that I'm getting close. That this is almost done, for good or ill. I haven't had this feeling in fifteen years.

The fact that I'm slowly turning into a statue isn't why I'm doing this. Sure it helps, but even if I wasn't, I'd be on this same road making the same plans.

When my parents were killed I hunted the man down who did it. I waited for him with a car full of leaking propane tanks and when he stepped out of a warehouse in San Pedro I shoved a brick onto the gas pedal, ran it into him and set off the propane. It didn't kill him. I fed him to the ghosts for that.

I'm doing it again. This feels like sitting in the dark, packing the car full of propane. Santa Muerte murdered Lucy knowing I'd come looking for revenge, knowing she could steer me in whatever direction she wanted. My sister's murder was nothing more than a means to an end. I don't even care why, anymore. Or even what happens to me. I just want Santa Muerte destroyed, Mictlantecuhtli back in the ground where he belongs, and Tabitha, my one, big loose end tied up and squared away.

Revenge is one hell of a motivator.

The Adderall burns in my nostrils and a few minutes later I can feel the buzz starting behind my eyeballs. My mouth goes dry and my sinuses open up. I get that jittery feeling of fake confidence. I can drive all night. I can outpace the cartels chasing me down. I can get to Tabitha, get to Mictlan, set the world on fire. Everything will be just fine.

I know it's all bullshit. I have to remember that. Have to force myself. Confidence in this game is dangerous. The second I think I know what I'm doing, give in to that screaming Adderall voice and its promises, the euphoria, the confidence, I'm fucked. The Adderall focuses me, keeps me awake, but it's a lying sonofabitch. Tomorrow I'm going to pay for it. Right now I need it.

The next five hours go by in a blur. I crank the volume on the one tape stuck in the car's dilapidated cassette deck, a regrettable collection of Norteño music I picked up in Tijuana. I can't get the damn thing out of the machine.

Half the tracks are narcocorridos, songs glorifying the cartels, making them sound like fucking Robin Hoods instead of mass murderers. If I weren't tripping balls I wouldn't be listening to this crap. So I'm rocking out while I speed down the highway to Movimiento Alterado's "Sanguinarios del M1," a peppy little number where some narco in Culiacán goes on about how awesome it is to kill people. The accordions really tie the song together.

I pass small towns separated by miles of nothing. Truck stops, gas stations, bars. The terrain becomes more mountainous as I get closer to Mexico City, the population denser, the world more modern.

The magic changes, too. The taste and feel of the magic shifts based on location and people. New York doesn't taste like New Orleans. St. Paul doesn't taste like Miami.

My entire time here, the magic has tasted old, like dirt and clay and ashes. It's peasant magic, mostly, spells that come from the earth, magic tinged with the wrappings of faith, either for the Catholic god or some of the older ones. The magic in rural America has a similar feel, if not as wild.

And not nearly so full of death. I've occasionally seen a few shrines to Santa Muerte on the road and in those areas the magic tastes off. Not bad, evil, or anything stupid like that. Those aren't things that apply to magic. That's like calling water evil.

No, it feels resigned, stoic. Like it's given up. Magic takes on the characteristics of the lives around it. So much violence, so much corruption, I'm not surprised. And when I pass those areas I feel a surge of power. Death is death, and whether I like it or not, that's what my magic's tuned to.

That's never bothered me before. It's just something I accepted. But lately, especially here where the body count is in the tens of thousands, where there's this much suffering, I'm not sure how I feel about it.

As I get closer to Mexico City the magic starts to feel more modern, colder. Steel girders and old world marble. Electricity and blood. As the seat of the Aztec empire before the Spanish came along there's a lot of blood. It wants it. Demands it. The murder rate doesn't compare to places like Acapulco or Ciudad Juárez, but it's got a deeper history of it. Murder here has its roots in ritual and the city feeds on it.

Pulling in to Mexico City proper and the magic competes with itself. It wants to be ancient and modern at the same time. A constant back and forth struggle as the people embrace the future and cling to the past.

Everything about Mexico City has that same sense of old and new. Cobblestone streets and modern day traffic, glass-skinned skyscrapers and five-hundred-year-old cathedrals. The whole city is built over the ruins of Tenochtitlan, the seat of Aztec power before the Spanish came, while just to the north lies Teotihuacan, a city pre-dating the Aztecs by a thousand years. No one knows who built it. No one knows where they went.

It's a strange city, even by my standards. Hell, a strange country. It's easy to be swept up in this idea that it's nothing but a murder party 24/7. But it's not. There are people pushing back. People living their lives. When all you see is the fucked up parts of a place, you start to think that maybe that's all there is. But most people aren't really that bad.

All that goes out the window, of course, as soon as I start crossing the city toward Tepito. I sit in gridlock for more than three hours trying to go less than twenty miles. Makes Fridays on the 405 back in Los Angeles look like an empty four lane highway. This is not a city built for cars. Or people with anger management issues.

I finally manage to park the Cadillac a few blocks from Tepito proper. Almost the entire barrio is taken up by a massive open-air market and trying to get the car in there is an exercise in futility.

I dig through the messenger bag past bullets, cans of spray paint, locks of hair from convicted murderers, grave dust and ground up bone, salt for barring doorways and drawing circles, extra Sharpies and "Hi My Name Is" stickers. You know, the usual.

For about a year all this stuff was stuck in the Caddy's trunk where I couldn't get it. Restocking took forever and there are some things that I just couldn't find. One of a kind items, reagents that would take me a couple of years to get more of. I'm lucky the trunk is warded as well as it is, or most of it would be useless by now.

The dead side sucks, sure, but if you do it right it's a great place to stash your stuff.

After a minute I find what I'm looking for. A pair of handcuff bracelets with the chain connecting them removed. I check the cuffs. One of them has a large M engraved on the side, the other an S. It won't do to mix them up.

I bought the cuffs about eight years ago off a

dominatrix who works sex magic in Brooklyn. Goes by the name of Mistress Morgana. Has the phrase "a touch of the exotic" on her cards for her normal clientele. Real name's Eunice. She's a peach.

I put the cuff marked M around my left wrist and close it. I can feel a small pop of magic as the spells in the cuff activate. I slip the other into a pocket.

I've modified these heavily over the last six months from their original purpose as a bondage toy. Each cuff has spells engraved into the surface. I blurred out a bunch of them and added new ones with a Dremel.

I just hope they work.

I secure the Benelli in the trunk, check to make sure the Browning's loaded, and sling the messenger bag over my shoulder. I'm jittery and worn out, adrenaline replacing the Adderall.

I cross a couple of boulevards, dodge traffic and then I'm in Tepito. Here the streets are clogged with people shopping at makeshift stalls covered in blue and yellow tarps, folks selling their wares on blankets in the street. It's a massive twenty-five block swap meet of vibrant color and noise, thick smells of food and sweat, gasoline and rancid garbage.

Clothing, bootleg DVDs, computers, luggage, TVs, boomboxes, guns, drugs, second-hand odds and ends, people. If you're looking for it, chances are somebody in Tepito has it.

And throughout it all is Santa Muerte. There are shrines to the Bony Lady in half the stalls. You can buy small resin statues of her, candles, incense burners. Every botánica has prayers to her printed on fake parchment, rolled up and tied with a bow. Spells for love, vengeance, money, happiness. She is death and sex and magic and salvation. A dark reflection of the Virgin of Guadalupe, her only promise being that one day she will come for you. Even if there were no shrines to Santa Muerte in Tepito she'd be in the very fabric of the place.

I get stares as I wander through the streets. The out of place gringo. Some are curious, some sizing me up. To the ones who look like they might be trouble, I lower my sunglasses and give them a good, long look at my eyes. They scurry along like rats after that.

I don't know where Tabitha might be in this chaos. I gravitate toward the shrines, the stalls with life-size statues dressed in hot pink wedding dresses, gold and black fabric, dollar bills pasted to their plaster robes.

I ask about a Korean woman and get pointed in half a dozen directions. To the locals anyone Asian is Chinese. A while back a slew of Chinese immigrants showed and started buying up stalls and storefronts. Now they own most of the place. None of them are Tabitha.

A couple hours of wandering and my body tells me it's either time for food or more Adderall. I opt for the food. I hit a cart and pick up a Coke and a bowl of migas, garlic soup with pork bones and day old bolillos. I'm leaning against a light post, staying clear of the wires and cables snaking up from the stalls into the lamp to pirate power, finishing my second bowl when I see it. A small, unobtrusive carving in the post of one of the permanent stalls across from me. A tiny pentagram with two wavy lines beneath it. If you didn't know what it was, you probably wouldn't notice it.

The stall is a botánica selling folk remedies, prayer candles. But the carving tells me it sells other things, too. A woman, old, with skin cracked and brown like gnarled teak, sits behind the table watching me run my finger over the carving. I toss the paper bowl and plastic spoon in a trash can, or at least I hope it's a trash can, it's a little hard to tell out here, and walk over to her.

The magic set likes to keep things quiet, so when practitioners sell to other practitioners they use symbols based on old hobo signs. The pentagram with the wavy lines means this woman sells potions. It's only about the width of my thumb.

Of course, she could just be manning the stall and the real mage is out. There's a simple way to get to the bottom of that. I take a sip of the local pool of magic, taste its tang of chaos, its thickness of human sweat, the draw of money. Her eyebrows shoot up as she feels the pull on the magic. She does the same. It's a quick and easy way to identify other mages. It's not like we walk around wearing robes and pointy blue hats with stars and moons on them. And it's more polite than acting like dogs and sniffing each other's butts.

Now that we've established our bona fides I pull a wad of 200 peso notes out of my pocket and put them on the table. She smiles when she sees the bills, showing cracked and yellow teeth. "I'm looking for someone," I say. And the smile goes away.

"I don't know anybody," she says. She looks away from me.

I ignore and press on. "I'm looking for the type of someone who might be interested in your sorts of wares." She doesn't have any other customers, but the stalls are so close to each other that anyone could easily overhear our conversation so I keep it cryptic. Above all else, we don't want to scare the straights.

Her eyes lock onto mine, and I can tell she's pissed off. I've crossed a line. "I don't talk about my customers." I pull a U.S. hundred dollar bill so that only she can see it and slip it under the peso notes. The last thing I need is somebody trying to jump me for my cash. I already stand out, I don't need to grab more attention.

"How about a slightly different question? Have you seen anyone around recently who you think might be a potential customer? Somebody like me?" I lower my sunglasses so she can get a look at my eyes. She scowls at me. She knows I'm human. When something that isn't draws power from the pool it feels different.

She thinks about it a second, then sweeps the bills to her side of the table making them disappear faster than you can say abracadabra. "End of the street. Girl's got a storefront. She does fortunes. Felt a draw on some power coming from that direction a little while ago. So if it's not her, it's somebody close."

"Much obliged."

"Don't tell her I said anything," she says. "She frightens me."

"Why?"

"She smells like death," she says, crossing herself. "The same way you do."

Yep. That's Tabitha.

Chapter 7

The storefront is right where the woman said it would be, in a white brick building with blacked out windows. Hand-painted in bold, red letters above the door is a sign that reads ADIVINADORA. Fortuneteller.

Well, then. Let's go see what the future holds.

A little bell rings when I open the door and step inside. The sounds and sights of Tepito disappear behind me and it takes me a minute for my eyes to adjust to the gloom. When they do I can see what look like carnival sideshow banners hanging from the walls, brightly colored paintings with words beneath each one. LA LUNA showing a smiling, crescent moon, LA MUERTE showing a skeleton, and EL CORAZÓN showing an anatomical heart with veins and everything. I've seen these before but I can't quite place them.

Pedestals line the walls holding softly glowing veladoras, prayer candles inside tall, glass cylinders. Each one stamped with an image that could be mistaken for the Virgin of Guadalupe in the gloom if they weren't all surrounding different effigies of Santa Muerte on each pedestal.

There's one in her traditional wedding dress holding a scythe in one bony hand, a globe in the other. Another of her in a red traje de flamenca, a green cocktail dress, a long, flowing quinceañera dress. Almost a dozen Santa Muerte statues, none more than a few feet tall, stare out into the room through empty eyes.

Through an open door on the other side of the room sits a table covered with a dark tablecloth. A single light shines down from the ceiling. Two women sit at the table, one a young Latina girl in a black t-shirt and jeans, the other an Asian woman wearing a blue flannel shirt over a tank-top.

Tabitha's black hair is longer than the last time we met and falls down to the small of her back. It looks good. I push that thought out of my head.

She places cards in front of the girl, saying something too quietly for me to hear. She glances up, sees me, gives me a slight smile and returns to her cards.

I stay quiet, not wanting to intrude. Better to wait until the girl's gone. She's not a part of this and I need some time alone with Tabitha.

As Tabitha puts each card down I can feel the slight tug of magic in the air. This isn't some sideshow con game. Is she actually telling this girl's fortune? Or is she doing something else?

Why would the avatar of Santa Muerte be telling two-bit fortunes in a shithole barrio in Mexico City? What does she want from this girl?

A few minutes go by as Tabitha lays down each card and says a few words I can't make out. The girl begins crying and Tabitha puts a comforting hand on her shoulder. When con artists give you bad news it's tinged with hope, a solution. It's that hope that keeps the mark coming back. Maybe she's just really good, but this doesn't feel like that. I'm thinking Tabitha's telling this girl something she doesn't really want to hear.

I have a thought I don't want. What if Tabitha doesn't want anything from this girl? I push it aside as unproductive. I'm not here to analyze her motives.

After a bit the girl stands to leave and starts to hand Tabitha a wad of pesos with shaking hands. Tabitha takes the girl's hand in her own, leans in and whispers something to her.

There it is. The catch. The girl doesn't brighten, but the shaking stops. She tries to hand the money to Tabitha again, but she won't take it. Finally, she nods, puts the cash back in her pocket and leaves.

I step further back into the shadows and push out a little I'm-not-here magic. It won't keep the girl from seeing me, it's not as powerful as the Sharpie magic, but she won't really notice me or care that I'm here. She shuffles out of the building, drying her tears on her arm, disappearing into the chaos of Tepito.

"Eric," Tabitha says when the girl is gone. "It's good to see you."

"Tabitha. Or do I call you Santa Muerte? You should try some of that half-face calavera makeup. I think it'd suit you."

I want the words to bite, but they just come out flat. It's weird seeing her. I've been hunting her down for months and now, after all this time, here she is.

I thought I'd be furious, angry. Told myself I'd have to keep control. She's important for right now. If I kill her, and I'm going to kill her, it can't be until I have what I need from her.

But all I feel is sad. Used up.

"That's still a few weeks off," she says. "You can call me Tabitha."

She waves at the chair opposite her. "Have a seat. Want your fortune told? Find out what your future's like?"

"I already know it."

"Do you now?"

"It ends badly."

She picks up her cards, shuffles them. "Everyone's ends badly, Eric. But let's take a look, maybe see how you get there. Really, have a seat. I won't bite." She shows me a wicked grin. "Unless you want me to."

"What'd you tell the girl? She seemed pretty upset." I slide into the chair. I can feel the weight of the unconnected handcuff in my coat pocket. I have no idea if this plan will work, but if it's going to, it depends on me getting close to Tabitha. She doesn't seem to have a problem with me doing that.

"The truth, of course," she says. "Her father's dying. Cancer. He'll be gone in a day or two. But I gave her hope."

"Telling her he wouldn't suffer? That you could save him? What's Santa Muerte looking for from her?"

"She's not looking for anything," she says. "He's got pancreatic cancer. Believe me, he's suffering. No, I told her that his death isn't the end. It's just a change. You know this better than most."

"I also know that sometimes it is the end."

"Sure. If you arrange it that way. You'd know that better than most, too." She shrugs, continuing to shuffle her cards. "It's cancer, Eric. Nobody's feeding him to ghosts. Nobody's destroying his soul. Normal, everyday death. The kind that happens to most people. His soul will go wherever it's supposed to go."

It's weird seeing Tabitha like this. She's either played cold, cryptic death avatar, or friendly confidante and lover. Before I knew she was the avatar of Santa Muerte she acted confused. Magic was a new thing to her and she didn't understand what it was, or how it worked. Sad, lost, little Tabitha. And I ate it the fuck up. It was all bullshit. She knew the whole time, and I bought into the act.

But her vibe is different now. Calmer. More centered. I had wondered which of those two roles was the real her. Now I know it's neither of them.

I'm not sure what it says about me that I never caught on.

She fans the cards out face down in front of her. "But let's talk about your future. Pick a card."

"I'm not here to play games," I say. "I'm here to take you with me."

"Oh, my," she says, her hand to her chest, eyes going wide in mock surprise. "An invitation from a man! Whatever will I do? I may swoon! Or is this a kidnapping? I can do kidnapping. Do I have to ride in the trunk? Fine. I'll come with you. But first, pick a card."

This isn't what I was expecting, and I don't trust it. "You're making this way too easy," I say.

"If you like I can make a scene when we leave. Have you throw me over your shoulder, kick my feet? Squeal like a Disney princess?" Her voice goes flat. "Help. Help. No? Not convincing?"

"What's the catch?"

"The catch is that you. Pick. A. Card."

"All right." I tap a card on the left.

"And you said you weren't here to play games." She flips over the card and I feel a tiny flush of magic in the air. The card is of a man in blue pants and a red shirt, a knife in his hand, blood on the blade. EL VALIENTE at the bottom. The Brave.

"Por qué le corres cobarde, trayendo tan buen puñal," she says.

"'Why would you run, coward, you brought such a good knife,'" I say. Now I remember where I've seen the pictures on the walls. "These aren't tarot cards. These are Lotería cards."

"Move to the head of the class."

"Aren't you supposed to play bingo with these?" I say. From what I can remember Lotería is a game where everyone gets a board with a set of images on it, and a caller pulls a card from the deck, announcing it with the card's catch phrase, a short little nonsense saying. The first person to fill a row, column, or square on their card wins.

"What, you can't do divination with playing cards or tea leaves?" she says.

"Point. So, what, that's me? The guy with the knife?"

"I'd say it fits. Kind of looks like you. Angry, impulsive, easily distracted by shiny objects. And, hey, you do have a knife."

She's talking about Mictlantecuhtli's god-killing obsidian blade. I almost murdered her with it the last time we met when she revealed herself as Santa Muerte's avatar. I'm still not sure if that was a missed opportunity or not.

"Except the card says I'm running," I say.

"What makes you think you're not?"

I ignore the comment and point to another card. "Great. I picked a card. Let's go." I start to stand.

"What's the hurry, lover?" she says. "Slow it down.

Take your time. A lady doesn't like to be rushed. It's bad form. Pick another."

"You said pick a card. *A* card."

"And now I'm telling you to pick another one."

I put my finger down onto one of the cards without looking. I feel that same tug of magic.

"Now that wasn't so hard was it? These are the things that oppose you."

"If that's not a picture of you or Santa Muerte I'll be awful surprised."

Everybody who practices cartomancy has their own way of doing it. I've known diviners who can tell your life story from a single card, and others who'll go through half a deck. It's not so much a matter of talent as it is of style.

She flips a card, LA MUERTE. A skeleton with a scythe. "That's—"

"Oh, look. I was right," I say.

She glares at me until I pick another. She flips it over. LA CORONA. A red and gold crown. "El sombrero de los reyes."

"The king's hat," I say. "Santa Muerte and Mictlante-cuhtli. Tell me something I don't already know." I tap another and she flips it.

EL ALACRÁN. The scorpion. "El que con la cola pica, le dan una paliza."

"'The one with the tail that bites, beat him'? The hell is that supposed to mean?"

She shrugs. "Could be anything. A warning? A command? Beat on the one who betrays you? Maybe it's not even talking about you."

"Oh, it's talking about me," I say. These days that's my whole raison d'être.

She gives me a considering look. "Be that as it may," she says, "these are the things that oppose you. Death, the Crown, the Scorpion. One card to go. Do you want to see how it all turns out?"

Death and the Crown I understand. Or at least I think I do. But the Scorpion? Betrayal? Triumphing over betrayal? Which betrayal? Whose? Christ knows there's plenty to go around.

That's the problem with divination. It's a tiny view of a larger picture. Like trying to get the layout of a house by looking through the front door keyhole.

I touch another. "Hit me."

Now I'm honestly curious. If I hadn't felt the magic when she flipped the first card I'd call bullshit on this. But it's there and that third card was unexpected. Why that image? Scorpions are betrayers. Hitting you by surprise with their poisonous tails. It's in their natures. And a beating, not a killing.

She flips the final card.

EL CORAZÓN. The picture is an anatomical heart, bright red. For a second it looks as though it's actually pumping. "No me extrañes corazón, que regreso en el camión."

"'Don't miss me love, I'm coming back on the . . . bus?'" I'm returning to something? Something's returning to me? Love? I have a hard time believing that. And how the hell does it fit into any of this?

"Lotería isn't exactly known for its stunning poetry, but it sounds promising," Tabitha says. "There are all kinds of love, you know. Maybe it's not all bad news."

"A bus trip?"

"It's a metaphor. Unless it's not. You never know with these things."

"Why are you doing this?" The room suddenly fills with the scent of cigar smoke and roses. I know that smell. I was wondering when this was going to happen.

"I'm trying to help you do what you agreed to do." Tabitha's voice shifts, goes hollow, her face goes gaunt, skin caving in to press against bone. Her eyes go as black as mine. "Husband."

"Oh. Hi, honey. Fancy meeting you here."

"You delay the inevitable," Santa Muerte says through Tabitha's mouth. Or maybe it's hers now. I'm really not sure. "You have Mictlantecuhtli's blade. You are tied to him and he to you. In the blink of an eye you can find his tomb and kill him. Why haven't you?"

"I work in mysterious ways," I say and waggle my fingers at her. "And, you know, his tomb's full of demons."

A while back I found myself looking for a place to stuff a bunch of demons that got loose in a storage unit in L.A. The only thing I could think of at the time was to open a hole into Mictlantecuhtli's tomb and dump them there. It was a dick move, but it wasn't like he was really using all that space.

Didn't occur to me at the time that that might be a problem for me later. Well, now it's later and it's a problem. Going in there to take him out is going to be a bit of a challenge.

"I don't need you watching over my shoulder while I crack that particular nut," I say. "Seriously, I got this covered."

She cocks her head to the side, black eyes regarding me with silent judgment. "You do not trust me," she says.

"The hell you say! Me? Not trust you? Killing Lucy, locking me up in this jade prison, getting Alex killed, threatening Vivian, duping me with Tabitha. Honestly, what's not to trust?"

"I would know your plans."

I reach over and give her a condescending pat on the hand. And I'd like to know hers. "Don't you worry your pretty, little death goddess head over it, sweetie. I got this."

The obsidian blade is heavy in my coat pocket. It would be so easy to pull it out and stick it in her throat right now. But that wouldn't kill Santa Muerte, just kill Tabitha. Tempting though it might be, it's not the right time. I still need her.

She gives my hand a sour look and I'm not sure if that's Santa Muerte doing it or Tabitha. "Why are you so interested in my avatar?" she says.

"I'm curious, how much of her is left in there?" I ask. "Anything? Or is she just a shell? A puppet for you to talk through?"

"We are joined," she says. "That is enough. How else should I speak with you? You've inscribed so many wards against me on your skin I can't see you except through her eyes."

The last time I spoke with Santa Muerte was on the side of the road outside of Los Angeles after talking to the Wind. She was able to track me down then, though she couldn't see me. I've added spells to my tattoos, found a couple of charms to hang from my neck to bolster the effect, try to push her further away. But I haven't been sure they really worked. Now I know.

"Thanks for the confirmation. I was hoping you'd say that." I clamp down on her hand with mine. She jerks back with inhuman strength, the muscles of her wrist wasted so that the bones show through, but I hang on. I pull the handcuff from my pocket with my other hand and slap it around her wrist.

The effect is immediate. The black fades from Tabitha's eyes. Her body puffs out from its skeletal shape and goes rigid, snapping her out of her chair to hit the floor hard. Her limbs jerk like she's having a seizure, while a thin whine escapes her lips. A moment later she lies still, staring blank-eyed at the ceiling.

On to stage two.

Chapter 8

Tabitha bolts awake in the passenger seat of the Eldorado, looking around confused. I've been driving through Mexico City for the last half hour waiting, hoping she'd wake up. She's no good to me dead.

"You got the Caddy back," she says.

"That's what you're gonna open with?" I say. "No, 'what the hell did you do to me, Eric?'"

"I know what you did to me," she says, pinching the bridge of her nose. "You've cut me off. Hidden me from her. The way you've hidden yourself." She inspects the cuff around her wrist, traces the runes Dremelled into its surface, the conspicuous S stamped on its side. "Wish I'd known your kink sooner. We could have had a lot more fun together. I assume you've got the master for this slave?" I lift my arm and show her the matching cuff on my wrist.

She says nothing for a long time, just stares at my wrist. I realize what she's looking at and drop my arm. The sleeve of my jacket covers the jade poking out from beneath it.

"I hadn't realized you were so far gone," she says.

"Not so far gone I can't do something about it."

I keep my eyes on the road, but I can feel hers on me. The silence stretches between us until she says, "I can't hear her. I've had her in my head for so long and now I can't hear her. It's very . . . quiet."

"I thought you were supposed to *be* Santa Muerte," I say.

"And I thought you were supposed to be Mictlante-cuhtli," she snaps. No matter how calm she tries to come off, she's on edge. "I'm her as much as I need to be. I have a piece of her in me. Just like you've got a piece of him in you."

"I don't—"

"Please. You might not be able to hear him but you still have some of his power. You're still turning into jade. You and I might be different in the particulars, but we're not that different. You've blocked my link to her, but you can't pull her out of me. Just like you can't pull him out of you."

When I had Mictlantecuhtli talking to me he took the form of my dead friend Alex. As I got more ensorcelled ink, spells in my tattoos to block him and Santa Muerte, he'd appear to me less and less. Soon he was nothing more than a hint of a whisper I could ignore. Eventually I blocked him entirely.

I did the same thing to the handcuffs. As long as she's got that on, and it's not coming off without my say so, she's cut off from Santa Muerte.

Getting rid of Mictlantecuhtli didn't really affect me. I'd only had him in my head a short while. But Tabitha, she's been linked to Santa Muerte a lot longer. Years. No wonder she's on edge.

She worries at the cuff with her hand. "So where to

now, lover? Or are we just going to drive around Mexico City until you turn into a piece of pottery?"

"Need a good way into Mictlan."

"You've got a good way into Mictlan."

"One that doesn't end with me turning into a green garden gnome."

"Okay. Muerte could have taken you there. Hell, she could have dumped you right in front of Mictlante-cuhtli." She pauses, chewing her lip in thought. "Unless you didn't want her help."

"Hey, you're quick."

"So that's what this is about? You kidnap me, break my link to Santa Muerte and, what, make me tell you how to get into Mictlan so you can kill my goddess?"

"I haven't decided if I'm going to kill her, yet."

"Oh, horseshit," she says. "You decided that a long time ago. I told her not to go after your sister. She was just going to piss you off by doing that."

"I thought—"

She tips her head back, closes her eyes. "That I don't have my own opinions? That's not how this works. Our lines blur, but it doesn't mean I don't have my own iden-tity. Christ my head hurts."

Tabitha tried to dissuade Santa Muerte from killing Lucy? I don't know how to feel about this information. I don't even know if I trust it. And I'm not sure how much difference it makes if it's true.

"Goddammit, you're fucking with my head," I say. "Why?"

She cracks one eye open. "I'm fucking with *your* head? I'm the one with a migraine over here. Muerte didn't strip me out of this body. I'm not a puppet. She's not like that."

"I meant why did you tell her to leave Lucy alone? Just because you thought I'd come after her?"

"Because Lucy was innocent," Tabitha says. "Because this wasn't about her. Hell, it's not even about you and I."

"Then what is it about?"

"You know there are bigger things than us, right? There's a lot of fucked up out there and some of us would like to change it. But I wouldn't expect you to know anything about that."

"Okay, what the actual fuck are you talking about?"

"It's about the souls scraping in the dust of Mictlan," she says. "It's about the countless dead from half a millennia ago. It's about the spirits she's responsible for since she became Santa Muerte. Mictlan's broken, Eric. Can you even conceive of that? A decrepit heaven that might as well be Hell. She has a responsibility and she takes it seriously. And she'll do anything it takes to make it whole."

"And why do you care about that? And what the hell do I have to do with any of this?"

"Because there are a lot of broken things and this is one I can fix. And you? You're not some Chosen One, Eric," Tabitha says. "That shit doesn't happen. You were just the right person at the right time. There aren't that many necromancers around, or hadn't you noticed? Santa Muerte needed someone tuned to the Dead. Someone with enough power in them that they wouldn't burn out. She's been waiting for you for a very long time."

Necromancy is an exclusive club inside an exclusive club. Doesn't mean it's better. Psychopaths are a pretty exclusive club for humanity, too. You don't see anybody signing up for that action. There just aren't a lot of us around. No idea why. I'm sure there's some enterprising mage out there who's tried to answer that with math.

But it's not like I'm the only one around. Or necessarily the most powerful. We don't exactly work together. I only know of a handful, though I've heard rumors there are more of us around than I've met. Why would Santa Muerte need to wait five hundred years?

"What about you?" I say. "She just happened to come by some girl dying in a ditch by the side of the road and thought, 'Yeah, she'll do'?"

Tabitha gives me a smirk. "She's been waiting for me for a very long time, too."

It takes me a second to realize what she means. "You are fucking kidding me." She wasn't waiting for one necromancer. She was waiting for two. "Fucking prove it."

"In the last five minutes we've passed twelve Wanderers, three Haunts and at least two Echoes. I've always called them Playbacks, but I like Echo better."

I think back. She's right. "Playbacks, huh? Okay. How'd the last one we pass die?" This isn't something you can guess at. She could have made up the numbers and I could have miscounted. But no matter how similarly people die, we all go out in our own way.

"Shot in her car waiting at a light. I only caught a glimpse of the car around her, but I'd say, late 1940s? Her hair was up in a bun. She was smoking a cigarette."

"I didn't see the cigarette. And you're saying you didn't get that ability from Santa Muerte?"

"You disconnected me from her, remember? This is all me, baby."

"And I disconnected myself from her and Mictlantecuhtli, too, but I can still use his power. I still have the abilities being married to her got me."

"Believe it or not, Eric. I don't really care. I know what I am. I don't need to prove it to you. And I know why I'm doing what I'm doing."

Interesting. So Santa Muerte needed two necromancers at the same time. One for her and one for Mictlantecuhtli? Did Tabitha get the same treatment I did? Did she get lured into it the same way?

When I'd seen her last, Tabitha, or maybe it was Santa Muerte talking through her, I don't really know, told me that she'd been killed and brought back by Santa Muerte putting a piece of her essence into her. Was that true, or just a convenient lie? And if it was true, and Tabitha knows it . . .

"Santa Muerte didn't murder you, did she?" I ask.

"Oh, she killed me," she says. "Forced my car off the side of the freeway, just like I told you."

"All right, but that's not what I asked. You knew it was coming. You agreed to it."

She looks defiant. I've hit a nerve. This is important to her. "Yes," she says.

"And she didn't kill me because . . . ?"

"She didn't have to kill you. Just marry you. And despite what some people might think, they're not the same thing. For me to be closer to her, linked more directly as her avatar, I had to connect with her more fully."

"Which meant you dying," I say. "So you signed up for this. Did you know what was going to happen?"

"Of course I did. She talked to me about it. Explained the whole thing. She needed an avatar. She asked me to be it. I chose this, Eric. Just like you did."

"I didn't—"

"Nobody put a shotgun to your head and made you do it."

She's got me there, though I'd argue I was manipu-
lated and didn't know what I was signing up for. I don't,
though. What's the point?

She did it for a cause. People who care. My parents
were like that. Always wanting to do the right thing.
Been running into that a lot, lately. I can never quite
figure out why. It's like some puzzle box I can't get open.
I mean, I understand why people care about things,
about making the world better. I'm just not sure why I
don't.

"I just don't get it is all," I say.

"Figure it out. Or don't. I don't owe you an explana-
tion, Eric. I have a thing to do. A thing I believe in. And
I'm sorry you got roped into this the way you did. I really
think if you'd known beforehand that it was all of Mictlan at stake, you'd have signed on all on your own."

"Yeah? Well, I didn't. And I'm not gonna be a part of it."

She laughs. "It's too late for that, lover," she says. "Too
late by a long shot."

I drum my fingers on the steering wheel in annoyance,
silence stretching between us. Finally I say, "So are you
going to show me a way into Mictlan or what?"

"Go to Mitla, south of here. It's—"

"The entrance to Mictlan," I say. "Yeah, I know. It's
the fucking front door. I need something a little more
discreet."

Mitla is a site in Oaxaca that dates back to the Zapo-
tecs almost three thousand years ago until it fell to the
Aztecs in the late 1400s. Not quite a city, not quite a palace, not quite a temple. When Cortés showed up it was
the seat of their religious power where their highest
priests lived and worked. He compared it to the Vatican,
compared their high priest to the Pope.

And it holds the entrance to Mictlan.

Most people can't see it, of course. Otherwise tourists and old archaeologists would be falling into the goddamn thing all the time. Instead of pyramids like in Chichén Itzá, it's all low, flat buildings. Closer to the ground. Fitting for a hole to the underworld.

I don't know if souls bound for Mictlan pass through there or if they go in some other way, but it's the main entrance. I go through that gate it's a good bet Santa Muerte's going to know pretty goddamn quick.

"You could always kill yourself."

"Ha."

"Why should I help you?" she says. "I don't agree with what Muerte did to you, and I'm sorry it happened. Lucy shouldn't have been killed. But you're siding with Mictlantecuhtli. We both know that. I won't help you kill Santa Muerte for revenge."

"No, you'll just use me as a convenient fall guy for her plan to fix Mictlan."

"Yes," she says. "I will. It's important. And I won't let you jeopardize that by murdering her."

"Just because I don't want her looking over my shoulder doesn't mean I'm going to kill her." She arches an eyebrow at me. "Okay, fine. Yes, I'm going to kill her. But I'm going to kill Mictlantecuhtli, too. She wants that, right? So if you get me in there, I promise I'll go after him first." Not a difficult thing to promise. I'm already planning on doing that.

She runs her hands over the red, leather seat of the Caddy, the cracked dashboard. "You haven't taken very good care of this thing."

"It was sitting in the land of the dead for a year. Don't change the subject."

"Yeah, sitting over there would do it." She traces her fingers across the windshield. "Wards on the glass kept the worst of it out, then?"

"More or less."

"Must have been a pain in the ass getting it back."

"It was. Took forever to find it. Somebody put a shipping container over it on the living side. I had to push the goddamn thing twenty feet before I could bring it over. At least I finally got all my stuff back."

"You're determined."

"Stubborn as a bulldog."

"I was going to go with jackass, but sure. Even if you kill Mictlantecuhtli you're still going to try killing Santa Muerte."

"But if you come with me maybe you'll be able to stop me."

I knew there was no way to convince her that I was on the up and up. The cuffs allow for a certain amount of compulsion. It's what they're designed for after all. She won't want to get too far away from me.

So I figure if I give her the thing she wants, Mictlante-cuhtli dead, and dangle the opportunity to keep me from doing the same to Santa Muerte in front of her, maybe she'll bite. She thinks about it, fingers tapping against her legs.

"And if I don't, you're stubborn enough to find another way to do it." She lets out a sigh and shakes her head. "I'm so going to regret this. Isla de las Muñecas. South of here in the canals of Xochimilco."

"Island of the Dolls? Sounds creepy."

"Heh. Yeah, that's a word for it."

Chapter 9

The sun is setting by the time we get out of the more modern parts of the city center and into Xochimilco. A deep orange glow in the western sky fades into blue.

Things change fast here. Fifteen minutes ago we passed a modern football stadium. Now we're in a dense sprawl of narrow, potholed streets, weathered cinderblock buildings.

As Tabitha directs me through the winding streets, barely more than alleys, the cinderblock sprawl gives way to canals where ramshackle huts and small gardens share space with strawberry trees, squat tepozanes, massive Montezuma cypresses and ocotes. The air smells green and swampy, the only sound the thrumming of the Eldorado's V-8.

"So, what, is there a bridge or something to get to this island?" For a short bit we parallel one of the canals, a wide, dark green river of slow moving water. Brightly painted trajineras, tourist gondolas for lazing down the canal, are heading back to their docks. Boats with vendors selling food and drinks aren't far behind them.

"Nope," she says. "Take a left there and park the car.

You'll have to leave the Caddy here." I do as she says, stopping at a dirt track that heads toward a small dock at the edge of the water. A small dinghy is tied up at the end of it.

"You're kidding me."

"It's that or swim. Come on." She gets out of the car. I grab my messenger bag out of the back seat, get out, pop the trunk to retrieve the Benelli. Tabitha stares at me as I come down to the dock slinging the shotgun over my shoulder.

"What the hell do you think you're going to do with that?" she says. "Everybody in there is already dead."

"Better to have a shotgun and not need it, than to need a shotgun and not have it." She shakes her head and unties the boat as I get in and grab the oars.

"All right, which way?"

"Just follow the current. You'll know when you get there."

She pushes us off and I row down the canal. No sound but the water lapping against the boat, the buzz of insects. The night comes on quickly and soon we're traveling in almost complete darkness, the only light coming from the shacks on the shore.

Is she leading me into a trap? And what would that even be? She's not going to try to kill me. Run away? She won't get far with the cuff on her hand. The only thing I can think of is that she'll somehow contact Santa Muerte before I can stop her and tell her where I am and what I'm doing.

That's a risk I'm willing to take. I can't do anything out here. I need to get into Mictlan. Once I get inside eventually Santa Muerte will figure it out, whether I try to stop Tabitha or not. All I can do is delay it a little.

If Tabitha's telling the truth, and there's a gate to

Mictlan on this island, then once I get inside the rest is going to be a whole lot of luck. My only exposure to the place has been driving through an extension of it in Los Angeles and standing in Mictlantecuhtli's tomb. It's not like they make maps for the place.

All I have to go on are legends and stories. And not all of them agree with each other. Some stories, the dead are ushered through the gates of Mictlan by Quetzalcoatl. Others say the dead are accompanied by a dog who helps them on their way. It takes four years of hard travel to reach their final judgment.

I find myself wondering what happens to the Dead now that Quetzalcoatl's on the outs. Do they show up on their own without him to push them through? Maybe he's not really needed and he's pissed off things are working fine without him. Wouldn't surprise me. He seems pretty bitter about things.

Mictlan has nine levels each with their own challenges and passages; a mountain made of obsidian blades, a terrifying wind, a rain of arrows, wild beasts and more. And at the end of that journey the soul finally comes to rest in a place called Chicunamictlan.

Honestly, that sounds like a pretty fucked up afterlife. I don't plan on going through any of it.

My plan, such as it is, is to get through the gates, get my bearings and find Mictlantecuhtli's tomb. I'd hoped to take the Caddy, but that's not happening. So I expect a lot of walking. Worst case I give in and tap into Mictlantecuhtli's power, open a hole to his tomb and shank him. Yeah, I know. It's a shitty plan.

"You sure you want to do this?" Tabitha says, breaking the silence. All I can see of her is her silhouette against the night sky and the glow of lights along the canal.

"I don't see how I have much choice."

"You always have a choice," she says. "You chose to come down here. You chose vengeance."

"I'm choosing to stay alive."

"By destroying two beings thousands of years old."

"Maybe they shouldn't have fucked with me, then."

"Do you know why I'm showing you this way into Mictlan?" she says.

"So you can jump me the second it's convenient?"

She laughs. "That, yes. But more so you can see for yourself what Santa Muerte's trying to save. It's a broken place. Even when the dead reach their end it's nothing but suffering. She wants to change that. Wants to make it what it's supposed to be."

"And you? Is that what you want? Or is that what she wants you to want?" She gives me a flat stare, says nothing, so I drop it.

"How close are the legends to the reality?" I say. "A mountain of obsidian knives? Wild beasts that tear your heart out? Is that worth saving? How is that not suffering?"

"It's suffering with a purpose. The trials are meant to cleanse the soul," she says. "When they're done there's supposed to be an end to it. But they don't get that end now. It might as well be hell."

"Yeah, well, that's not my problem."

"I know you well enough by now to say you're full of shit, Eric."

"Dead is dead," I say. "It happens. People die, souls move on. It's natural. If that's where they're supposed to end up, then that's where they're supposed to end up. I don't have a problem with people dying."

"You act like you don't care, but we both know that's

an act. You might not have a problem with death, but you sure as hell have a problem with suffering, don't you? If Lucy had just died, would you be here? If she'd been in a car accident, say, or even murdered if it was quick? I don't think so. I think you're here, I think Santa Muerte caught you, because she made your sister suffer."

I stop rowing, say nothing for a long time. We float in the current, lazily heading down the canal, my hands tight on the oars. I want to beat her, throw her over the side and leave her there.

"Strike a nerve?"

"How much further is this place?" I say.

"Not far. Can't you feel it?"

I tune out the background of magic, the whispers of old dead. And then, just on the edge of perception, there it is. Haunts. A lot of them, but weak. And at the edge of my hearing a sound I can't quite identify.

"Is that crying?" I look over my shoulder and see a dim glow in the distance. Tiny pinpricks of light swarm the far shore like hovering fireflies. I start rowing toward the sound.

The closer we get, the louder the sound and the more I can feel the dead. The light becomes brighter, the noise a cacophony. A constant wailing of anguish, torture, agony. What the hell is over here?

I let the boat bump against a row of tires tied to short wooden pilings to hold the shore together. I stare at the scene in front of me.

True to its name Isla de las Muñecas is covered in dolls. Perched in the crooks of trees, wrapped to branches with wire, duct taped to a couple of tiny shacks, strung from the timbers of a decaying, log fence. Large and small, weathered and cracked and coated with grime.

Kewpie dolls, porcelain dolls, clown dolls, rag dolls, troll dolls, bobbleheads, marionettes, puppets.

And nailed to each doll is a child's screaming ghost.

Like the dolls they're all different types. Some look to be infants, some toddlers. None looks to be more than five or six years old. Their phantom light casts everything in a pale, blue glow that casts erratic shadows as they writhe in their plastic prisons, struggle against their bonds.

"Jesus fucking Christ."

"I'm pretty sure he's not here," Tabitha says, sadness and resignation in her voice. Even she's not immune to this psychic onslaught. She steps out of the boat and onto the shore.

"What the hell is all this?" I follow her, consider tying the boat, but don't see anything to secure it with. Suppose it doesn't matter. I doubt I'll be coming out this way again. If I ever come out at all.

"It's a side door to Mictlan," she says pitching her voice above the ghostly noise. If anyone else were with us they would wonder why we were shouting. "The man who built this place didn't know what he was doing. Story goes he found a little girl drowned in the canal. Tried to save her and couldn't. Later he found a doll floating in the canal and stuck it in a tree. Then he hung more and more dolls. Did it for fifty years. Folks figured he was still trying to save that girl, I guess."

We walk past the walls of shrieking ghosts staring at us from the trees, the doll heads swiveling to track us. Some of them twitch against the wires holding them in place. One of them falls to the ground.

Tabitha kneels to the ground and picks up the doll, and the child's spirit inside stops screaming. She gently places it back into the crook of the tree, holds it for a moment in place, her hand against its porcelain face. When she steps away its screams rejoin the cacophony of the damned.

"So what's the real story?"

"Pretty much the same thing," she says. "Only he killed the girl in the canal and then went on to murder the rest. He'd lure them with promises of candy or money. And then he'd bring them here and drown them. He kept pieces of them, a lock of hair, a finger. There are a few eyes around here, I'm sure. He'd put them into the dolls as trophies. I don't think he knew the dolls would trap their souls. But if he did, he probably would have gotten off on it."

"What happened to him?" I hope somebody strung him up and used him as a piñata with a machete.

"Drowned in the canal. Ironic, when you think about it. Here it is." We stop at a wide break in the trees overgrown with vines. I can see a light shining through. She parts the vines to reveal a shimmering wall of red light wide enough to walk through hanging between the branches.

"Well, that doesn't look ominous at all."

She cocks a thumb over her shoulder. "All that suffering back there? All those ghosts? It made this. It called to it and the door opened. That's what Mictlan has become. Their suffering tore a hole into it."

"Sounds like a great place." I can't wait to burn it down.

"It was. A long time ago. And there are a couple of spots that still are."

"You're okay with all that back there?" I say.

She looks past me at the strung up dolls, the shrieking ghosts of children. Her face goes flat, she chews her lower lip. Picking her words? Rationalizing what this island is so she can keep this back door open?

"No," she says finally. "I just can't do anything about it."

"And how does Santa Muerte feel?"

She ignores the question, and I think that's answer enough. She steps closer to the portal. All sly smiles and snark again. "Well, we're here. Care to carry me over the threshold, lover?"

"Ladies first," I say.

"Sure you trust me? I might run off. Track down Santa Muerte. Throw a wrench in your plans."

"You won't," I say. "Not until I've killed Mictlantecuhtli."

"You're awfully trusting."

"No, just banking on the selfishness of human behavior."

"Fair point. See you on the other side."

She steps through, the red light swallowing her up. I don't think she'll take off, and if she does she won't get very far with that cuff on her wrist. I don't want her waiting any longer than necessary in case she gets ideas. It's a risk, but I have to do this.

The wailing ghosts of murdered children stare at me with hungry eyes, mouths working like gasping fish. Who knows how far gone they are, trapped in this hell? I doubt they remember who they are, where they're from. All they know is pain and hunger.

Tabitha might not be able to do anything about it, but I sure as hell can.

The dolls are the key. They hold the tortured souls in as if they're wrapped in barbed wire. I could free them. But I'd have to do it one by one and with this many it could take hours, maybe even days.

I don't have time to let them loose one by one. But maybe I have another way. I pull Quetzalcoatl's lighter from my pocket. He said it would burn anything. I wonder how far the flames will spread. Far enough, I hope, to clean this island. Far enough to set them free.

I flip it open and flick the striker until I get a low, blue flame. It doesn't look any different from a normal one. Quetzalcoatl said in Mictlan it would burn the whole place to the ground. I really, really hope it doesn't spread quite so far on this side of the veil.

I touch the lighter to the ground where it catches on dead leaves, engulfs them in blue fire. The flames spread with unnatural speed, crawling across the moist earth, up into the trees.

The screams of the children rise in pitch and volume and I wonder if I've made things worse. Panicked shrieks as the flames tear them from their prisons. Plastic melts, porcelain cracks. The dolls explode from the heat. Twisted wires holding them in place crumble to dust. Thick gouts of black smoke belch toward the sky and the shacks and fence are consumed.

The screams die as each ghost pulls itself free from its prison, only to be replaced with a terrified mewling. Shredded souls trapped so long with their murderer they don't know what to do. They swarm me, buzzing around me like bees.

I don't know where they need to go, either. Like all ghosts, they'll fade away, bleed off to whatever promised land awaits them. But it could take time. Until then they're going to be miserable and afraid. I don't know how to help them. I could do an exorcism, but that takes time and materials. I don't have enough of either. Setting them free is the best I can do.

The flames hit the water, lapping at the shore, and set it to boiling before dying out. It's persistent, I'll give it that. In the wrong hands the lighter could really fuck things up.

I watch the island burn until the flames threaten to turn back on me. I wait as long as I dare, smoke making my eyes sting, making it hard to breathe. I cover my mouth and wait. The final doll cracks open and the tormented child's soul inside it bursts free.

This island of trapped children is just the portal to Mictlan. Jesus. Is it this bad inside? Am I walking into Hell here? Have I bitten off more than I can chew?

Suppose it doesn't matter. I'm committed. I step through the portal, letting Mictlan swallow me up, shaken and afraid. Is this whole thing just a stunningly bad idea?

Guess I'll find out.

Chapter 10

The oppressive heat from the flames gives way to the dry, cracking heat of a desert at high noon. Instead of the stink of smoke and burning plastic the air is filled with the fetid stench of blood and rot.

Like when I went to Mictlan by way of Los Angeles the landscape is almost identical in structure if not form. The canal behind me is a thick river of blood. The ground is made of shattered skulls, the trees are bone. Flaps of desiccated skin and sinew hang from the branches in a sick mockery of leaves. Nearby I can see the buildings of the barrio we drove through to get here, each building constructed from bones.

In the distance where Mexico City proper should be are tall, bone pyramids that rise toward the sky. I can see a shimmer of red along their sides, light reflected up from something I can't see. The buildings surrounding it are low and compact, crazy sprawl of the city nothing like the one on the living side. Beyond that I see a landscape of bleached bone, mountains of black glass.

Tabitha sits on a bleached pile of skulls waiting for me, the bone trees swaying their flesh leaves in the breeze. "Took you a while," she says. She stands, frowning at me. Comes close and runs a finger across my forehead, coming away with it covered in soot. Behind me the portal to Isla de las Muñecas shudders, the light changing from a deep red to a pale blue.

It shatters like glass, exploding shards of light over us with a sound like a bomb going off. We both instinctively duck, but when the light hits us it fades into nothing.

"What the hell did you do?" The way she says it doesn't sound like an accusation.

I wipe soot from my face with the back of my hand, spit ash out of my mouth. "Set something right. So where are we?"

From the look on her face she wants to ask more but doesn't. She's not stupid. She knows what I did. Even if she doesn't know how I did it.

"Past some of the rougher spots," she says. "We have the obsidian mountains to get through, but the worst of those are behind us. No knives flaying the skin from our bones."

"That's a plus."

"It's not an easy hike to get to Mictlantecuhtli's tomb. All the buildings this far out are obstacles more than anything. Window dressing and not much else. I know a bit of a shortcut nearby. It sucks, but it beats slogging through all this crap."

I nod toward Mexico City and the bone pyramids. "And that?"

If I'm oriented right, on the living side that area would be either Tenochtitlan or Tlatelolco, two Aztec cities that sat where Mexico City is today. But these pyramids here are larger than I recall from the books I've read about them. Instead of clean lines and geometric steps, these are misshapen, lopsided, twisted in weird ways.

"A joke," she says. "Mictlantecuhtli built those to 'honor' Huitzilopochtli. Tenochtitlan was his home and he demanded sacrifices at his temples. Sun god, warrior god. Mictlantecuhtli thought he was an asshole, so he made a mockery of his temples and the city."

The landscape isn't exactly based on the area today, and it isn't exactly from five hundred years ago. Out here on Isla de las Muñecas it's largely the same as it is in the living world. But further afield, with the pyramids in the distance, it's clearly Tenochtitlan. Which means that red reflected light is probably Lake Texcoco where the city sat on an island before the Spanish started draining the water.

A canal full of blood is one thing, but a whole lake? Ugh.

"Nothing for Tlaloc?" Huitzilopochtli and Tlaloc, sun god and rain god, ruled in this area, sometimes sharing space, certainly sharing sacrifices. I think back to the map of Mexico City. I passed their twin temples out by the Mexico City Cathedral. That gives me a reference point. I feel a little better knowing roughly where we are.

Tabitha shrugs. "Mictlantecuhtli didn't much care about him."

"Isn't Quetzalcoatl supposed to be here to usher the dead into Mictlan? I don't see him." And of course I don't expect to. He wants this place to burn. If he were here, he'd do it himself. But I'm curious about why.

"At the main entrance down in Mitla, not here. And

he hasn't done it in about five hundred years. There was a disagreement. He sided with the Spanish."

"Why? Domestic disputes between gods seem to be a thing around here."

Interesting. Mictlantecuhtli told me about how a Spanish priest led an army of Conquistadores into Mictlan in the hopes that they could use it as a springboard to take the other lands of the Aztec gods. He said he lured them into a trap, cut them off from their weapon, but never said what that weapon was.

Was it Quetzalcoatl? It might explain how the Spanish did so well against the Aztec gods, if not the Aztecs themselves. But why side with the Spanish? Did he see the way the tide was turning?

I remember reading about a battle at Cholula, where the Aztecs had a small force and were hoping to use Quetzalcoatl's power against the Spanish. They got their asses handed to them.

Did Quetzalcoatl forsake them? Or was he powerless to help? That's the funny thing about gods. So much of their power is smoke and mirrors. Real world influence is sketchy at best. They're much better with belief and magic than they are with cold, hard fact.

Trying to figure out the motives of gods gives me a headache so I shut down that line of thinking. I'll figure it out. Or I won't. He's not really my problem. I have an agreement to keep with him. That's all.

"Shit happens. Isn't that true for everybody?" She stands up from her pile of skulls, stretches until her back pops. "Come on. It's a long way off."

"You said you know a shortcut?"

"Yeah. It'll get us up into another mountain range near Teocoyocualloa."

My head spins as she pronounces it. So many Nahuatl words give me a headache. "That's the part of Mictlan where wild animals try to eat your heart?"

"Yeah. Don't let them do that. Hope you've been keeping up with your cardio. Come on." She leads me to the banks of the blood river. The thick, coppery stink of it is overwhelming.

"We are not swimming through that."

Tabitha makes a face like she's just bitten into a cockroach. "Ew. No." She puts her hand out over the shore, palm down. Then jerks it up while making a fist.

The air fills with the scent of roses and smoke and I feel . . . something. It's not magic like I normally know it, and it's not the same energy that I feel when I call up Mictlantecuhtli's power. I've never felt this with Santa Muerte, but it's obviously her power Tabitha's tapping into. The scent gives it away.

The bones at our feet shudder, leap into the air like they're on strings. They clack together, strands of sinew wrapping themselves around connections, joints snapping into place like some nightmare museum exhibit. A few moments later the bones stop dancing.

"It's a boat," I say.

"You're very perceptive. I can see why La Señora chose you."

It's less a boat and more a barge, like the trajineras that take tourists down the canals, only not as large or as colorful. A pole made up of linked together femurs wrapped in tendons leans up against its side.

"Help me get it into the canal," she says. We push and it slides easily off the shore. Tabitha hops in and I follow, picking up the pole and pushing us off.

"Which way?" I say.

"Back the way we came." The barge glides through the river of blood.

Tabitha sits on the gunwale staring silently out at the shore, frowning at the landscape. I can't tell what she's thinking. I try not to care, but I'm having trouble with that. I leave her alone and don't say anything.

Occasionally I see something break the surface behind us, a fin or a piece of flotsam. I can't tell. I don't want to know what could possibly live in this.

"Think you can push the barge a little faster?" Tabitha says, eyeing a patch of bubbles in our wake.

"This boat isn't the most stable thing to stand in. I'd really rather not fall in and have to swim through a river of blood, thanks."

"No, you really don't." Tabitha puts her hand out and a few long bones disengage from the side of the boat and click into another barge pole. She dips the pole into the river and shoves.

"Should I be worried?"

"You ever hear of the Ahuizotl?"

"Sounds vaguely familiar," I say.

"It's a sort of cat-dog with hands instead of paws and a prehensile tail that ends with another hand. About the size of a jaguar. It's pretty unpleasant."

"And that's it behind us?"

"If we're lucky."

I don't want to know what it might be if we're not lucky. I put my back into pushing the boat faster, my eyes on the bubbles frothing behind us. Between the two of us we gain some distance and soon the bubbles disappear. Whatever's been following has lost interest. I spend the rest of the time watching out for anything that might come leaping out of the blood at us.

We come ashore at a dock that juts out into the canal. Bleached white bone like everything else here except for the red stain from the blood lapping at its pilings. Further back is the Mictlan version of the streets we drove through to get here.

When we get out onto the dock Tabitha gestures at the boat with her hand and it rapidly deconstructs itself and sinks beneath the blood.

We walk through the bone streets, past buildings that would make H.R. Giger cream his jeans. Our feet crunch through shards of skulls like gravel. The heat is more oppressive here than out on the boat. Sweat spreads black soot from the island fire streaking down my face, soaking my shirt. Great. I get this far and I'm going to die of dehydration. I pull off my coat, roll up my sleeves. I catch Tabitha looking at my arms when I do it, no doubt wondering how much more of me has been invaded by jade.

"Shouldn't there be, I dunno, more Dead here?" I say. "Seems kind of empty." We haven't seen anyone since we came through the portal. Even when I drove through the part of Mictlan that extended up to L.A. there were souls around. Not many, but enough that I noticed them. Here there are just empty buildings, silent streets.

"Trust me, that's a good thing. There are some things we don't want to run into out here. I told you Mictlan is broken. Just because Santa Muerte rules doesn't mean she has complete control over it."

"What, like the locals do? They're dead." I try to keep the tone light, but after the Ahuizotl in the river I know this is serious. Besides the challenges I've read about, I don't know what else is here. And if Mictlan is in as bad a shape as she says it is, there's no telling what kind of nastiness is running around.

I don't know how much of my magic I can tap into. I can feel a trickle of power in the area, but it's faint and tastes sour, like spoiled milk. I'm not sure what will happen if I tap it and I don't trust Tabitha to tell me the truth.

Plus there's the problem that if I only have my own power to use that won't last long if I have to do anything big. It'll come back, but slowly. And if I pull too much and end up inadvertently grabbing Mictlantecuhtli's power things will go south in a hurry.

"Most of the dead who came in after everything went to shit are Aztecs killed in the war with the Spanish," she says. "Lately, it's been devotees of Santa Muerte. But with Mictlantecuhtli out of the picture they can't reach the end of their journey. So they wander, waiting for things to get better."

"They don't sound so bad."

"Dead warriors?" she says. "The Narcotraficantes, or even the police who follow La Señora? Some of them are here, too. We do not want to run into them."

"And you said I wouldn't need the shotgun."

"Shotgun's gonna do sweet fuck-all, Eric. They're already dead. You're not."

We come out past the buildings, through the narrow, winding streets and onto a wide road heading toward the pyramids in the distance. Bone trees grow thick on either side.

I feel a weird rumbling through my feet. Does Mictlan have earthquakes? No. It doesn't feel like that. Too steady, too low. I can see a thin cloud of dust further down the road. "Anything else we need to worry about?"

"Too many to list. This is why Santa Muerte needs you. Look at this place. Before the Fall this was filled

with souls on their journey to their final rest in Chicunamictlan. It was a rough existence for them, being
judged by your gods is never easy, but it was more like
the world outside than this. There were plants, water.
Servitors of the dead to help the souls on their journey.
Now look at it. Discarded scraps of flesh and bone. The
rivers are blood for fuck sake." She bends down and
picks up a fragment of a skull and tosses it into the distance.

Does she really care? It's not like Tabitha is old
enough to have seen it. How much of this conversation
is Tabitha and how much is the piece of Santa Muerte
grafted to her soul? Is there any difference?

"And having a king in place would solve this?"

"This place needs two rulers," she says. "Mictecacihuatl and Mictlantecuhtli had their own duties in taking
care of this place. They can't do each other's job."

That dust storm is really starting to kick up. Tabitha
hasn't noticed it, yet, and I'm not sure if it's something to
worry about. I nod toward it. "Should we try to find
cover or something?" Not that there's any I can see besides the trees. And though there are a lot of them, their
threadbare trunks won't offer much protection. Maybe
we can dig a hole in the road and cover ourselves with
bones.

Tabitha squints at the cloud. "Shit."

The dust is spreading in a wide column on the horizon. Instead of the whistle of wind there's a rumble that
sounds like car engines. It takes me a second to realize
that that's because it *is* the sound of car engines.

"What the hell is that?"

Tabitha starts running toward them. "The narcos I

was talking about. Probably some of the Aztecs they've roped into joining up with them."

I break into a run and follow her. Oddly, we're running toward the column of dust.

Of all the things I was expecting about Mictlan, this is so not one of them.

Chapter 11

"They're in cars? Where the fuck did they get cars?"

"How the hell should I know? I told you things have gone to shit around here."

She cuts sharply to the left through a break in the trees, kicking up pieces of skull that clattered behind her. Not far off I can see a low hill. At first I think it's just another bone pile, a wrinkle in the landscape, but there's a hole in it that becomes apparent the closer I get to it.

"Jesus, Tabitha, what is this? Mad Max?"

"In some places, pretty much. Hurry up, we're almost there."

Wherever we're going we better get there fast because the people chasing us are almost on us. I look over my shoulder and see five vehicles that can only be called cars from the fact that they've got wheels and move fast. They burst through the trees, scattering the trunks like tenpins.

The cars look handmade. Sheets of stitched together skin lashed over bone struts. Wheels made out of, shit, I don't know what the hell they're made out of, but it's sure as hell not rubber. Black smoke belches out the back. The cars are bone and sinew like everything else in this nightmare land. And for all that they're terrifying, there's an absurdity to them I just can't wrap my mind around. These things are more Flintstones than they are V8 Interceptor.

"You know, if they're looking for us," I yell over the noise of the engines, "the only hole that's visible for miles might be one of the first places they look." The engines are getting louder. What the hell do they use for fuel?

"It's an entrance," she yells. "To the shortcut. They won't be able to go in there."

"Why not?"

"Because they're not us." She ducks into the hole and the blackness swallows her up. Behind me the cars are speeding closer, throwing up a wake of shattered bone behind them, the engines a deafening roar.

I don't know what I'm doing, but I know I don't want to deal with a bunch of post-Apocalyptic cosplayers with war wagons. I jump after her, but a line shoots out from one of the cars and wraps around my ankle, biting deep into the skin, pulling taut. I hit the ground about a foot short of the entrance and get yanked back as the car fishtails into a U-turn.

More trees go over, the car dragging me along and back onto the road. I pull together a small fire spell that I hope won't cost me too much power and tip me over the edge. A pinpoint of the line holding me begins to smolder.

It's hard to concentrate when you're being dragged across a field of broken bones by a car that looks like it should be driven by a nightmare Barney Rubble, but I make do. The spot begins to glow, then flame. As the line burns I can smell cooking meat. Of course. This stuff is made out of flesh.

The car fishtails again, whipping me around just as the flame burns through the line, severing it. Momentum shoots me across the ground, and I skip over the skull landscape like a rock across a pond. Where my skin hasn't turned to jade it's getting the mother of all road rashes.

I hit one of the trees hard, fight back the dizziness and pain. I pull myself up onto my knees, hope to Christ I haven't broken any bones. Blood seeps into my eyes, the skin on the back of my left hand is shredded. I grasp for the shotgun over my shoulder, but it's gone. I look around wildly for it as the cars circle me, closing in like sharks. I might not be able to kill them with it, but I bet I can make their day suck.

I find it about five feet away from me and leap for it, but one of the cars peels off from the pack toward me to cut me off. I try to move out of the way but I'm too slow and maybe even a little concussed.

It veers off at the last moment, missing me by inches and knocking over a tree. For a brief second I think maybe I'll get out of this okay. But then somebody in the passenger seat reaches out and swings a massive bone club at me and clocks me over the head. The blow throws me backward hard into the ground and everything goes dark.

Chapter 12

When my friend Alex, whom I'd known since he was a kid using magic to run penny-ante scams on normals, had his soul consumed and replaced by the same man who'd killed my parents, I put a bullet in his brain.

I told myself he was already gone. That this wasn't my friend. This was some monster using his face. I didn't believe it.

When I saw him again months later I thought I was going insane. He couldn't be a ghost. Ghosts are remnants of souls, leftovers, images. His had been eaten. No soul, no ghost.

It turned out that it was Mictlantecuhtli choosing his face to get to me, his dark power running through my veins. I kicked him out, blocked him from my thoughts, from contacting me, from even knowing where I was. I pushed until I couldn't hear him anymore, and then I locked him out with more spells inked into my skin.

I didn't push hard enough.

"You look like hell," Alex says from the driver's seat of my Cadillac. It's night in Mictlan. I can smell the dry, desiccated air, feel the strange heat, the smell of flesh and ash and bone blasted by searing winds.

There is no moon in Mictlan and so the only light is from the Caddy's headlights casting strange shadows along the bone-paved road to who knows where. This has happened before, me being in the car with him like this. Not quite a dream, not quite reality.

Of course, it's not Alex. And it shouldn't even be Mictlantecuhtli.

"I kicked you out," I say. "And barred the door. Why are you here?"

"What, no hello? No, hey buddy, how ya doin'? I'm hurt. Come on, man. It's been months."

"It's the power I have from you, isn't it? And being here in Mictlan. That triggered something."

"And they said you were stupid," he says.

"Why are you here?"

"Why are any of us here, really?"

I don't bother answering him.

"No sense of humor," he says after the silence becomes uncomfortably long. "I'm here because you're here. I'm not Mictlantecuhtli. I'm your idea of a piece of him stapled onto your own soul. It's all very meta."

"I didn't think it was possible, but you're just as big a pain in my ass as Mictlantecuhtli. So I'm talking to myself? Awesome." Mictlantecuhtli was always like this with me, so I guess it makes sense that this piece of him has the same personality.

"Sort of? Not really? Think of me as fake Mictlantecuhtli. Mictlantecuhtli Lite. I'm just the piece left over in your head. Stuck in here with your self-loathing and shitty self-confidence. All the death god with fewer calories. Fake me, real you. After a while we'll just be us. Make sense?"

I rub my temple where I got hit. My head is starting to hurt and I'm not sure if it's this conversation or the bone I took to my skull. I'm assuming I'm unconscious and this is all going on in my head, so feeling pain is probably a sign I'll be waking up soon.

"Not really. Is this the same thing as what Tabitha has with Santa Muerte?" I'm still having trouble figuring out what Tabitha really is. Is she Santa Muerte? Is she Tabitha? If what he says is happening to me is also happening to her, then the answer is yes.

Tabitha told me that she and Santa Muerte had merged but she has her own opinions, her own thoughts. She was connected to Santa Muerte, had her voice in her head, until I cut it off with the handcuff.

I knew Tabitha had a chunk of Santa Muerte in her soul, and I wasn't entirely sure she had any of her own. Santa Muerte killed her to make her avatar, after all.

He frowns. "Pretty much, yeah. I'm a little sketchy on the details. I don't know everything real me knows. A lot, but not all of it. I've got holes. But if you're asking if she's her own woman? Yes."

My head is really starting to throb. I press the heels of my hands against my eyes. Christ, when I wake up this is gonna suck. "Okay, so why are you here now?"

"At the moment you being unconscious is the only way I can talk to you. The longer you're here in Mictlan, the faster we'll sync up. Eventually I'll just be a voice in your head. And then we'll be one mind. Anyway, I wanted to talk before you kill real me in the hopes that you'll flush out fake me and stop turning into a yard ornament."

"Figured that out, huh?"

"I'm in your head," he says. "Mictlantecuhtli Lite, remember? Everything you know, I know."

"You gonna try to stop me?"

"Well, duh. We both know the second I can connect to the real me outside of your skull, I'll do it in a heartbeat."

"Fantastic."

"I think so," he says. "But that's not really why I'm here."

"Oh? Do tell."

"Quetzalcoatl."

There's no reason for playing coy or trying to deny I know what he's talking about. If this piece of Mictlantecuhtli's soul knows about my plan to kill the real Mictlantecuhtli, then he knows about my arrangement with Quetzalcoatl. "I did make a deal with him. And I try to keep my promises."

He laughs, a braying, mule-like guffaw that goes on so long he starts to wheeze. "Oh, that's rich. Promises. You." He wipes a tear from his eye. "Have you stopped to think what burning down Mictlan would do?"

I look out at the bone road speeding by in the headlights. "Raise the property values?"

"You'll destroy hundreds of thousands of souls."

I stare at him. How had that not occurred to me? The answer comes to me immediately. Because I didn't want it to. I've been thinking of any souls I might run into as the same as ghosts. Just remnants that haven't moved on to their respective afterlives. Only this *is* their afterlife.

I came here to save myself, exact revenge for my sister's murder. Fully prepared to take out anything that got in my way. But this? I burn down Mictlan, I destroy everything in it. I destroy those souls forever. This is mass murder.

But if I don't burn down Mictlan, then when I get out

of here Quetzalcoatl's going to make my life a living hell. Scratch that. *If* I get out of here.

"Shit."

"And here I thought you didn't have a conscience," he says.

"What the hell is Quetzalcoatl's deal, anyway? Why's he got such a hate on for this place?"

"Oh, the usual. Jealousy, ambition, he's a dick."

"Sounds like there's a story there."

"There always is."

"Christ, I hate talking to you."

The car shudders. I know what that means. The last time I had this vision the car crashed, and I woke up covered in blood, in a storage room of an electronics store, a couple of demons arguing about whether they should eat me or not.

"I think you're going to have to wait on that story," he says. "I'm sure I'll see you again soon, the next time you get the shit kicked out of you."

The car rocks as something unseen hammers it from the side, it goes into a skid. Mictlantecuhtli pulls hard on the wheel, looking suitably surprised. Is he really, I wonder, or is it just my brain's interpretation of things?

The car wobbles, hits something in the road and goes end over end like something out of a bad, seventies TV show. Whatever. I've been here before. I sit back and enjoy the rollercoaster.

Because whatever is happening here, it's going to suck so much more when I wake up.

———

I come to, my right eye snapping open, my left too crusted over with blood from a cut on my forehead to do more than twitch. I'm lying on the bone ground staring up at the ceiling of some kind of tent that, it takes me a moment to realize, is stitched together panels of human skin.

Where the jade hasn't covered me, bruises and scrapes have. There's a goose-egg of a knot on my forehead where I took that femur to my skull. It takes a few tries to sit up and when I finally make it I wish I hadn't.

"Manuel," I say, seeing the dead Bustillo sitting cross-legged in front of me, skin sallow, the upper left side of his head from the cheekbone up sheared away from when I shot him with the Browning. And he ended up here. Huh. Guess he really is a true believer. "You're looking good."

He smiles, a sick rictus that only goes up on one side, his push-broom mustache twitching. "Better than you, I bet," he says.

"Yeah, I get that a lot. Little surprised to see you here, though. Shouldn't you be a little further back in line for your journey to the Promised Land?"

I'm also surprised to see I'm still breathing and haven't been tied up. My bag is missing, as is the shotgun, and I can't feel the weight of Mictlantecuhtli's blade in my pocket. But nobody's shanked me so far, so I'll call that a win.

"I'm told it normally takes a few years to get to this point," Bustillo says, "but as you can see there is a certain lax enforcement of protocol. Quite the cottage industry has sprung up at the gate from Mitla to get souls this far. And I am resourceful."

"Oh, I don't doubt that."

We sit under a makeshift pavilion constructed from long bones wrapped in tendons and flaps of skin for a tarp. Around us are bone buildings that look like they were put together by a toddler with a poor understanding of architecture. They have no doors, windows are thin, crooked slits.

And then there's the twisted pyramid to Huitzilopochtli.

Up close it's even more messed up than I thought. The stones aren't just poorly cut and ill-fitting, they sag as though they're made less out of rock and more out of Jell-O. A thick green slurry drips from the cracks and it has a faint but undeniable stink to it. But it's the perspective that really does the trick. Like an Escher drawing it seems to twist in on itself, angles folding into other angles that don't make sense.

"You probably don't want to look at that too closely," Bustillo says. "It gives even me a headache. And I don't have much of a head left."

I tear my eyes away from it, turn back to Bustillo. Behind him I can see men and women, some in far worse shape than Bustillo here, wandering around the area. Some look lost, aimless, others are tending to the bone vehicles. Old and young, some killed violently, others from disease or old age. Most of these people look modern, but a few are wearing loincloths or skirts and simple cloaks.

A few wear the armor of Aztec Jaguar or Eagle warriors, macuahuitls, wooden swords with flat slabs of razor sharp obsidian embedded in the sides, hanging from their sides. I even spy a few men wearing dented Spanish cuirasses. Every one of these soldiers shows the wounds that killed them.

I scan the crowd for Tabitha. She should stand out like a neon sign, but I can't see her anywhere. I guess that hole she jumped into really could keep them out. "Quite the crew you got here. Kind of surprised, though. Shouldn't the warriors and soldiers be with Huitzilopochtli? Riding with him to the sun?"

He cocks an eyebrow in surprise. "You've done your homework."

"When you take a trip to Hell it helps to read the brochure. How'd you pull this together? You've been here, what, all of two days?"

"Has it been?" Bustillo says. "Seems much longer than that. Years, even. I think time moves differently here. Or we perceive it differently." He stands and holds his arm out to help me up. I'm wary, I did put a bullet in the guy's head after all. He obviously wants something. Otherwise why not just shank me while I was unconscious? Finally, I take his hand.

I stand, wincing from the pain in my left leg. It's not broken but it's pretty banged up. My left knee is swollen, making it hard to bend, and the bottom of my pants leg is stiff with blood. I wipe at my eye, clearing some of the crusted blood away, but it's still too swollen to open.

"Some of these people have been here more than half a millennium," he says. "Up the mountains is Izmictlan Apochcalolca, the blinding fog. It's their final challenge before they reach Chicunamictlan. This is as far as any souls have gotten in the last five hundred years. They enter the mists, and they're spit back out. Mad, lessened. Every time they try to pass through it takes more from them. So many have stopped trying or have not made the attempt at all out of fear." He walks toward the row of bone vehicles and I follow him, limping.

"Isn't that the point of a challenge? That it isn't easy?"

I catch the souls giving me furtive glances. Anger in

their eyes, fear. I know they're not ghosts, or they would have eaten me already, but I don't know what they're capable of. I shift my weight and feel a sharp pain in my ribs. Well, I know some of what they're capable of.

"This is beyond that," Bustillo says. "No one has gotten through for as long as anyone can remember. It seems once the Aztecs lost to the Spanish everything shut down. Can you imagine how frustrating it must be for them? To be stuck here for centuries knowing that on the other side of those mountains are their families, their friends. Some of them have lost all hope. But I've given it back to them."

"Yeah?" I can see where this is going and I don't like it. "How'd you pull that off?"

We come to one of the vehicles. It's actually more disturbing up close like this than seeing it barreling down on me. It's vaguely car-like. Four wheels, a chassis, seats, steering. But that's where the similarities stop. Like the trajinera Tabitha created it looks like it's built from some child's nightmare TinkerToy set.

The tires are round, more or less, with femur spokes and flat slabs of bone for treads. The seats are rough frameworks covered in flaps of leathery skin and a raised platform in the back holds the driver's seat and the steering wheel. Skulls are perched all along the sides. For the life of me I can't see how the hell it runs.

"I told them you were coming. The reincarnation of Mictlantecuhtli who will bind this world together again."

"You know that's not technically true, right?"

"It's true enough for them."

"Let me guess. They think I'm going to lead them out of here. Over the mountains and through the mists to grandmother's house we go? I was wondering why you hadn't killed me. I get you through the mists, you're hailed as the good guy. And then it's an eternity of blowjobs for the guy who saved the souls of thousands of desperate dead."

"You catch on quick."

"And if I don't want to do it?"

He pulls Mictlantecuhtli's blade from his pocket and holds it in his palm as though he's weighing it. "Then you don't get this back."

"I was wondering where that went." I figured he had it the moment I laid eyes on him. It's an interesting threat. He's not saying he'll take my skin. We both know he can't use it anymore. And he's not threatening to kill me, either. I wonder if he thinks I can't be killed here. I could make a play for it, but to be honest I'm not sure it would work. I'm limping, I'm slow and even if I can get it from him, what about all the rest of these people? It's not like I've got anywhere to run.

"I assume you have the rest of my stuff."

Bustillo reaches into the vehicle and lifts out my messenger bag, hands it to me. I look through it. Everything's there as far as I can tell, the powders, the charms. Even the Browning and my pocket watch are in there along with a box of bullets and a couple of loaded magazines. All of this had been sitting in the trunk of the Caddy for over a year. It's good to have it back. I'd hate to lose it again.

"No shotgun?"

"Sorry. It got run over by one of the cars. It didn't survive."

That's impressive. Benellis are tough. But looking at the bone wheels on these cars I can believe it. Pity. It was a nice shotgun. I got it off a guy in Tijuana who tried to ventilate me with it. But like Tabitha said, shotgun's gonna do sweet fuck-all out here.

"So aside from threatening to not give me back my toy, what makes you think I'm going to help you?"

"We both know you're going that way, anyway," Bustillo says. "And when you get where you're going you're going to need the knife. We both win."

I almost ask him how I can trust him and then realize that's a stupid question. I can't. He knows it, I know it. It would just be insulting to ask.

"How could I possibly refuse such a generous offer," I say, putting my hand on the side of the nightmare Flintstones mobile. "When do we leave?"

Chapter 13

The bone cars, a dozen at least, rattle across the desert toward the mountains, engines grinding out a low rumble. Plumes of shattered skulls kick up like gravel behind them. Each car is so packed with the dead they hang off the sides.

The lead car that Bustillo and I are in contains just us and three nasty looking men who I don't doubt would be excellent at committing just about any sort of violence you'd care to try. They certainly look as though someone did it to them. Like Bustillo one of them was shot in the head, another was opened from throat to gut with a blade, ribs pulled out and his organs hanging like Christmas tinsel, a third had his throat sliced open and his tongue pulled down through the hole. I wonder how he talks with a Colombian Necktie.

I have to wonder how effective muscle like these guys are here, though. Do these dead feel pain? Fear? Bustillo had to have done something to gain status with them so quickly. Nobody just walks in to a group like this and just says, "Hey, I'm in charge now!" Could it have been as simple as them thinking I can open the mists for them?

"Who built these things?"

"No idea." He yells over the engine noise. "I don't even know how the damn things work. They were here when I arrived. You say I've only been dead a couple of days?"

"Yeah. I put a bullet in you . . . Tuesday? I think it was Tuesday."

"Feels like months. Did you find the Avatar?" Does he not know? I didn't see him when I was captured so maybe he wasn't in one of the cars and doesn't know she's here. I'm okay with that.

"Nope. Haven't seen her. So what's with this mist we're going to? All I know is that it's a challenge that souls have to pass through."

"Izmictlan Apochcalolca. There are supposed to be nine rivers that the souls have to wade across in the fog, but no one here knows if that's true. They've all taken to calling it 'Devorador de Memoria.'"

I can hear the capital letters in it. "Eater of Memories? How come?"

"Everyone who enters returns, but they come back diminished. They know they've been confronted with some horrifying truth, but can't remember what. They can't remember other things, either. The more they go, the more they lose. Their memories, their names. After five or six times there's nothing left. I suspect the rivers are metaphorical."

"A metaphor for what? A memory-eating monster waiting to ambush you in the fog?"

"That or something in the nature of the fog itself. When I was alive I studied as much of it as I could, but there's only so much one can do on the other side. It's still a mystery."

I'm not surprised that Bustillo was looking into it. Even the most ruthless and nasty of mages are digging into the mysteries of the universe. At their core, mages are just academics who found something practical to do with a philosophy degree.

"And we're heading into it?" I look behind me. "All of them are heading into it?"

"All of them. And more." He points toward the mountains and when I squint I can see them. There aren't just this handful of dead. There are hundreds. Thousands of them. A sea of people at the base of the mountain have built a makeshift city. The thick fog shrouds the peak high above them.

And they're all going to do it because they think I can get them through. He's brought them a Messiah. Talk about backing the wrong horse.

"So how is this gonna work?" I say. "I lead them through the fog and into the Promised Land?"

"Something like that," Bustillo says.

"And if I can't?"

"Then I guess we nail you to a tree like all good martyrs."

"Fantastic."

The city that's sprung up around the mountain is a sprawling mess of slapped together buildings of bone and sinew like some macabre art installation at Burning Man. It's had hundreds of years to grow, its population getting bigger and bigger and no one ever leaving.

Bustillo drives the car through the center of the city, slowing down to almost a crawl. Souls openly stare at us, fall in behind as we drive by. Creepy as all that is, it's nothing compared to the fact they're not making any sound, just silently marching behind us.

"Are they always this chatty?"

"You can only scream in despair for so long before it all becomes routine," Bustillo says. "And what would they talk about? Nothing ever changes. You're the biggest thing that's happened here in five hundred years."

"There's a path up the mountain that we'll be taking," Bustillo says. "The car will get us most of the way there. But then we'll have to walk. From that point it won't take long to get to the mist."

I'm not sure what he's expecting me to do. Stand there and part the fog like it's the Red Sea? When we get to it maybe I can make a run for it. I can't bail without the knife, so I'll stick close to Bustillo and grab it when we get up there. I don't doubt he'll come after me, but if it's as weird as they say it is I might be able to lose him in it. Provided I don't get lost in it myself.

Bustillo doesn't stop the car. The bone houses disgorge their occupants and the mob swallows them up, growing like a tick on a dog's nutsack. By the time we reach the base of the mountain and the road winding up its side we have a trail so long behind us that I can't see the end of it.

By the time Cortés showed up there were over five million Aztecs. Between him, smallpox, and typhus, they were annihilated in just over fifty years. By the look of things, most of them are right here.

"The road gets a little bumpy," Bustillo says. "I'd say buckle up, but these things weren't exactly built with safety in mind."

He isn't kidding. The cars have no suspension. The bone road was bad enough, but at least that was relatively smooth. Once we hit the mountain it turns to rock and dirt, cratered with potholes. My teeth rattle as

Bustillo takes a turn too fast, hits a crater in the dirt that almost sends me flying.

"So you've been up there?"

"We all have," he says. "Stood at the edge and stared into the abyss."

"And nobody goes in anymore?"

"I know what you're thinking. How do we know what happens if nobody goes in? There are people who do. Or, more to the point, people who get pushed in."

"Must be hard to punish somebody if they're already dead."

"Exile would be pointless. We're all exiled. There's no hardship to it. But going into the mist, well, just the thought of it keeps order in place. More or less."

"You've seen this happen?"

"Half a dozen times since I've been here. Tossed a couple of them in myself. A few . . . days? Weeks? Hard to tell time around here. They come back out, missing pieces of themselves."

"What was your knack?" I say. Every mage has a knack, a specialty, something that they really shine in.

"It is . . . it *was* aeromancy. Why?"

When Bustillo flipped the desk to block my shot I knew it was magic, but there are so many different ways to move an object I had no idea what kind it was. He probably just used the air to move it.

"Just curious."

Curious how much he actually knows about necromancy. I'll go out on a limb here and say not much. There are things I'm still learning about it, and I was born into this shit. For example, I picked up a little tidbit last year on why ghosts deteriorate over time.

The theory is that when most people die they just go

where they're supposed to go. But ghosts get stuck like water in a plugged up toilet. Over time they fade, losing bits of themselves as more of their soul slowly drains away to their particular Valhalla.

Which sounds an awful lot like what Bustillo's talking about when somebody walks into the mists.

I wonder what it will do to me.

The drive up takes a couple hours and by the time the road disappears my back feels like I've been running a jackhammer. The fog isn't far off. It hovers just above a wide plateau above us. The walk gives me a chance to stretch my legs, unkink my back.

The silence from the amassed dead following us is maddening. Even Bustillo, who was such a Chatty Cathy when he was alive, says nothing. His three goons are just as silent, though I suppose that's understandable with the guy sporting the Colombian Necktie.

"What's their story?" I say, breaking the quiet.

"Lieutenants of mine," he says. "Loyal even unto death."

"Loyal? Sure they weren't just bored? I have to wonder how long it will be before they turn on you. Loyalty might keep them going for twenty years or so, but eternity? I'd watch your ass if I were you."

"You should probably be more concerned about your own," he says, acid in his voice.

Ah, there it is. I know that at some point Bustillo is going to try to kill me. He hasn't yet because he either thinks I can get him through the fog, or he's got some plan to use my not getting through to his advantage. Can he use the knife to take my skin? Or does his being dead prevent that? If he thought he could, he'd have done it while I was passed out.

We reach the plateau and I get to see the mist up close. The mountain ends here. What looked like a pointed peak down below turns out to be a pyramid of black fog. Thin lines of lightning shoot through it, arcs of electricity dancing in its roiling depths. It smells of rain and wet forests, dank with the scent of rotting wood.

And then the scent changes. Car exhaust and oil. The metallic tang of a desert wind in summer. The salt air of the beach. Every breath I take smells different. But one thing remains constant. It scares the shit out of me.

I see why they don't want to go in. A sense of dread comes off it like a static charge. Like standing on the edge of a cliff and looking down and knowing that if you step off you're not going to survive it.

The assembled dead fan out around us. The plateau's nowhere big enough to hold them all, so they spread down and around the side of the mountain, staring at me.

Panic crawls up my spine. I do not want to go in there. I am not putting myself through whatever meat grinder that place is. I wrestle the fear into submission. No, I don't want to go in. Yes, I will go in. I don't see as I have much choice.

I catch a flash of movement behind me. I've been waiting for Bustillo to make his move and it seems this is it. He steps quickly behind me, pulling out Mictlante-cuhtli's blade. He slashes at my neck. One swift movement and he'll easily sever my spine.

Only I'm ready for him. The spell I cast isn't even so much of a spell as just a thing I can do. A while back it would actually have taken some thought, maybe even a full-on ritual with blood and everything. But the last couple of years I've been getting better at this sort of thing. I used it on a bunch of corpses on a subway train in L.A. after a crazy Russian lady killed them all with a spell.

This is a little different, of course. Bustillo's not a corpse, or a ghost. I'm not really sure what to call him. The important thing, though, is that he's dead.

The blade stops centimeters from my neck.

I won't be able to hold it long. But then I shouldn't have to. It's still magic and I'm burning my reserves. Go too far and I bump up against that other power. I could tap into the local pool of magic, odd that Mictlan would have one, but it feels even more sour and rotten up here than when I crossed over. Drinking that power in would be like gargling maggots.

"Oh, Manuel. I thought we were friends." I turn to him. He's frozen in place, his face straining as he tries to move. "You do recall the bit about necromancy, right? And that you're living impaired? You seeing the connection here?"

His three bodyguards move toward me and I lock them in place with a wave of my hand. I can feel my reserves draining. They'll replenish over time, even without tapping the local pool, but I don't have time.

"This was your plan?" I say. "Kill me, hope you can take my power and stroll through the mists on your own? What makes you think you can even wear my skin?"

"I wasn't going to skin you," he says. "Just kill you. No one's gotten through the mists in hundreds of years. Killing you will send a message to Santa Muerte, to Mictlantecuhtli, that the dead will not stand for this. They will let us through to Chicunamictlan. We have power and we're not afraid to use it."

"Seriously? Since when did the dead unionize? You're

acting like you're a bunch of striking workers. Jesus, I blew out more of your brain than I thought. What the hell is that going to accomplish? You can't tell me you don't know that there's something seriously wrong with this place. They're not keeping you out here because they don't like you, dumbass."

I'm beginning to feel like Sergeant Howie at the end of *The Wicker Man*. Bustillo didn't promise them a Messiah to guide them through the mists. He promised them a sacrifice.

Bustillo's not stupid. I doubt he even believes what he's telling me. But he does believe he can put himself in charge. He's already gotten partway there. All these people wouldn't be here if they didn't think he could deliver.

And now that it's looking like he can't, there are murmurs in the crowd. An ugly, angry muttering that spreads from person to person like a virus. It begins to sound like rain, then a storm, then a flood.

"I will see this through!" Bustillo yells. It's not for my benefit. He's trying to regain control. But it's not working.

Problem is I can feel my control slipping, too. Keeping four dead souls locked in place isn't taking a lot of juice, but it's taking enough. Sustaining spells like this isn't easy. It's like lifting weights. Sure, you might be able to bench a few hundred pounds, but for how long?

Bustillo struggles against the hold I have on him. He slips a fraction of an inch. Not nearly enough for anyone to see it. But I know it happened, and from the grin on Bustillo's face, he knows it, too.

I pluck the knife from Bustillo's quivering hand. "It's been fun, Manuel, but I really gotta go. Thanks for the lift."

"He's escaping!" he yells. "Kill hi—" I reach behind him with the knife, grab his hair with my other hand. I slice the blade from the back of his neck and out through his throat, the blade passing through muscle and bone like it's pudding. His head pops off and hangs in my hand, mouth twitching, eyes rolling like marbles. His body falls bloodless to the ground.

The blade is supposed to be able to kill anything, even gods. Can it destroy souls? Bustillo's head has stopped twitching, so I'm gonna go with probably.

The crowd surges forward like a tidal wave. The grasping hands of the dead reaching out. I release my control of Bustillo's goons just as they're overwhelmed. The rage coming off the crowd is palpable.

"Hey, here's the guy who fucked you over," I yell and toss Bustillo's head into the crowd. They fall on it like wolves.

Time I was leaving then. Unfortunately, the only way out is through. I don't know what's waiting for me, but I suspect it won't be good.

I turn and step into the mists, the gray haze swallowing me up. I have a second where I think I've made a huge mistake and then everything fades away.

Chapter 14

I blink at the too-bright lights, my ears ring at the too loud noise. Something's not right, but I can't remember what it is. I remember a knife and . . . smoke? No. Fog.

"Are you listening to me, Eric? You have to stop doing this," Vivian says, pouring sugar in her coffee. Her red hair's long, down to the small of her back. She hasn't worn it that way in years. Last time I saw her she had it cut in a bob.

Wait. That doesn't make sense. That would have been this morning? No. Months ago. I haven't seen her since I stopped her from being killed in her apartment last year. But she doesn't live in an apartment. She lives with her mother in Beverly Hills.

What the hell is wrong with me? There's something but I can't figure out what it is. The memory I had slides off my brain like it's Teflon. I try to grasp at it, but it pulls away just out of reach.

We're in Canter's Deli on Fairfax in Los Angeles. The place is full of late night diners, people getting out of clubs and bars. In a few hours the crowd will shift to people stopping in to get a bagel on their way to work, old Jewish men and women from the neighborhood coming in for breakfast.

I'm beat to hell again. Bruised ribs, left eye swollen shut, knee feels like it's been stomped on by a sumo wrestler. Road rash from ... something. I can't remember how I got this way, but it's not like it's the first time.

"And for god's sake, put that knife away."

Knife? The hell— Oh. Huh. I'm clutching a black, obsidian blade tight in my hand, some antique thing. It feels familiar but for the life of me I can't remember where I got it. I find a sheath for it in my coat breast pocket and put it away.

I've got two images of Vivian competing in my mind. My girlfriend for over five years now. We've been dating since I was fifteen. But I also see a woman who moved on after I disappeared, leaving everyone I knew and loved so that hopefully they wouldn't be killed because of my own mistakes. But I haven't gone anywhere. Have I?

"What happened?" Something slips. The diners around me go hazy for a second then snap back into focus. I'm forgetting something important.

"You tell me," Vivian says. "This is getting bad, Eric. Every couple of weeks you do this. Going out and getting the shit kicked out of yourself isn't healthy. Look at yourself. You need a hospital."

"I thought you liked bad boys," I say. Slowly because the words feel strange in my mouth. I've said them before. A weird sense of déjà vu hits me. I've had this conversation.

Vivian and I met because our families were in the life. When you're in the magic club your dating pool isn't exactly what you'd call deep. And since dating normals is such a pain in the ass, we don't do it much. Lying about who and what you are is second nature to us, but eventually anybody you're fucking's going to find out. It was nice to know that Vivian and I at least had magic in common.

That's not necessarily bad. Lots of normals know about us. But those are the ones who know not to talk about it in public. The ones who don't tend to have short lifespans.

"Well, yeah," Vivian says, "but I prefer the type who doesn't get into constant fistfights with drunks. Do I have to get the first aid kit out?"

"Not this time." I know she's right. I've been doing this crap for a couple years now. I'll go to a club and find the biggest, most piss-drunk asshole there. Words will be exchanged. Voices will be raised. Eventually we'll get tossed out by the bouncer and take it out to the parking lot.

Sometimes I lose. Sometimes I don't. But I don't use magic. Just fists, a head butt, an occasional kick to the nads. Vivian tells me I've got anger management issues, problems with authority.

Yeah, no shit. Ya think?

My parents had me talk to a therapist once when I was twelve. Another mage, of course. We spent a lot of time talking about my feelings, how I view death, what I think comes afterward. He wasn't really helpful. If he'd been another necromancer, maybe he'd have been some use.

He annoyed me when he kept arguing with me about ghosts and things he called "theory" and I called "my every waking moment." So I summoned the ghost of his dead grandmother and let her yell at him for half an hour. That was my last appointment.

"I've missed you," I say. I have. I screwed things up so badly with her that I don't know if I can fix them.

"You saw me this morning," she says.

"Yeah," I say. "But . . . I just miss you." I put my hands on the Formica table, touch the silverware in front of me. It all feels solid, but it doesn't feel substantial. Like it's all a plastic shell. "I feel weird."

Something snaps in my mind and I don't know what I'm feeling weird about. This is Vivian and me. I went out and got into a fight and now I'm sitting with her here in Canter's and goddamn it she's beautiful. I marvel at how lucky I've gotten the chance to be with her. And I wonder what she could possibly see in a train wreck like me.

"Well, yeah. Things are weird right now," Vivian says. "This shit with that Frenchman is making everybody nervous."

Jean Boudreau. A mage who's trying to be like some mafia don, shaking down lesser talents, mages who don't have a lot of power. Making their lives difficult if they don't pay up. Or worse.

My parents have been standing up to him and his goons, organizing people to do the same. Getting mages to work together is like herding cats on meth. But they've been doing it.

"It'll blow over," I say. Every few years some asshole tries this kind of thing and a bunch of mages will decide to stomp on them. This isn't any different.

"What if it doesn't?" she says.

"Are you scared?"

"That's not the point," she says. "They killed some hedge witch down in Alhambra last week. And the week before that they burned down an airplane mechanic's business over at the Torrance airport."

"That was the aeromancer, right? Guy who was charming planes to keep them running better?"

"And they went after him because he couldn't protect himself. If we had an actual community, this shit wouldn't happen."

"Look at you getting all liberal activist."

"Dammit, Eric, I'm serious. Your parents are doing something about it. My mom is too damn scared to help."

Vivian's dad died a couple years ago. Massive heart attack. Nobody found him for over an hour. A little sooner and somebody probably could have brought him back, but there's only so much magic can do.

I tried finding his ghost, even though Vivian told me not to. Just as well, he didn't leave one. A good sign, actually. Meant he probably died quick and painless.

"What do you want me to do, Viv? I'm not my parents. They're good people, but come on. This is their cause, not mine."

"Do you even have a cause?" she says. "They could use your support, you know. You've got more cred than you realize. People talk about you. They could use your help. What if something happens to them?"

"Yeah, they talk about me because I'm one of the two freaks who talk to the dead in this town and the other one's a fucking psycho Nazi. What's going to happen, Viv? Boudreau's not going to do anything to them. He'd get a royal ass-kicking and he knows it."

"What about Lucy?" she says. My sister. The black sheep of the family. The one with no magic. The one we don't talk about.

At the mention of her name my mind snaps back and I know what's happening. It's the mists. Whatever the mists are they've decided I need to see this particular evening.

March eighteenth, three in the morning. Everything is about to go to shit.

"This isn't real," I say.

"What are you talking about?" she says.

"This already happened. Nineteen ninety-five. Alex is going to come through that door any second now and he's going to tell me that I need to get home. My house is on fire. My parents are inside. He's going to break every rule we have and use a one shot teleportation charm he bought out of the back of some guy's Buick in Vegas to make me disappear in front of all these people. It won't get into the news because mages have people in the papers and the networks and they'll block it."

Vivian looks at me, eyes wide. "I—What?" Alex runs into the restaurant right on cue.

"Told ya. So, is this all in my head? Or are you actually a thing?"

"Eric, I'm your girlfriend," she says. "What are you going on about?"

"No, you're not. And god, I wish you still were. But we both know that boat's sailed. You're a memory, maybe. Or something that's tapped into my memories?" I pull the obsidian blade from my pocket. "Let's find out, shall we?"

I lunge across the table, grabbing the back of her head and pulling her forward as I shove the knife deep into her chest. She tries to scream, but I've punctured a lung and all that comes out is a wheeze.

For a sick moment I think I'm wrong. That I've had some weird hallucination and it really is nineteen ninety-five and I've just murdered the woman I love.

No. I'm right. I have to be right. Even now the magic of the mists are making me doubt. Making me forget. Why I'm here, what I'm doing, who I am. I twist the blade hard and everything comes back into focus.

"How fucking dare you use Vivian against me. I don't know who you are or what you are, but goddamn it I am not letting you win." Vivian looks up at me, wide-eyed and horrified. The diners around us are staring at me, frozen in fear.

And then Alex begins clapping.

"Bravo!" he says, walking across the restaurant toward our table. Vivian, the diners, the waitresses, they all evaporate into smoke. Silence crashes down around us. In seconds it's just Alex and me in an empty restaurant.

"So which one are you?" I say. "The real Mictlantecuhtli, or just the piece of him stuck in my soul?"

"Neither, actually," he says. "I'm here to guide you. Everyone who comes through here faces their demons. They win against them. Or they don't."

I can guess what happens when they don't. They get kicked out of the mists, diminished, stuck. All those souls out there who tried and failed and tried again only to come out missing chunks of themselves. So why didn't any of them make it through?

"And you're my demon?"

"One of oh, so many," he says.

"You do this for everybody who comes in here?"

"Everyone gets a guide. I didn't exist until you came in here, and I'll stop existing once you're gone. Your own personal Virgil."

"Personalized concierge service for the dead? Nice."

When Mictlantecuhtli took Alex's form he was indistinguishable from the real one, flaws and all. But this thing isn't quite right. It looks like Alex, talks like Alex. Except . . . he's a little too Alex. Skin too clear, teeth too straight. Some details are off and as I think of them they clarify. He becomes more like the real Alex the more I remember him.

"You're pulling all this from my memories," I say.

"Yes."

"I have some pretty fucked-up memories."

He smiles the way a hungry wolf that's just cornered a rabbit might smile. "Oh, yes, you do."

"Why hasn't anyone else gotten through?" I say, trying to change the subject and keep him talking. Maybe I can find a way through here that doesn't involve me reliving the past.

"The mists were locked when Mictlantecuhtli was imprisoned," he says. "And now you've unlocked them."

"So all those souls backed up out there? They're going to finally get through."

"Some of them. Possibly even most. They still have to go through their challenges. Everyone who comes through here does."

"Even the king of Mictlan?" I say, hoping a little bit of name dropping will get me to the front of the line.

He nods. "Even the king. This is the last stop before reaching Chicunamictlan. There are nine rivers you must traverse. Each one is a window to your past."

"Nine rivers, huh? Real ones? Or, like, metaphorical ones?"

"Depends on the person. Some people, it's rivers. Some people, it's snakes. Some people, it's all the regrets and mistakes they made in their lives that they can't take back."

"I'm in that last category, aren't I?"

"Do you have a problem with snakes?"

"Not particularly."

"Then yes, you are. And the sooner you continue the sooner you can finish."

"You're like Mister Roarke on *Fantasy Island*. Where's your midget?"

"That's an interesting way to put it," he says. "I'm a greeter of sorts. A facilitator. We usually don't explain what's happening to the dead who come through here. You're special."

Maybe that's my loophole. "If I'm so special why am I going through this?"

"Because you're here. Alive, dead, mortal, god. Everyone pays their way in pain, here, Eric. Everyone." He snaps his fingers.

And I fall.

Chapter 15

My house is on fire.

I'm standing in the driveway of the home I grew up in, staggering from a sudden wave of nausea. One of the joyous effects of Alex's teleportation charm. I'm glad he had it. Driving would have taken me an hour even in late night traffic, but I'm still too late.

There is something I'm forgetting. Even through the terror and realization that there's nothing I can do, there's the sense of something vital that's just out of reach. It surfaces briefly like a whale breaching the waves and then just as quickly sinks back down again, disappearing completely at the sight of the house engulfed in flames.

It takes everything I have not to go running into the fire. The entire façade of the building has burned away. The living room, foyer and kitchen are gone. The second floor collapses as I watch crews of firefighters desperately try to put it out.

I can tell already they won't make a damn bit of difference. I can feel the magic in the air, residue of massive spells. Some of them undoubtedly my parents'. The rest of it is from a thing I catch out of the corner of my eye, dancing in the flames of what used to be my living room.

Then there's the death. No ghosts, but the sense of death lingers. Not quite a smell, not quite a sound. Just a feeling I get when someone nearby has kicked the bucket.

My parents and Lucy, I'm sure. I can't see bodies. The untouched garage is still closed. I can't tell if their cars are in there or not, and much as I hope they took off for some late night errand, I know they're in the house.

All this devastation has been caused by a fire elemental. Not a big one. I can see it flitting from flame to flame, hiding in the fire, disguising its shape. The firefighters, normals every one of them, won't see a thing, but I know what to look for.

I catch a glimpse of another one that hasn't hatched yet in the remains of the living. They start as eggs, tiny things made of fire that grow to about the size and shape of an ostrich egg before cracking open and letting loose a nightmare beast of flame. They're good for burning things, nothing else. And unless you're into arson for insurance purposes, and believe me there are better ways to do that, you only use them to kill.

And I know who set them off in my house.

Jean Boudreau. He's been fucking with mages and lesser talents for months now, and my parents were pushing back. Vivian said something about an aeromancer whose business burned down. I doubt an elemental was used there, too. A can of gasoline and a match would be less indiscriminate.

I've moved on from panic, straight through grief and horror and hit the brakes firmly at rage. I know the way I know that the sun rises in the east and sets in the west that I will kill this man. I will tear him to pieces. I will make sure he knows I'm the one who's doing it to him.

And I will make it hurt.

A car pulls up into the driveway, screeches to a stop. I don't recognize it, don't know who's driving. I ready a fire spell of my own in case it's Boudreau come to gloat. He wants a fight, I'll give him a goddamn fight.

But it's Lucy. She jumps out of the passenger side in sweats and sandals, brown hair pulled back with a scrunchie, sleep still in her eyes. She's running on adrenaline. Relief that she's safe, horror that she's going to see this. I run to her and pull her close, turning her away from the flames.

I can't shake this feeling of déjà vu, as if this has all happened before. It has an almost hazy feeling, like a memory I can't quite grasp.

Lucy's with a woman I don't know, something strange about her. The feeling that this is a memory stops at her. She feels familiar, but I can't place her. It's like she doesn't belong here. Her face is blurry. Smoke in my eyes, I imagine. Who the hell is she?

"Oh, god, Eric, what happened? Alex called and we came right over." We? What is this woman's name? I know her, don't I? That doesn't sound right. A memory tugs at me and all I can think is that she feels wrong. Lucy should be alone.

I'm not the hugging type, but I can't seem to let go of my sister. I should be feeling grief but all that I can seem to grab is anger. My insides are a knot, competing emotions tearing me up from the inside. Relief that Lucy's safe, rage that my parents are dead, that Boudreau murdered them.

I don't know what to say. There's been an accident? I

don't know yet? She'll see through anything less than the truth, so I don't bother hiding it.

"Mom and dad were in there," I say.

At first there's confusion. The words aren't registering. And then understanding floods into her, and she pulls away from me, tries to run. I hold on tight, don't let her go.

"We have to get them out." Her voice is ratcheting up to a scream. "We have to go in there and get them out."

"Lucy, they're gone," I say. She knows what I can do, knows the things I can feel. She's got to know I'm telling the truth. "Someone let a couple of elementals loose in the house. They're still there. If we try going in there we'll die, too."

The fact that the elementals haven't come out of the house to look for Lucy and I is, if not a good sign, then at least a thin, silver lining. That means Boudreau went looking for our parents and not for us. We should be safe from them as long as we stay out here. Once there's nothing left of the house to burn they'll put themselves out and fade back into the void.

All the color drains out of Lucy's face. "Do something," she says. "Do something." Her voice pitches higher as she repeats herself. It's a command, a plea. Her voice echoes like a banshee's cry. She pounds my chest but I don't let go. I know what kind of person she is. She'll run in there looking for our parents. She'll die if she does.

She knees me hard in the crotch and the shock of it makes me loosen my grip. True to form she bolts for the house. I'm running behind her, ignoring the lightning pain in my nuts and the nausea crawling up into my gut. I need to get to her before she gets herself killed.

I manage to, but barely. I get my arms around her and lift her off her feet. She's kicking and screaming.

"Why won't you do something?" she yells.

"I am doing something, goddammit. I'm saving your life."

"You're a fucking coward. You have magic. You can bring them back."

"I can't. Dammit, Lucy, you know I—"

A look of determination clamps down on her face, and I can tell she's feeling some of the same anger I am. Only directed at me. "Bring. Them. Back."

I can't. I can't do a goddamn thing. I have never felt so powerless in my entire life than at this moment. I have no control over anything. I am too late, too weak and too vulnerable.

I am less than nothing.

Everything freezes. The fire engine lights stop strobing, Lucy stops beating against my chest. Even the water from the firehoses and the flames in the remains of the house go stock still. Then slowly fades into a hazy gray of nothing. I am holding empty air.

I snap out of the memory and back into the present. Like in the recreation of Canter's I suddenly realize what's happening. Like a switch that's been thrown. Maybe this is what Hell is. Living the horrible things that have happened in your life over and over again. I had no idea it wasn't real.

Wait. No, I did. A little. That woman who was with Lucy. She hadn't been there when it happened. That's why she felt wrong. Was that the guide who's walking me through?

"Why didn't you save them, Eric?" says a voice. It's not a man or a woman, just a flat, androgynous sound. "Fear? Surely you could have done something."

"Is this where I talk about my feelings?" I say. "My inner demons? Is this seriously one of my regrets? Saving my sister?"

"She didn't feel that way, though, did she?"

No, she didn't. She saw it as letting our parents die. For the next couple of weeks as we picked up the pieces, prepared for the funeral, paid lawyers, greased palms and cast spells to move things along, she either wouldn't talk to me, or outright accused me of murdering them.

And the hell of it is, I felt the same way. If I'd been a few minutes sooner I could have saved them.

Lucy didn't ask, but I knew she wanted me to look for their ghosts. I didn't want to, and I tried to avoid it as long as I could. And when I finally did there was nothing. No Haunts, no Wanderers. Not even Echoes. I know that was the best possible outcome, but not finding them just added to my failure.

"So what am I supposed to do with this?" I say. "Tap into my inner child and cry about it? You know you're a shit therapist, right? It's been more than fifteen years. I got over it. I made a choice."

"Was it the right one?" says the voice.

Like I haven't asked myself that question. Look what it led to. Exiled from home, leaving what was left of my family in the care of Alex and Vivian, who I selfishly assumed would take care of her. Running away with my tail between my legs. No contact with anyone for fifteen years.

I still don't know the answer. And then the world snaps around me like a rubber band.

I'm standing outside a San Pedro warehouse at night, a smoking hole of twisted metal in its side from a burning car that's been run straight through. One man is on the ground, the other is slumped over the hood.

I'd loaded the car with a bunch of propane tanks and opened the taps, wrapped the whole mess in detcord. And then, when the man who killed my parents came outside, I stuck a brick on the accelerator. A small fire spell, once the car hit the warehouse, took care of the rest.

This time I'm not reliving the memory, I'm watching it. I can see myself walking across the parking lot from behind a shipping container, full of piss and vinegar and unending rage. Younger me grabs the man on the hood, Jean Boudreau. Punches and kicks him.

This is different from Canter's or at the house fire. This is watching myself instead of being in the middle of it. The actions might feel distant, but the rage is white hot and present. Even now I'm getting a sick sort of glee out of watching myself beat the living fuck out of Boudreau.

I remember every one of those blows. How my hand kept creeping toward the Browning in my waistband. I wanted to drag it out, make him hurt. How I eventually decided that I could do something so much worse than shoot him.

I remember being glad I hadn't killed him, that he was conscious. I wanted him to be awake. I wanted him to know what was happening to him. I watch myself slap him hard and his eyes jerk open. He tries to go for a gun, but it's kicked out of his hand to go skittering across the pavement.

Boudreau's weak, disoriented. Broken bones for sure. If he'd been any more aware of his surroundings he'd have killed me. I gave him the mother of all sucker punches, and it didn't even occur to me that I had no idea what the hell I was doing. I knew a handful of spells. He could have wiped the floor with me.

Younger me drags Boudreau away from the wreckage, bunches his fists in the man's shirt collar. I remember that moment. The spell I'd only tried a few times before. I knew it was possible the way I knew I could tie my shoes when I was a toddler, but I still had trouble doing it.

But that's how most magic works. We don't write much shit down. There's no point. We learn from experimentation, picking up tips from other mages, doing what feels natural.

And much as it strained me and took forever to cast as I tried to get it right, I remember it feeling like the most natural thing in the world.

Then they're gone. No flash of light or weird noises. Just there one second and gone the next. I took him over to the ghost's side. Took him there and called to any ghost who cared to listen.

And then I fed him to them like I was chumming sharks.

"I'd do it again," I say. And I would. Hell, I did. When I came back to L.A. a shred of Boudreau's soul had somehow reconstituted itself, sucking ghosts in to rebuild. I put him down pretty much the same way. Only I'm the one who ate his soul.

"No regrets?" says the voice. It's changing. Becoming more feminine. Out to the side of the warehouse, standing among the shipping containers I can see someone. Blurry, like the woman who got out of the car.

"Not a one," I say. "Why do you care, anyway? If you're trying to make me feel remorse about this, that's not happening."

"Not even for the consequences?"

"Me leaving L.A.? Small price to pay to protect Lucy and my friends."

"But it didn't. What do you have left, Eric? You got a short-term gain for a long-term loss. You won the battle, but you lost the war."

I can't take my eyes off the figure in the distance. It's becoming more distinct, more solid, but I still can't make out enough detail to know who it is.

"Is that you over there?" I start walking toward the figure. She, he, it's hard to tell, is standing in the shadows, watching me, not moving. I pull the obsidian blade from its sheath in my pocket. This whole thing is bullshit and I'm tired of it. I'm tired of gods and afterlives and getting dicked around. I'm tired of cryptic non-clues.

"Actions have consequences, Eric," says the voice. It's all around me. Louder now. Definitely a woman, but there's a distortion to it.

"Yeah, like my boot up your ass." The figure still hasn't moved. If I shank this observer, or concierge, or whatever the hell it is, maybe it'll pop me out of this place.

The scene shifts again, shimmering around me like water rippling after a stone thrown in. The warehouse, the parking lot, the figure in the distance, they all fade away to be replaced with a brightly lit house. White walls, white carpet, modern lines. The art on the wall a series of black and white photos, the decor modern and minimalist. I can smell sea air wafting in through an open window and the slight sewer scent of the canals off Venice Beach.

I know this house and everything inside me starts screaming.

The last time I was here it had been a crime scene. Furniture shattered, blood on the walls. The white carpet was so soaked through with blood it crunched under my feet as I walked across it.

I saw Lucy's Echo here. Forced myself to watch her murder replay itself so I could find some clue to who killed her. She lasted a long time before finally dying and I sat there and witnessed the whole thing with no way to do a goddamn thing about it.

When she finally died after being beaten and tortured and brutalized, the murderer wrote a note in her blood using her body as a paintbrush. Then they wiped it out so the only way anyone could read it would be if they could see her Echo. If they could watch her die.

In other words, it was tailor-made for me. I spent the next half-hour being violently ill in the sink.

I walk down the short hall and come to a den that fits the same motif as the rest of the house and stop dead.

Lucy sits curled up on the couch wearing yoga pants, her brown hair dyed black. She walks a familiar looking silver dollar back and forth across the back of her knuckles with a practiced air. I've only ever seen her dressed like this in a handful of photos and when I watched her Echo. I left L.A. too early to see her grow up into this woman.

"Hi, Eric," she says. "Come to murder me again?"

Chapter 16

When Lucy was a kid I tried to help her find her magic. Pretty much a pointless endeavor. She didn't have enough to register, but we did it anyway. I bought her an old silver dollar and we worked day and night trying to see if she could manipulate a coin toss.

For most mages that's dirt simple. Pretty much the first thing we learn. It's also one of the reasons we don't usually lack for things like money. But she couldn't get it. She'd get frustrated, have a tantrum for a bit, cry about it. But then get back to it. She'd gnaw at it like a dog with a bone. Never giving up. I found out after she died that she finally got that coin toss. Took her years to do it, but she got there.

I wasn't around to see it.

"You're just pulling out all the stops, aren't you?" I say.

"What, this?" she says, tossing the coin in the air with a flick of her thumb and catching it in the palm of her hand. She smiles and it's a smile I remember from when we were kids. Seeing her with the coin hurts. Seeing that smile hurts more.

I know she's not really here. It's not her soul. She's not in Mictlan. Why would she be? Santa Muerte might have killed her, but unless she was a follower she should have gone somewhere else, though where I have no idea.

That's one of the biggest problems with necromancy. I know how ghosts are made, I can talk to them, influence them, control them, even. I know there are afterlives, but before I met Santa Muerte I'd never actually seen one up close or figured out how to get to one. I mean, besides the obvious way, of course.

Mages are surprisingly agnostic. Yes, we know there are gods, we deal with them all the time. We just think they're largely irrelevant and mostly assholes. In case you hadn't figured it out, yet, we're pretty fucking arrogant.

Gods have limits, boundaries, rules. We exploit those, twist them to our own ends. Or don't and end up a smear on the floor if we're lucky.

So where did Lucy end up? The most popular guess, and that's all we've got, guesses, is that we go to what we're most drawn to. Gods don't choose it. We do.

Christian? Go to Heaven. Norse Pagan? Valhalla. Hate yourself and everything you've ever done and have a vague idea that there's probably a God, but you're really not sure and if there is boy howdy are you ever fucked? One of a thousand random Hells, probably.

Point is, when you die you'll go somewhere. Even if it's only to be recycled into the universe.

So Lucy's out there, somewhere. But she's not here.

I sit down in an easy chair opposite her. I wonder what would happen if I stabbed her with Mictlantecuhtli's blade. Would it kill the thing that's impersonating her? Or is she just an illusion being fed to me the way Vivian was and it wouldn't do anything?

I'll do it if this thing starts to piss me off, but otherwise I might as well see how things play out. I slide the knife back into the sheath in my coat pocket.

"So what's the point of this exercise?" I say. "I mean in a cosmological sense? There's got to be a reason for putting people through this crap. Did all the Aztec gods get together and say, 'Hey, let's fuck with our believers and make them relive their individual horrors'? Or did they just do that whole carving out human hearts thing?"

"It's a challenge, Eric. That's the point. This is Izmictlan Apochcalolca, the mists that blind, the place of nine rivers. The final stop before reaching your destination. By the time they get here, most have had their devotion tested by the crushing mountains of Tepectli Monamictlan, their sins carved away by the obsidian mountains of Iztepetl, their fears flayed from their souls by the scouring blade winds of Izteecayan. There's only one thing left."

"I figured with the river metaphor it had something to do with swimming."

"Why'd you kill me, Eric?"

"I didn't—"

The room flickers, blood blooms on the carpet, streaks across the walls. Lucy's head lies on her shoulder, cocked at an insane angle, bones poking out her arms. Her fingers are ground down stubs of blood and meat, her face purple and swollen.

"Yes, you did. You murdered me as much as the man who burst through the window to beat me to death," she says, her voice thick around a slurry of blood and ground up teeth. "As much as Santa Muerte used his hands to break my bones. Everything you did brought this down on me. Letting our parents die, killing Boudreau, running away like a whipped dog and staying away like a coward. And even if you hadn't done those things, I'd still be dead because of you. Because of what you are. You'd have brought Santa Muerte or some other freak to my doorstep just to get at you."

I can't speak. I want to. I want to argue with her, but I know she's right. It's all true. Every word.

"You always thought you were the freak of the family because of all the death that surrounds you. You were wrong. It was me. It was always me. I was the family embarrassment. I was the shame you all needed to hide."

She shifts her weight and her head lolls over to the other shoulder on a neck so broken it's just a bag of shattered bones.

"I was that thing you all hated, Eric. I was normal." She spits the word out, blood dripping from her devastated jaw.

"I never felt that way," I say. "I loved you." Only I did feel that way. I'm ashamed of it and horrified by it, but I did. She was a thing that shouldn't have happened. A normal in a family full of mages. She was a target for anything that wanted to get to us.

One time as a kid I even thought it would have been better if she'd never been born.

"You say you loved me. And that's why you killed me, Eric. You were always going to kill me. Just like you killed Alex. Just like you've killed all the other good things in your life. That's what you do. You kill the things you love."

"I did not kill you," I say, trying to put a conviction into my voice that I don't feel. "I tried to save you."

"Hell of a way to save someone," she says. She peels herself slowly off the couch, congealed blood sticking her to the seat. Her body jerks around like a badly controlled marionette and steps toward me.

"You're guilty. We both know it. If you weren't, why won't you go back into my house? Why won't you exorcize my ghost? You're just letting me replay my death over and over and over again. Because you're too cruel and too cowardly to make it stop."

Doubt engulfs me. I try to fight against it, but it's too strong. It pulls me down and every argument I have is washed away by self-loathing. Guilt and shame fill me up. She's right. It is all my fault.

I can't breathe, I can't move. What the hell's the point of even being here? I should just let everything play out and swap places with Mictlantecuhtli. Become a stone at the bottom of a hell I have no business being in. I deserve nothing better. I deserve so much worse.

Wait. That's it. I made a smartass joke about the nine rivers being something to swim in. I was closer than I thought. These rivers aren't for swimming.

They're for drowning in.

Self-doubt, guilt, shame, regret. That's what this place is for, that's the challenge. That's the trap. The dead come in here, confronted with their own failings and it eats them up. Like they're eating me. The more I fight it, the more it sucks me in. Maybe there's another way. Maybe I do the opposite.

"Yes," I say, standing up from the blood soaked chair, my feet squelching in the gore soaked into the carpet. "I killed you. If it wasn't for me, you'd still be alive. If it hadn't been Santa Muerte it would have been something else. I chose not to run into a burning building to save our parents. I chose to kill Jean Boudreau and got this whole shitstorm started. I chose to leave and not come back. I pushed away Vivian. I shot Alex. I got suckered in by Tabitha. I've cut a swath of corpses through Mexico to get here. All of that's true."

Lucy pauses. I step in close. She stinks of rot and blood. Her eyes are filmed over and gray, green pus running from the corner of her mouth. Her hair falls out in clumps to drift lazily to the floor. I have to remind myself that this isn't her. This isn't the girl I grew up with, the woman she became who I never had a chance to meet.

"So fucking what?" I say, and for the first time ever I feel like I'm telling the truth about it. "I've been hanging onto this shit for years. I made choices in shitty situations. Do I regret what happened? Yes. Would I love to take it back? Absolutely. But I can't. So if you're trying to get me to wallow so you can feed off my guilt then you're going home hungry. Because I am fucking done with that."

"Do you mean it?"

"Fuck you. I don't have to justify a goddamn thing to you."

The room shudders around me, bends and distorts like it's being run through a taffy machine. Lucy's neck straightens, her bruises and cuts fading, her broken bones sliding back through the jagged tears in her limbs. Her skin fades from suppurating green to an ashen gray and finally back to normal.

"You have a chance to fix some things, Eric," Lucy says. "Don't waste it."

She shatters like stained glass, the room going with her. Shards spray out in a shotgun blast of color and light blinding me. I cover my face with my hands as my vision goes white, my ears fill with a blast furnace roar. Pain wracks my body, a cold burn from the inside out that shoots through my limbs. It drives me to all fours and it takes everything I have just to stay conscious.

When the light and the sound clear I'm lying on a flat plain, the pain fading from my body. I roll over onto my back, catch my breath. The sky is the same, cold gray as when I stepped into the mists, but the mountains rising in the distance tell me I've come out the other side.

"That took less time than I expected." Tabitha sits on a rock nearby, eating an apple. The landscape is less paved with bone here so much as scattered with it. Even the scrub brush and distant trees look more alive, less desiccated. Actual plants.

"Where the hell have you been?" I say. And where the hell did she get an apple?

I'm exhausted. And raw. Lucy's image floats in my mind, neck snapped, bones shoved through skin. Her body a wreck of trauma and blood and rot. I want to throw up. I want to pass out.

But that's not the thing that's gnawing at me. I am done with feeling guilty. I am done with feeling responsible for shit I have no control over. I'll take my lumps, I'll admit to my role.

But I'm not responsible for everything, and giving up that belief feels like I'm giving up my memory of her.

Why haven't I been back to Lucy's house? Why haven't I exorcized her ghost? Do I really think this isn't all my fault? Or did I just bluff my way through the mists?

She said I had a chance to fix things. How the hell can

I do that? How can I possibly fix anything? Goddamn, doubt's a cold-hearted motherfucker.

"Close by," Tabitha says, holding up her wrist to show the handcuff. "This thing wouldn't let me get very far from you."

"Yeah," I say. "Kind of by design. That's why I got it for you. Figured I got this fancy wedding ring out of this arrangement, why not get you some jewelry, too? How'd you stay close and not end up on Bustillo's radar?"

She couldn't have blended in with the crowd. Now that I've met the dead in this place it's obvious how much Tabitha and I stand out. There's a solidity, a real-ness, to us that none of the souls have. For all their seeming physicality they still feel insubstantial in comparison.

"The Crystal Road," she says. "That cave I ran into leads to a network of tunnels that run all through Mict-lan. If you'd managed to keep up you wouldn't have had to go through all that." She takes another bite of her apple. "When's the last time you ate?"

"Tepito," I said. "I had a couple bowls of migas."

"Want some of this?"

"I don't have much of an appetite, thanks." I don't want to eat, and I'm sure as hell not accepting food from her here. Persephone and Hades come to mind. But I need to do something. Exhaustion is yanking at me and there's no way in hell I'm going to take a nap in this place.

I root around my messenger bag until I find the bottle of Adderall. I don't really relish the idea of dry swallowing these things, but the only thing I've got in here is a flask with some whiskey in it that I haven't opened since before I lost the Cadillac in San Pedro.

Ah, what the hell. I haven't had anything to drink

since that Coke in Tepito. I toss back a couple of the pills and take a swig from the flask. The whiskey burns on its way down.

"Do that a lot?" Tabitha says, concern on her face.

"The fuck do you care?"

"I—You're right. Forget I said anything. Now that you're adequately fortified you want to get going?"

"The sooner this is over the better off I'll be." No matter what the outcome. I stand up and wince at the pain in my knee. "Where are we, anyway? I thought the mists were the last stop before Chicunamictlan." If this is the Aztec's idea of paradise they're more fucked up than I thought they were.

"It is, but there's still a lot of distance between Izmictlan Apochcalolca and Chicunamictlan. As we get closer things will look better, too. Fewer skulls on the ground, that kind of thing."

"So no more challenges?"

"Not like the mists were, no. I'm sure you've got plenty still ahead of you."

"I saw someone in there," I say. "Thought it was this guide who talked to me. It was you, wasn't it?"

"Maybe. I was in there, but I couldn't find you. I kept stumbling around in the fog. Eventually I decided to wait for you out here."

"You ever gone through it?"

"Not like that," she says. "I know how to skirt the edges."

"Good for you," I say. "What's the point of it, anyway? Weed out the weak? Toss 'em back like fish that are too small?"

"It tests a soul's resolve," she says. "Burns away, well, not sins. They don't really have a concept like that here.

But your doubts, fears. It's to prove that you have the courage to continue."

"I can see why Mictlantecuhtli locked himself up if he had to deal with judging that crap all the time."

"He didn't. The point is to prove it to yourself," she says. "Just because he ruled here, doesn't mean he told people what choices they could and couldn't make. It doesn't work like that. If you're going to get through the mists, you have to want to get through the mists."

"Jesus. Tell me that's not what kept everybody from getting through."

"No," she says. "That was just Mictlan being broken. But now that you've gone through you've cleared the way for them."

"So I was the plumber who fixed the backed up toilet." I wonder how many of those souls who kept trying and failing, slamming their heads against a door that couldn't open, aren't even going to try. And what about the ones who will, but won't get through anyway. People whose wills are too broken to pass through.

Makes me wonder if maybe I should burn the place down like Quetzalcoatl wants me to. Might be a mercy.

"So where to now, lover?" Tabitha says, finishing her apple and tossing the core over her shoulder into the dirt. Seriously, where the hell did she get an apple?

"Stop calling me that," I say. I know she's doing it to get under my skin. "Depends. Who's closer? Santa Muerte or Mictlantecuhtli?" My knee is in pretty bad shape, and I can't help but limp. Really wish I had one of Bustillo's bone cars right about now.

"You still want to kill her?" she says. "Mictlantecuhtli tried to kill her and got caught in his own trap. All those

souls stuck out there outside the mists? That was Mictlantecuhtli's doing. She's trying to help them."

"Killing my sister kind of trumps all that."

She starts to say something, then looks away, won't
meet my eyes. Whatever argument she might have dies
on her lips. "I told you I'm not going to help you kill
her."

"You're really struggling with this, aren't you?" Is she
just as caught up in this mess as I am? I don't want to feel
sympathy for her. I don't really want to believe her.
That's already screwed me.

"What? No. Don't be stupid. I don't want her dead."

"No, but you want her different," I say. "You argued
with her about my sister. What else did you argue
about?"

"I don't . . . Look, I'm her avatar. I don't get to like
everything she does. And no matter how I feel about it,
I'm not going to let you destroy her."

"I'm not asking you to," I say. "You're here because I
needed someone to get me in here. I need a guide. I'll
find her eventually. With you, I'll find her faster."

"And then you'll kill her. I don't see how that's any
different."

"I haven't decided what I'm going to do, yet," I say.

"That was bullshit the first time you said it and it's
bullshit now." Her face goes hard. If there had been any
doubts about her before, they're gone. "You're going to
kill her and then you're going to kill me. We both know
it. So stop fucking lying about it."

"Fine. Mictlantecuhtli, then. Or do you have a problem with me killing him, too? I don't know who's telling
me the truth. You? Him? Her? And since when do you

care about dying? I don't know if there's even a 'you' in there. So tell me, Tabitha, who do I kill? I'm gonna shank somebody. At this point I'm not sure I care who it is."

She says nothing for a long moment and then stands up from the rock, her face grim. She turns and starts walking away. "We take the Crystal Road," she says over her shoulder. "There's another entrance nearby. We can reach Mictlantecuhtli's tomb that way."

Chapter 17

The Adderall doesn't do anything for the pain in my knee, the road rash on my hands, my swollen eye, but it does make me care less about them. I've been popping these pills so long I barely even notice the jitters. If Tabitha does she doesn't say anything. It's probably not that different from how I've been since before I got here, anyway.

There are no roads, no paths. The bone landscape has mostly receded into dirt and stone. Actual plants dot the ground, a smattering of madrones, ficus and copperwood trees, not their sick mimics of bone and stringy flesh. Sickly looking grasses poke up through the dirt, wasted and thin, but alive or however close to alive this place gets. The sky is still a flat, uniform gray, though. No clouds, no sun. Does it ever become night here?

When I came here I was absolutely certain what I was going to do. Kill anything that gets in my way until I sever whatever connection I have to Santa Muerte and Mictlantecuhtli.

But now, I'm having doubts. I still want those things, but I'm wondering what will happen when I get them.

My stepping through the mists re-opened them to the souls trapped on the other side. If I kill Mictlantecuhtli do they shut down again? If I kill Santa Muerte does something else fall apart here?

I still want to kill her for everything she's done and I want to kill Mictlantecuhtli whether it will stop this transformation or not because he annoys me and he's kind of a dick.

But what about Tabitha? I thought I wanted to kill her. To clean up a loose end if nothing else. But is she just a meat puppet for a chunk of Santa Muerte's consciousness? Is she actually still in there?

When I discovered that she was Muerte's avatar she told me she didn't care if I killed her or not. It wouldn't destroy the goddess. It'd just leave me with a corpse I'd have to dispose of.

But now I have to wonder. She ran from Bustillo's crew. She accused me of wanting to kill her as if it mattered. This shit is giving me a headache. I need a distraction to keep my brain from eating itself. Mictlan delivers.

"Hold up," I say. I squat to get a closer look at the dirt. "You see this?" Depressions in the dirt that look like handprints spaced the way an animal might leave them. Something that walks on its hands.

"Shit," Tabitha says. She looks along the ground. "I think it looped back behind us."

"Ahuizotl? Or is there something else with feet like hands around here?"

"I'll be honest, I'm actually kind of curious to see this thing. It's one thing to be chased through a river of blood and not wanting to take a swan dive into it, it's something else when it's on solid ground where I can see it coming."

"Yeah. Come on. We're not far from the entrance to the Crystal Road. I don't want to be here if it notices us."

"If it's looping back around it's a safe bet it knows we're here." I don't see it among the trees and brush, which is surprising because there just isn't that much. "It's got good camouflage, doesn't it?"

"You ever see that *Predator* movie?"

"Huh. Yeah, that could be a challenge. Do they travel in packs or singly?"

"There's only the one."

"So if that's what was following us in the river, then it's hunting us. Awesome."

"Which is why I'd like to get out of here. It never gets too far from its prey. And if it's been stalking us since we got into Mictlan it's probably getting impatient."

"You're no fun," I say.

"Hey, if you want to be eviscerated by an ancient Aztec horror, knock yourself out."

And again with worrying about her own safety. It's clearly got her spooked. But why? The only difference I can think of from before is that now she's been disconnected from Santa Muerte. Is that what's doing this? Is she Tabitha now? Or is the piece of Santa Muerte in her trying to keep its own hide intact?

Interesting, if it is Tabitha. I just don't know what to do with it, yet.

"Lead the way."

I follow her through the trees. They cluster together closer to each other the further we go until it's an almost impenetrable forest of madrones.

"How the hell are there trees in the land of the dead?" I say, pushing my way through a tight bundle of branches.

"They're not trees," Tabitha says. She picks up a rock

from the ground and strikes a sharp corner against one of the trunks. The tree visibly shudders and bright red blood walls up from the cut. "They're Cihuateteo. Women who died in childbirth and brought here by the goddess Cihuacoatl. They're warriors and they're given one of the most important jobs, guardians of Mictlan. Try not to piss them off."

Tree warriors. Something tells me that they're not nearly as immobile as they seem.

"Cihuacoatl. She's a fertility goddess, right? I remember reading that somewhere. Where is she now?" But I hadn't heard of this thing with the trees. I wonder how much of the histories and myths I've read are actually true. Like so many of them around the world, they're never quite what you think they are.

"One of several," Tabitha says. "Dead. Missing. So many of the gods scattered, disappeared, or flat out died. Hard to say." She pushes past another tree, squeezing through its branches. It takes me a little longer to get through the tight space.

"Any of the other gods still around? Quetzalcoatl?"

"Quetzalcoatl's been missing ever since he got his ass handed to him by Mictlantecuhtli. You know about that, right?"

"I know he sided with the Spanish," I say. "But that's all."

"He'd been lending his power to the Spanish. Hitting the other gods while the Spanish took on the Aztecs. Mictlantecuhtli and he got into a fight and Quetzalcoatl lost. But by then it was already too late."

Pieces are beginning to fall into place. Mictlantecuhtli told me he'd been trapped in his tomb when he did something to a weapon the Spanish were using. So maybe that weapon was Quetzalcoatl and that's why he's got such a hard-on to burn this place down?

It fits, but is it right?

Tabitha disappears past a tree and I struggle to keep up, tree branches snagging at my clothes, as though the Cihuateteo are actively trying to slow me down. And who knows, maybe they are.

I get past one more tree and stumble out into a massive, stadium sized amphitheater of carved stone steps leading down into a pit a good forty feet deep. An arch of thick bricks carved with stylized skulls sits at an angle at the bottom, a dim, yellow glow emanating from inside.

Vines crawl down from the tree line. Tall wooden scaffolds of horizontal poles dot each level of the amphitheater all the way down to the bottom. Each pole in the rack pierces a dozen skulls, their lower jaws missing, tattered skin hanging loose off the bone.

"Tzompantli," I say. Racks filled with the skulls of sacrificial victims. "The drawings don't do them justice. There's gotta be, what, couple thousand skulls here?"

"Easily," Tabitha says. "Come on." She starts down the steps, navigating past the rows of tzompantli. I follow her down.

"So what's with the Cihuateteo? Why are they here and not around the entrance to the Crystal Road out in the bone desert?"

"They used to be," Tabitha says. "Cihuacoatl has a thing for crossroads. Groves surrounded all of the entrances. But like everything else, once Mictlantecuhtli was locked up it all went to shit. Cihuacoatl disappeared, the Cihuateteo died off. Only ones left are on this side of the mists."

"And the tzompantli?" I stop to look at one of the

racks. Most of the skulls are bare, but a good third of them are still covered in skin and muscle. I poke at one with my finger and its eyes pop open, milky orbs staring at me.

"Ambiance."

The trees above us groan as though twisting themselves into shapes they weren't designed for. Creaking. A snapping of wood. And then a guttural howl shatters the air.

"That's our cue to leave," Tabitha says. She hurries down the steps, taking them two at a time.

"Hold up, I want to see it," I say.

I watch the trees weave together into a twisted bonsai wall. The howling grows louder, a guttural shriek of anger and frustration, a tearing of wood. That thing is pissed.

"Stick around and you can see it up close and from the inside."

A dark shape pokes over the tree line. The Ahuizotl scrambles to get over where it can't get through. It looks to be about the size of a lion. A dog's face with a wide slash of a mouth filled with enormous teeth. Hands where paws should be, finger tipped with razor sharp claws. Its tail whips up over its head and another hand at the end of it grasps the top of one of the trees to help it climb.

It catches sight of me, its eyes flashing a bright red. It doubles its efforts, tearing and ripping through the trees. The trees retaliate by growing more branches to block it.

That thing is fucking terrifying.

"Okay, I've seen it," I say and run to the archway where Tabitha is waiting for me.

"Great. Can we go now?"

"Yeah, I think that's a good plan. Wait. Can't it follow us in there?"

"Eventually, yes. The arch will resist it, but it won't last forever. I want to get as much distance between us and it. With any luck we'll lose it inside."

"Luck really isn't my strong suit," I say.

"Yeah, I'd noticed. Come on." She steps into the arch and disappears in a flash of light. I hesitate at the entrance. So far my track record with being in Mictlan is not exactly stellar. Is this going to work? Is this a trap?

I steal a glance toward the trees and see the Ahuizotl climbing ever higher. It swings one of its massive hands at a branch that has shot up to block its path, tearing it off the trunk in a shower of splinters.

It rips through the trees like a cat in a bag, clearing the trees and crouching on the edge of the amphitheater. It pulls back its lips in a Cheshire Cat grin of shovel blade teeth.

If the archway's a trap, at least it's not some Aztec horror trying to eat me. I give the Ahuizotl the finger and step backward through the arch.

Chapter 18

The arch isn't just a hole into a tunnel. I can feel the magic before it hits me and I feel myself stretching like a rubber band, my mind pulling in multiple directions. A moment later it all snaps back into place and I come through the arch into a cavern that looks like the inside of a geode.

Crystals thick as tree trunks shoot up from the ground, down from the ceiling. A soft white glow emanates from deep inside them, smaller crystals in the walls throwing back sparkling rainbow light.

A road paved with stone blocks has been carved through the crystal forest. It stretches out in two directions, twisting and disappearing behind massive crystal columns.

"The Crystal Road," Tabitha says.

"I can see that. The Aztecs were pretty literal, weren't they?"

"They weren't big on superfluous language."

"How long do we have before our friend out there breaks through the archway?"

"Should be a while. Hours, at least. Maybe a day,"

Tabitha says. "But I'll feel better if I'm not right next to the entrance." She starts to head down the road and I fall in step beside her.

"I'm more worried about why it would try to get through at all," she says. "I've run into it before but I give it a wide berth and it leaves me alone. It's a hunter, but I've never heard of it going very far for prey. It usually stays in the rivers on the other side of the mists and takes souls on their way to Chicunamictlan."

"So, you're saying it doesn't like me."

"Does anybody?"

"Ha. Funny. Okay, it wants to eat me. Why? I'm gonna go out on a limb here and say Santa Muerte doesn't control it, or you wouldn't be freaking out about it. So Mictlantecuhtli?"

"No. And why would he? He wants you to get to Chicunamictlan to kill Santa Muerte as much as you do. No one controls it as far as I know. It's associated to Tlaloc. But Tlaloc's gone. Quetzalcoatl killed him in the war."

Could Quetzalcoatl be behind this? That doesn't scan, either. He wants me to burn Mictlan down. Is this his way of warning me to keep my agreement? Or has he decided I'm not the guy to make it happen so he's sent the Ahuizotl to take me out?

"What about Quetzalcoatl, then? Could he have gotten control over it after Tlaloc died?"

"I suppose, but I don't think it's likely. What would he have against you? He's not able to come into Mictlan anymore, so I'm not sure how he could even be directing it."

"Yeah. I don't get it, either."

It hesitated at the top of the amphitheater. Why? It could have jumped down from the top of the amphitheater and gotten to me. It probably wouldn't have gotten me, all I had to do was fall backward and I'd have gone through the portal. But did it know that?

Or does it not want to kill me?

If Quetzalcoatl sent it to keep tabs on me, that might make some sense. Quetzalcoatl was banished from Mictlan. So how did he give it orders? How did he tell it to come after me? There's more here I'm not seeing, yet.

"How far until we hit Mictlantecuhtli's tomb?"

"Not too far. But you won't like it when we get there."

"I don't like anything about this trip, so why change now?"

"It's sealed behind a circular door that has to be rolled out of the way."

"Oh, is that all? So I put my back into it. I thought you were talking about the demons."

"Putting aside that it's about twenty tons, rolling it aside isn't the tough part," she says. "Hang on. What demons?"

"The ones I dumped in there. A bunch of them got loose in a storage place on Santa Monica, and I didn't have anywhere else to put them."

"So you dumped them into Mictlantecuhtli's tomb?"

"Seemed like a good idea at the time. And it's not like he was using all that space."

"How many did you put in there?"

"Twenty? Thirty? I wasn't exactly counting at the time. Don't worry about it. I have a plan to deal with them. So what's this about this door?"

"Okay. I guess we're done talking about the demons," she says. "The door's locked. I can't open it."

"Goddammit." Do I have anything that explodes? Maybe I can blast it open.

"I said *I* can't open it."

Ah. I get it now. Shit. "I can but I have to use Mictlan-tecuhtli's power to do it, don't I?"

"Sorry."

I wave it off. "Whatever. I'll burn that bridge when I get to it." A wave of dizziness hits me and I stagger. I steady myself against one of the quartz crystals. Tabitha grabs me.

"What's wrong?"

I shake her off. "I'm fine."

I knew this was going to happen eventually. I need sleep and food. The Adderall is only going to carry me so far and any spells I know that can keep me going have a nasty price. The drugs are actually safer.

"No, you're not. How long have you gone without sleeping? Days? And what about food? You need rest."

"I am not sleeping here. Or near you."

"Eric, I'm not going to— You know what? Never mind. I'm going to take a nap. You do whatever the hell you want to do. Sleep. Don't sleep." She puts out her hand and an apple appears in her palm. "And maybe have something to eat."

"I was wondering where you got that apple." I don't make a move to take it.

"Jesus, Eric." She rolls her eyes and puts it on the ground in front of me. "You're not Snow White, I'm not the Wicked Witch." She goes over to one of the larger crystals on the side of the road, sits down against it, closes her eyes. "And it's not a goddamn apple. Wake me up when you pull your head out of your ass."

"That could be a while."

"Don't take too long. That Ahuizotl's still out there. And you're not getting any less jaded."

"I see what you did there." She doesn't say anything in response. I pick up the apple, look it over. I've never been good at conjuring. Not a lot of mages are. We're great at bending reality around but making something out of nothing is a whole other level.

Knew a guy in Philadelphia who made a killing on the séance circuit by conjuring watches, rings, bracelets, shit like that. He'd do this 'Spirits, show me a sign,' shtick and make them rain down on everybody. Inevitably somebody would insist that one of the pieces had been buried with their dead grandmother.

I worked with him for a few weeks. I'd be behind the scenes talking to actual ghosts and feeding him information. Made a lot of money for a while. But then he ran into a demon he'd tried to cheat twenty years before and ended up as a wall decoration.

I take a bite. She's right. It's not an apple. The consistency is like an avocado, but it tastes like custard. Before I know it I've finished the whole thing. I don't seem to be in any danger of passing out until a prince kisses me, but I am damn tired. Even with the Adderall buzzing through my skin exhaustion is threatening to pull me down.

To hell with it. Tabitha's right, whether I like it or not. I need sleep. I lie down against one of the crystals, bunching up my jacket to use as a pillow. I'm out in seconds.

———

"Jesus, not you again," I say.

Alex / Mictlantecuhtli sits across from me in a dimly lit bar that I know I've been in, but can't quite place. Strong 1930s vibe, jazz quartet playing on a stage. It isn't until I see the guy behind the bar, a massive black man with arms like tree trunks hitting on some redhead, that I figure it out. Darius.

"Why are we in Darius's bar?" The bar was the last place I saw the Djinn back in Los Angeles. I'd only been there twice when it looked like this, and not for very long either time. It's a pocket universe inside his bottle that he changes around from time to time and lets people in by opening portals scattered around Los Angeles. Just because he's trapped in his own little world doesn't mean he can't be social.

Before I left L.A. he'd had the place done up as CBGB's in New York. He was big into punk in the late nineties but he didn't have a great idea what the place looked like. I took a trip there and brought him pictures. During the time I was gone his tastes had shifted from punk, and vomit in the bathrooms, to jazz and speakeasies.

Alex looks around this recreation from my memory and sips at a glass of scotch in front of him. Balvenie '78 from the bottle sitting on the table.

I pick up the bottle. "Now that's just mean," I say.

"Got some memories about that, don't ya?"

A few. Tabitha snagged that bottle of scotch from Alex, and we said we were going to drink it together. Took a while before we got to that point. It was good. But now when I think of it all I can see are Tabitha's lies and Santa Muerte's face.

"So what are we doing here?"

"I like the vibe," he says. "Nice music. And it's good to see Darius again. Even if it's only by plucking him out of your head."

"You are really starting to— Say that again?"

"Darius and I. We go way back. He never told you?"

I was banned from Darius's bar once I got married to Santa Muerte. This was before Mictlantecuhtli started showing up to me.

I think about it and realize that Darius did tell me. When I met Santa Muerte he was the one I went to looking for information. He said he knew her back before she became Santa Muerte. Told me Mictlantecuhtli was dead, for a given value of dead, of course. Said he'd met them a long time ago.

I assumed that was all bullshit. Darius isn't known for being big on the truth, though he's not exactly a liar. I figured he heard about them through some kind of demigod grapevine or something. But if he actually did meet them . . .

"Anyway, I'm not here to dredge up old times and get all maudlin over some castaway Djinn," Alex says. "I'm here to tell you that what you're doing is a really bad idea."

"What I'm doing is trying to take a nap but instead I'm sitting here having to listen to your bullshit. Speed it up so I can stop dreaming and go back to sleep."

"You're going to open my tomb. You don't want to do that."

"Why, because I'll let out all the beasties I put in there? Or because it'll use some of your mojo, and I'll end up as a green garden gnome? Either one's a risk. And I'm okay with taking a risk."

"It's not just that. If you go in there and kill Mictlantecuhtli you're screwed."

"This is, what, the thousandth time you've told me this? Here's the thing. I don't believe you. I think you're trying to keep me from killing him because, well, he's you. So I'm going to ignore that advice, like I've been doing, and go carve out his heart. Maybe I'll eat it. You never know. I'm wacky that way."

"So you're siding with Santa Muerte, then."

"No, I'm not. This is not an either or thing. I'm going to kill her, too. In fact, I'm not just going to kill her, I'm going to kill her really, really hard. I'm going to tear those bones apart and build a hamster wheel or maybe an end table out of them. Then I'll feed the leftovers to dogs. I think she'd appreciate that, don't you?"

"You don't have to be sarcastic about this," Alex says, an offended tone in his voice.

"You keep trying to warn me away from this and it never works. You're not keeping me from going in there. I'm not getting any sleep. Neither one of us is getting what we want right now. So let's just end this. Cut the cord. Don't bug me, anymore. Pretty soon you'll either be out of my head or I'll be dead. Either way, I win."

"No," he says, "you won't. Because when you go in there, your body turning to stone, he'll kick your ass before you can kill him. Then you're stuck. Awake, aware and encased in jade for all eternity. I'm sure you'll just love it."

"I know what I'm getting into. But thanks for your concern, mom. It's really touching."

"You're an idiot."

"And you're just a chunk of bad memories stuck in my skull. I'm really looking forward to getting rid of you."

"Everything fine here, gents?" Darius looms over the table, two tumblers of amber liquid in his meaty palms. He sets them down on the table in front of us. "Heard me some raised voice over here. Thought, now that's not a way for good folks to conduct themselves in my establishment. So I thought I'd help smooth out the road. Drink up, take the conversation down a notch."

We both stare at him. "Are you making this happen?" I say.

"Not me," Alex says.

I've had plenty of these visions by now. Mostly with Mictlantecuhtli until I managed to block him out completely, and now with this leftover bit of his consciousness. But they've never had anyone else in them. It's always been me and him. That's it. When something has happened, a blown tire, a light bulb exploding, something that interrupts the conversation, it's been a signal that the vision is about to end.

But this one doesn't seem to be ending.

I sniff at the alcohol. Like the real Darius's drinks it's a weird concoction I can't identify. The real deal tastes like a hundred different things inside of ten seconds and all of them will be good.

I don't know that I trust this, though, so I don't drink it.

"Oh, don't look so surprised, gentlemen," Darius says. "I may be locked away and buried way up in the land of liquid sunshine, but that don't mean I can't put myself out there from time to time."

Holy shit. Now I get it. "Butthead over here didn't pick this place, did he?" I say.

"He might have been . . . influenced a bit."

"What are you talking about?" Alex says. "I—" He freezes, cracks crawling across his face and down his body like crazing on pottery. He explodes into fragments the size of sand grains and blows away on an unfelt wind.

"Ah," Darius says, as if he's just had the most satisfying shit of his life. "That's so much better." He slides into

Alex's empty seat. He's a big man but moves with surprising grace. "How you live with that garbage in your head I have no idea."

He gives me a big smile with too many bright, white teeth. "You and me, son, we need to have ourselves a conversation."

Chapter 19

"So it really is you?" I ask.

"You got no way to tell for sure, so you'll have to trust me. Or not. Up to you."

"You certainly sound like Darius. Only I thought I was persona non grata in your bar."

"You are. This isn't my bar. It's your dream. It just happens to be your dream of my bar. So it works. I've been waiting for you or that chunk of Aztec dickcheese floating inside your head to have this dream for months now. Finally realized I had to take matters into my own hands. Think of it as your dream with a little help."

"Okay. How? I mean, magic, obviously. But how'd you get a spell into Mictlan?" There's a lot I don't know about magic, that nobody knows about magic. The best we can really say is, "because it works." I haven't heard of any human mages figuring out how to cast in one plane and directly affect another beyond summoning spells. When I'm over in the ghost side of things nothing I do affects the living side and vice versa. Not that that means a whole lot. One thing mages are really good at is keeping our secrets.

"Son, when I say I'm from the old country I mean the *really* old country. I'm some grade-A, antediluvian shit over here. I know a thing or two about bending cosmic powers to my will."

"Uh huh. Sure."

"Okay, yeah. I mean, I am really goddamn old. But I been here before. I know my way in and out of Mictlan." He leers at me. "All I need's a hole." Yeah, that's Darius, all right.

Connections begin to click together. "Mictlantecuhtli told me when he was trapped in his tomb that he cut the Spanish off from some superweapon, but it was too late to save his people. I thought it was Quetzalcoatl. But it was you, wasn't it?"

Darius throws back his shot, gets a faraway look in his eye. "Seven? Eight thousand years ago? I was trapped by a Halaf wizard in Tepe Reshwa in Mesopotamia. Fucker stuck me in a clay pot. Stunk of spoiled mutton. Still can't stand the smell. Couple thousand years later my prison gets an upgrade to a gourd."

"A gourd?"

"A gourd."

"Livin' the high life, there."

"Oh, it was a nice gourd," he says. "As gourds go."

I knew Darius was old, but Jesus. Eight thousand years? And that's how long ago he was trapped. How long had he been alive before then? Does "alive" even apply to Darius? I'm afraid to find out.

I slam back my drink. It might not be real, but it still tastes good and if I'm lucky it'll make me just as drunk as the real thing.

"Eventually I ended up in al-Andalus. Berber general name of Tariq ibn-Ziyad. Bounced around, changed hands. By the time I ended up with Cortés I was in an actual metal and lead crystal bottle. Very swank."

"I thought you came across with Cabrillo. By the time he came to California, Cortés had already wiped the Aztecs out."

"Yeah, by the time he came to California, sure. But first he was in Mexico. Came over with Pánfilo de Narváez to kick Cortés' ass. Some political bullshit. Only Cortés heard about it and left Tenochtitlan to wait for Narváez and take him out. Once Narváez was out of the way, Cortés pulled his troops into his own army."

Something about this story is poking at the back of my mind. Then I have it. "Cortés already had Tenochtitlan when that happened. And when he left that's when things really went to shit."

"Yep. Left some yahoo in charge who panicked and ended up slaughtering a few hundred Aztecs. By the time Cortés got back it was a lot worse than when he left. Lost a lot of men trying to haul his gold out of the city. Had some help from the Tlaxcala, some locals who hated the Aztecs. Shit, everybody hated the Aztecs. After that it was a real war. Cortés regrouped. Months of fighting to take Tenochtitlan back. Tens of thousands of men dead."

"What were you doing during all this?"

"Keeping Huitzilopochtli, Tlaloc, and all the other gods off Cortés's ass. Weren't for me, they never would have made it half as far as they did."

"And Cabrillo?"

"He got put in charge of a bunch of crossbowmen. After the siege to retake Tenochtitlan Cortés stuck him on a fool's errand. There was this priest who wanted to take the fight to the Heathen Gods. Found some ritual to get into Mictlan. So Cortés hands him my bottle and tells him to go nuts. So it's me, this crazy-ass priest and Cabrillo and his men. And your buddy Quetzalcoatl. Gods are batshit, but him? Hoo-boy. He was a piece of work."

"No shit," I say. "He's running around Mexico as a wind spirit made of trash now." Darius cocks his head, looking like a cat that's wondering whether something should be played with or eaten.

"Huh. That's news. You'll have to tell me that story sometime."

"Let me survive this one first. So you killed a bunch of the gods and came into Mictlan to finish the job."

I play that sentence back in my head. Darius killed the Aztec gods. Holy shit. *Darius killed the Aztec gods.* I've gone drinking with this guy. He's in my goddamn city. Trapped, sure. But what happens if he gets out? What happens if somebody lets him out?

"Most of them." There's a dangerous gleam in his eye as though he knows what I'm thinking. And hell, maybe he does.

"That does explain why you were worried I'd come after you once I'd signed on with Santa Muerte. I can't imagine she likes you much." Though what the hell he thinks I can do to him I have no idea.

"Mother of all understatements, there."

"Why didn't you just tell me?"

"Partly because I couldn't. There's all sorts of things I can't talk about. Those two death gods saw to that. But mostly I figured you'd freak the fuck out."

I think about that for a second. "Good assumption. I

probably would have. So what the hell happened in that tomb? The place is littered with the bones of dead Conquistadores."

Darius takes another drink. Both our shot glasses are suddenly full. I remember this is a dream. I toss back a second one and watch it fill back up the second I put it back onto the table.

"Got ambushed. Mictlantecuhtli was waiting for me. Set a trap. Had some mojo all set in there to stick me back inside my bottle and lock it up tight. I don't know what the plan was after that. Whatever it was, it didn't happen. I turned him into a rock while he was sitting there working his magic to shove me back in my bottle. Everybody was losin' their shit about then. Dead soldiers. Priest just a smear on the wall. Lots of chaos."

"And that's when Cabrillo took the bottle," I say. The gaps are filling in quickly.

"Only thing that saved him. Took him weeks to get out of Mictlan. And I was no help. He couldn't open the bottle. I couldn't get out. He kept me around, afraid what would happen if anybody else got hold of it."

"And then he bounces around South America and twenty years later heads up to California, gets himself killed in the Channel Islands. And your bottle winds up where?"

"No idea. Somewhere on the mainland."

I know Darius well enough to catch when he's outright lying, something he doesn't do very often. He's much better at twisting the truth by simply not telling you all of it. But a flat out yes or no? That's not like him.

"This is fascinating and all," I say. "And it fills in some holes, but what does it have to do with why you're here now?"

"Shit's about to hit the fan, son. For you and that little lady you got snoring out there. You're both fucked and you got no idea how bad."

"Oh, I have an idea."

"No. No, you really don't."

"Then tell me. You know what Santa Muerte wants from me, don't you? You know her agenda. Which one of them is telling the truth? Which one do I kill to fix this?"

"Oh, it ain't nothin' that simple. But there's three problems with telling you what the real deal is and how to keep your ass out of the fire. The first is that I can't tell you. Not the important part at least. Mictlantecuhtli's magic locked me up, sealed my lips as much as it sealed my bottle. I can't get out even if somebody finds it. That shit lasts a long time. I've only been able to talk about this at all in the last hundred years or so."

"It's weakening?"

"Yeah, but not fast enough to do you a goddamn bit of good."

"Great. So, what, I play Twenty Questions?"

He taps the end of his nose. "Got it in one. Though I seriously doubt it'll take you twenty."

I haven't slept in days and the first time I get any shut-eye I get to spend it playing a guessing game with a Djinn.

"All right, what else?"

"Second one's more of a problem. See if I tell you, then you know."

"How is that— Oh. If I know it, this piece of Mictlantecuhtli in my head knows it."

"You keep this up, son, you may win yourself a cigar. Right now I got him asleep. He ain't eavesdropping on this conversation. But once you're awake, it'll be like normal and he can run his fingers through your brain like it's a Rolodex."

"But what does that matter? I've got it locked up in there. It can't talk to Mictlantecuhtli or vice versa. So what's the big deal?"

"We'll get to that. But trust me, it matters."

"So what do I do?"

"You forget," he says. "You'll get your answers and then I'll block them off."

"You're going to tell me and then make me forget. I'm seeing a flaw in this plan."

"Oh, you'll remember, but only when the time's right. We'll work out the details. Chances are, when you do remember, you won't have a lot of time to use what you know. Seconds, probably. So I'll make sure you at least remember that you forgot."

Takes me a bit to wrap my brain around that concept. "That way I'll be waiting for it to kick in and not just be caught by surprise."

"Right. Now that piece of ol' Mick you got in there with you, he'll know you learned something, too. But he won't be able to get to it until you do."

"What are you getting out of this?" I say.

"Revenge. Fix a problem should have been fixed a long time ago. I've been watching and waiting for this for five hundred years. And when I met you I knew that eventually one of them would come callin'. Truth be told, when you up and left L.A. I panicked a little. Wasn't sure you'd come back. But then she got her hooks into you and here we are."

"Why do I feel like the mark in a long con?"

"Because that's what you are. You're the mark, you're

the McGuffin. You're the boy they're gonna screw over, and you're the treasure they've been huntin' for."

Well, goddamn. "So this all started five hundred years ago?"

"Yep."

"And you're telling me that for five hundred years there were no other necromancers around?"

"None that were powerful enough, or weren't batshit crazy. I mean you got your moments, but you remember that Nazi who used to live in the Hollywood Hills?"

"Neumann, yeah. He was a prick. I heard somebody ate him."

"Somebody did. Friend of mine. For a long time Neumann was the only game in town. I think you can understand why nobody would want to throw in with him. Lot of you necromancers are just as crazy, or more so."

I'd met Neumann a couple times before I left L.A. Talked a little shop. But he was a condescending little fuck who always had these two bodyguards around who creeped me the hell out.

One was this body-builder, six-foot, easy. Real enforcer type. The other was his homunculus. Twisted, little, razor-toothed midget who followed him around on a leash. Homunculi are good places to store all your rage if you have anger management issues. Long as you can keep them from eating people they're not bad to have around.

"L.A.'s not the only place with necromancers. We're rare, but we're not that rare."

"Rare enough for their purposes."

"All right, what's the third thing? I'm not going to be asleep forever. I need to know everything."

"Son, we're in a dream. We got all the time in the world. But that third thing? It's maybe the most important one of them all and the one you'll have to fight through to do. And that is that you're really gonna hate it."

"I think anything that gets me out of this situation is a win. Hit me."

He tells me.

He's right. I hate it.

———

I startle awake, my head pounding and my mouth tasting like a rat just took a shit in it. The alcohol in Darius' bar might not have been real, but it still gave me a hangover.

The dream is still vivid and fresh in my mind with one massive exception. The entire conversation we had after he told me I was going to hate his suggestion. It's just a blank.

Now I only hope that when it's time for it to come back to me that it does. I pull myself up from the ground, stretch my back and hear it pop.

Tabitha sits cross-legged against a crystal eating another one of her not-apples. She sips something from a clay cup the color of a blood orange.

"Morning, Sunshine," she says. "Good nap?" She tosses another one of her not-apples at me. I'm slow and groggy but manage to catch it, anyway.

"It was informative," I say. And maddening. I keep poking at the hole in my memory. I get that it's for my own good. At least I think it's for my own good. "Don't suppose that's coffee you got in that cup."

"Water," Tabitha says. "I can't do coffee. Chocolate, though, if you like it bitter."

I turn the not-apple in my hands. "What is this?"

"White sapote. The Aztecs cultivated them."

"You picked this trick up from Santa Muerte."

"Came with the package." She puts her hand out, palm down toward me. There's a snap in the air and a red cup identical to hers appears in front of me. I take a sip of the water, and like the fruit I ate last night, it's gone before I realize it. "If you let yourself try you could do the same thing."

"Summon food of the Ancient Aztecs?"

"Other things. Like the boat I made to cross the blood canals."

"Useful trick, but I think I'm a little far gone for that to be a good idea. Don't suppose you could call up some tequila."

"Sorry, no. I can do pulque, though if you'd like."

"Oh, Jesus, no."

"Bad experience?"

"You have no idea. Okay, so I'm trying to get an address out of this guy in Chihuahua and he doesn't seem the type who's gonna break if I beat on him. So he says he'll tell me what I need to know if I drink some pulque with him."

"Oh no."

"Yeah. So I say, sure, let's do this. How bad could it be, right? He brings out this pitcher, pours this milky white gunk that looks like jizz shot out of a hippo and stinks like three-day-old fish."

"You still drank it?"

"And threw it all up right then and there."

Tabitha's laughing. "Did he tell you what you wanted, anyway?"

"No, I had to put his head through a wall."

"Of course you did."

We're both laughing now. Tension draining away. And then I think about where we are and what's going on, and the laughter dies and it all gets weird again.

"I want to ask you something," I say after a minute, "but I don't know who I'm talking to."

"We've been over this. I'm me. Part of me is Santa Muerte. Part of me is left over from when Tabitha died."

"I get that. But here's what I don't get. When I saw you last in Hollywood, you were different. More, I don't know, more Santa Muerte? She spoke through you and at the time she *was* you."

She rubs at her wrist just above where the handcuff sits. "But then you showed up and slapped this thing on me."

"The magic in that should have disconnected you from Santa Muerte and it's got a compulsion that forces you to not get too far away from me. But that's it. You're not fighting me all that much on killing her. You haven't beaten me over the head with a stick and tried to take the obsidian blade from me. You haven't let me get eaten by the Ahuizotl, or tossed me out of the boat into the blood river."

"I'm not hearing a question," she says.

"Are you your own person? Or are you still Santa Muerte's mouthpiece?"

"I've always been my own person," she says.

"Look me in the eye and say that and maybe I'll believe you. What are you, Tabitha?"

She taps the fingers of one hand against her knee. Doesn't answer me. I don't say anything, just let the silence grow more and more awkward.

"I've had her voice in my head for years," she says.

"Knowledge, memories. Not everything. There are gaps. Maddening gaps. I know I have my own opinions. I've argued with her. I argued with her about your sister, about you. When I would become her it was like I was filling up with power and knowledge and everything made sense. And even when that went away and I was less than that, I knew I was a part of something bigger, something important. And I wanted to always get back to that, stay connected to it."

"And now?"

"Now it's gone. When she came to me it was like finding a sister I never knew I had. But now I'm not sure I want that connection back. The piece of her inside me is just me now. And when I think about her voice it feels like—"

"Gaslighting?" I say. "She lies, Tabitha. You know that. She's lied to me. She's had you lie for her."

"She's the most honest thing I know."

"Yes. She's a *thing*. She's not human. She's death. Nothing more honest than that. But it's when she's not being death that there's a problem."

I consider my words. I feel like I'm talking to a spooked horse. There's a chink in Tabitha's devotion to Santa Muerte and I want to worry it open, a little bit at a time. Too much too fast and it could all break down.

"What would you do if you didn't get that voice back? That connection?" I say.

She gives me a sad smile. "What does it matter? It's not like I can stay away from her forever. Even with this trinket on my arm. This thing ends one of two ways and you know it. I either go back to her or you kill me."

"What if there was another way?"

"You mean kill her and let me live? I still have part of

her in me, Eric. If she dies and I don't, I don't know what will happen. But I don't think it will be good for any of us. I'm still not going to help you kill her."

"Will you stop me?"

"I don't know anymore."

"Fair enough." It's not much, but it's a start. I don't want to have to kill her. I don't know what she is or who she is, but she's not what I thought she was.

Of course, says that voice in the back of my mind, she could be lying now, too. I rub the bridge of my nose where the headache is growing. I'm tired of all this. Tired of the paranoia. Tired of the betrayals. I would like to be able to trust somebody. But something tells me that's not going to happen any time soon.

"She loves you, you know," Tabitha says. "As much as she knows how. I've felt it. She's been alone for such a long time."

"I know. I figured that out a while ago. It's fucked up, like Sid and Nancy fucked up. She's not human. She's not going to feel the way we do. The fuck does love even mean with her? Love the way a dog loves a bone? Love me enough to murder my sister to get my attention? That's insane to me. But it isn't to her. I think she loves me for what she can use me for. She's got a plan. And I'm a big chunk of it. You know that, too. Hell, you might even know what the plan is."

"I don't," Tabitha says. "That's one of those gaps I was talking about. I have some of her memories, but there are things she won't share with me. That's one of them."

I feel sorry for her. I want to tell her about Darius, but what would I say? An eight-thousand-year-old Djinn told me what's going on but he made me forget, and wow is that less than helpful, or what? Yeah, that'll fly like a lead balloon.

And say I could remember. Should I tell her? Probably not. Darius could be blowing smoke up my ass. Or he could have it wrong. Maybe he doesn't really know as much as he thinks he knows. Too many variables, too many risks, too many ways for things to go shit wrong. But at least it's a direction.

Instead I say, "Did she say why she chose you?"

"I told you, I've got the same kinds of powers you do. She needed a necromancer."

"For what?" I say. "What's the long game? You've asked, haven't you? Wondered?"

"Of course, I've wondered. I just—" Confusion in her eyes. "It never seemed important." The drumming of her fingers on her leg speeds up. She's questioning. Nervous.

"So you never asked."

"Once," Tabitha says, her voice cracking. "She wouldn't tell me."

I don't want to push her any more. I tell myself it's because that might force things too far too fast and it'll backfire. That all I need right now is for her to be questioning things. The seed's planted. Let her worry on it.

But I wonder if I just don't want to hurt her.

"How far to Mictlantecuhtli's tomb?" I say, standing up. My knee creaks and my back screams at me with a knot of pain. I ignore it as best I can. I put out my hand and she takes it. She holds my hand a little longer than is strictly necessary before I help her up. Or maybe I hold hers. I can't tell.

"An hour maybe," she says. "Are you sure you want to try to get in there?"

" 'Want' isn't exactly the word I'd use, but yes. I don't know if killing him will stop the progression of the jade, but I have to try."

"It could speed it up."

"So could all sorts of things. I'm trying not to think about it."

She starts down the road and pauses mid-step. "If nothing else," she says, not looking at me, "please know that I'm sorry that it came down to this. That it happened at all."

"Yeah. Me, too."

Chapter 20

I can tell we're getting close because I can feel Mictlante-cuhtli's power uncoil inside me like a snake catching the first rays of the sun. It's a big knot of want. It wants to get into that tomb, wants to reconnect with Mictlantecuhtli. It knows it's in the wrong body and it wants very much to fix that.

Weirdly, the raven tattoo on my chest is getting in on the action, too. It's been feeling off for months now, as if the change in me is changing the ravens. They might be magic, but they're still just ink. Even when the spell triggers and releases them, they're just phantoms. A last ditch weapon when the shit hits the fan. There's no thought in them, certainly no will. But I still can't shake the feeling that they're waking up.

We head around a bend and all my tattoos get in on it. The ones to ward me against being detected by Mict-lantecuhtli are beginning to itch and burn, even where my skin has turned to jade. The burning spreads. Each tattoo lighting up on my skin like they were drawn in fire. Searing pain engulfs my body and it takes everything

I've got to keep from falling to my knees. As it is I bend over double, gritting my teeth through it.

"What's wrong?" Tabitha says. She runs to me, trying to help but I wave her off. I lean against a crystal column, push myself forward.

"I'm fine," I say.

"No you're not. Tell me what's happening."

"Fuck, I don't know. My tattoos are rebelling, or something." Most of them are protection spells, shields to stop a bullet, misdirections to keep me hidden, spells to ward off magical attacks. They're all kicking into over-drive. There's a threat here and they're doing everything they can to protect me. But I can't tell what the attack is or where it's coming from.

"Mictlantecuhtli," Tabitha says. "He doesn't want you in there. We should leave."

"He can go fuck himself," I say. "Besides, I thought you wanted him gone."

"I do. He's dangerous. But not if you're going to end up dead before you get there."

I'm not crazy about the idea myself, but if I'd seen a way out of it without this I'd have done it already. I force myself to straighten up. What are these spells trying to protect me from? Something about the tomb? Something on the door?

"You're not feeling anything?" I say, gritting my teeth against the pain.

"No."

"Lucky me. I always knew I was special. Come on." I push myself onward, staggering with each step. It feels like walking through burning Jell-O. Tears fill my eyes and run down my cheeks and it isn't until I wipe them away with the back of my hand that I realize it's blood.

When I start bleeding from my eyeballs it's time to admit I might be wrong. I'm about to turn back and get away before this kills me, but then we make another turn and there it is. Set against one wall of the cavern is a circular, stone slab a good ten feet across. The door to Mictlantecuhtli's tomb.

I stagger against it and the moment my hand touches its surface the pain stops. Whatever it was it's gone, though I can still feel the ravens circling hungrily in their tattoo and Mictlantecuhtli's dark power seeping into my bones.

"Oh, look. We're here."

"What gave you the first clue? How are you feeling?"

"Better. Recognized." I tap the slab. "Like this thing knows me." I pull my hand away, waiting for the pain to start again, but it doesn't.

"That's good?"

"I don't know. I'm not sure it's me that it's seeing."

The stone looks a lot like the Aztec Calendar Stone sitting in a museum in Mexico City, a massive, twenty-ton calendar made of basalt that shows the different eras of the Aztec civilization. But instead of being split repre-sentations of jaguars, wind, rain, and water to mark out the different eras, it's covered in death iconography.

In the center is carved Mictlantecuhtli's face. His real face, not the one of Alex I've been talking to. A skull with eyeballs bugging out of the sockets, a feathered headdress, a necklace of human eyes.

Surrounding his head are carvings of different loca-tions in Mictlan. The mountains, the plains, the rivers, the mists. All the places where the dead travel to reach Chi-cunamictlan and claim their final reward. The work is stunning, cut with laser-like precision.

Behind that slab, inside his tomb, Mictlantecuhtli is waiting for me, encased in his own prison of jade. I wonder how the change is affecting him? As the stone takes me over, is his flesh becoming revealed? Skin hanging from bones, organs pushing out and visible against it? Is his skeletal face plumping out with muscle?

"What do you know about this?" I ask.

I can feel the power in my bones stretching out toward the door like a plant to the sunlight. I run my fingers across the stone, feeling for any kind of mechanism, a switch, something. Physically it's just a big rock. Dead, inert. Magically, it's lit up like a fucking Christmas tree. Even if I didn't have Mictlantecuhtli's power rolling through my veins I'd feel it.

"Only what I've picked up from Santa Muerte. Her memories are fuzzy about it. I don't think she liked thinking about it much."

"I don't blame her. It can't have been fun." I wonder if I'd stayed connected to Mictlantecuhtli would I have picked up his memories instead of his annoying personality popping up in my dreams?

She touches the stone. "I've always wondered why she never tried to do anything about it."

"What, like crack it open? That does seem kind of weird. What sorts of memories do you have from her, exactly?"

"Bits, mostly. Images, thoughts, knowledge. I've pieced together more than I've actually gotten from her. Like I said, there are gaps."

"Maybe gaps about him?"

"Some, yeah. I know she loved him intensely. They were married for thousands of years."

"Really? She seemed kind of bitter about it."

Tabitha frowns. "It's hard to tell with her, sometimes. They didn't always get along? How did you put it? It's fucked up, like Sid and Nancy fucked up?"

"Cemetery love. I've had a few of those relationships."

"You still do."

"Like I need reminding."

I tap at the stone some more. The magic in it traces along the carvings, stronger in some spots, weaker in others.

"You wouldn't happen to have any dynamite in that messenger bag, would you?" Tabitha says.

"Yeah. Just not sure I should use it."

"Wait, seriously? You have dynamite?"

"Better, actually." I dig through the bag, pushing past Zip-loc bags of grave dust, a vial of Four Thieves Vinegar to ward off disease, a chicken foot amulet for protection against demons and a severed thumb I got off an Icelandic Seiðmenn that I can't remember what the hell it's for.

"Here we go." I pull out a small green marble the diameter of a quarter. "I got this from a Bruja in L.A."

Tabitha's face turns sour. "Oh. Her."

Tabitha met the Bruja, Gabriela Cortez, when we went in to Tabitha's bar to find a shapeshifting Russian mobster. The mobster killed Tabitha, though if he hadn't there was a good chance Gabriela would have.

"You saw her for like two minutes," I say. "How much do you even remember from that night, anyway? You were dead for most of it." At least I thought she was. I also thought she was normal at the time.

"The night's fuzzy. I was less me than I was Santa Muerte at the time. I just know more about the Bruja through Santa Muerte's memories than you do, obviously."

"Yeah, I think I'm siding with the Bruja on this one," I say. "She didn't turn out to be Santa Muerte's avatar." She did try to kill me, though. Which, to be honest, is not that rare an occurrence. "Before we do this, I have to take some precautions. If those demons are still in there that's gonna be a whole lot of trouble."

I dig a depression into the dirt road about twenty feet in front of the tomb with the heel of my shoe. Another minute of rummaging through my messenger bag and I find a half-empty bottle of Stoli. It's an impromptu spirit bottle, a ghost trap. Some poor schmuck died in Darius's bar and left a ghost he couldn't get rid of. I did the old Djinn a favor and trapped the ghost.

I've been meaning to let it go, banish it to wherever it needs to be, but I keep forgetting. It hasn't exactly been high on my to do list. The volume of the bottle isn't important. When it comes to spirits you can fit a surprising number of them into a really small space. Demons, too.

I set the bottle into the depression and tilt it so it doesn't wobble and the opening faces the entrance to the tomb. I draw a circle around it in the dirt with my foot, unscrew the cap and set it aside. Finally, I pour salt into the circle, and add a couple of drops of blood from my thumb.

I can't see the ghost inside, but I can feel him. Small, insignificant, scared. I kinda feel sorry for him. I don't even know his name. Probably feels like an eternity in there. Trapped with nothing to do but bang around against the glass like a fish in a tiny aquarium. Suck it up, pal. Things are tough all over.

Normally I wouldn't have to go through this much trouble. But I need to set it for bigger game than just a ghost, and using my own magic to bait and set the trap might just be a really bad idea. This way I only have to tap a little bit and this small ritual does the rest.

"One makeshift spirit bottle half-filled with the finest Russian spirits a gulag chain gang ever had the misfortune to drink."

She bends down to look at the bottle. "If it works, it'll suck in all the demons?"

"That's the idea."

"What if it doesn't?"

"Then we won't have anything to worry about again ever. But don't worry. It'll work just fine."

The trap set, I turn my attention back to the door. There's a space in the carving of Mictlantecuhtli's mouth. It's not large, but it's deep. Deep enough for me to shove the marble into it and seat it firmly. The marble's keyed to me, so it won't just go off if I drop it.

"Might want to stand back," I say. We both get behind a column of quartz about ten feet away. I've been pretty close to these things when they went off, but I don't want to take a chance that the blast won't kill us, too. Maybe I'm paranoid, but these things can leave a hell of a mess. I prime and trigger it with a thought.

A tremendous flash fills the cavern as the marble explodes. When the blast fades Tabitha starts to look around the edge of the column and I pull her back. I learned the hard way that the show's not over yet.

A sound of rising wind punches through the air with a sonic boom that rattles my teeth. Dirt, dust, anything that isn't nailed down in this section of the road gets pulled in like a black hole to end with a muffled pop. I can feel the force tugging at my clothes, shifting the quartz column we've sheltered behind.

The wind and noise die down. I give it another minute and venture a peek around the column at the stone slab.

"Well, shit." Nothing. Not even a scratch.

The fifteen feet or so of ground in front of the door is polished clean. All the dust and dirt and crap got sucked into the blast. The only thing left is the spirit bottle and the circle of blooded salt. The spell binding it will keep it in place against anything short of a hurricane.

"There's got to be another way to open it," Tabitha says. "Maybe together we can push it aside?"

I'm out of ideas. If Gabriela's exploding marble trick can't put a dent in it, I don't see what else I've got that might. "I appreciate the sentiment, but I need to get in there and this is the only way in. I clearly can't blow it up. I can't roll a twenty-ton stone slab out of the way on my own. Even with you helping I don't see it happening. There's only one way to do this. It's locked. I've got the key."

"Let me try," she says. "Our powers are similar. Even the ones we've inherited. Maybe it will open for me."

"Be my guest."

She steps up to the slab, hand hovering just over its surface and stops. "What happens after you kill him?" she says.

"You know what happens."

She nods. "I'm going to have to stop you."

"Thanks for the reminder, Señora."

"Goddammit, Eric," she says. "I'm not Santa Muerte, all right?" She taps the side of her head. "I have a piece of her inside me, that's all. I have my own thoughts and my own feelings. I believe she's right and she's doing what she needs to. I'm not her goddamn puppet."

"Careful there, Pinocchio, your nose is growing."

"Oh, fuck you." Tabitha reaches up to the slab, fingers resting lightly on the stone. She closes her eyes and a soft radiance grows from inside her to an intense white light. I can see her bones, organs. It's like she's burning from the inside out. She takes her fingers from the stone, then slams them hard against it, unleashing all that built up energy into one massive strike.

Two things happen. The first is that Tabitha gets blown back into the road, hitting the dirt and skidding a good five feet before coming to a stop. The second is that the door doesn't open.

Tabitha stands, shaking dirt out of her hair. Aside from some burn marks on her clothes she looks fine. She brushes more dirt from her clothes.

"It didn't work at all, did it?" she says.

"Not even a little."

"You're sure you don't have some magical crowbar in that bag?"

"I wish."

"Shit. Just be careful, then," she says. "Please?"

"If I were the careful sort we wouldn't be here in the first place. Stay behind the bottle. Once this thing opens up those demons are gonna pour out like a burst pipe. And, uh, if any of them get past it, might want to duck."

"What do you mean if any of them get past it?"

Mictlantecuhtli's tomb isn't going to open up to anything less than Mictlantecuhtli's power. I had really hoped I could have avoided this.

There's a good chance that this is going to tip me over the edge, turn me into a permanent place for pigeons to shit on. That was the whole point of taking the long way through Mictlan instead of just using his power to pop inside the tomb. But I don't see any way around it.

I go back to the door, tracing the carvings with my fingers. There doesn't seem to be any obvious way to open it. No handholds, no keyhole. After a moment of looking and not finding anything I press my hands against the design of Mictlantecuhtli in the center of the slab and his energy takes notice.

"Eric," Tabitha says, "I asked you a question."

"It'll be fine," I say. "I've done this hundreds of times."

"Hundreds?"

"Okay, a couple. But they worked. Mostly."

"Eric."

My attention pulls toward the energy flowing out through my center, spreading down my arms, into my hands. There's an even greater hunger to it now. A need in it. Pain tears through me as the power rips through my fingers and into the stone.

My knees buckle, but my hands stay locked to the slab. The carvings glow with a sudden green flame that spreads across their surface, running through the channels between the designs.

The power won't let me go. It rips through me like high voltage through a penny. My legs give out and I collapse to the floor, my hands still stuck to the slab, smoke rising from them. Tabitha runs forward and yanks me back, drags me behind the bottle. I'm too weak to stand, so I let her. A deep rumble wells up from the slab. Slowly, with a sound of stone grinding on stone, it rolls to the side.

I can feel her crafting a spell, that same not-quite Santa Muerte magic I felt at the blood river filling my nostrils with the smell of smoke and roses. I'm not sure if she's doing it or if it's the piece of Santa Muerte in her soul reacting. The spell is sloppy, instinctual, less a spell and more an outburst of power.

Mictlantecuhtli's power responds to it before I can tamp it down. I can feel it intertwining with her own, the spell amplifying. I try to pull it back, but I've lost any illusion of control I ever had over it.

I can't tell where I end and she begins. The power inside knots together, pulls tight against the other and for a split second we're so deeply entwined. We're just the energy, just the spell. The will of Santa Muerte and Mictlantecuhtli merging together.

The spell tears loose from us with a sound like a cannon. A wave of blue fire rips itself out of our bodies and fills the chamber in front of us. My vision goes white, blinding me, and all I can hear is a high-pitched whine.

Tabitha and I collapse in a heap on the ground, neither of us able to do more than wheeze. Either it destroyed the demons in the chamber, or the spirit bottle got them. Or it did nothing and they're already coming for us but we're too blind and deaf to know.

I'm really hoping it's not that one.

Chapter 21

"Did it work?" Tabitha says after what feels like forever. I must have blacked out at some point because I don't remember my vision and hearing coming back.

We're not dead so I suppose something worked. "I'm not sure I even know what that was."

The spell wasn't one I've ever felt before. It didn't even feel like magic, not the way I know it. It was nothing but distilled rage. The phrase "wrath of god" pops into my mind and I realize that that's exactly what it was. The fury of the old gods channeled through their avatars.

I slowly drag my way to the bottle. Besides a very pissed off ghost and some tainted vodka there's nothing in it. I sniff at the air. Something's not right. When demons die there's a smell. Like rot and asphalt. Once you smell it you never forget it. It can last a few days.

But I'm not smelling it. So unless the spell we just unleashed destroyed every trace of them down to the stink, and hell, maybe it did, I should be able to smell dead demons.

"I don't think the demons were in there," I say. I

slowly manage to stand, my balance shaky. I steady my-self against one of the quartz columns. I look at my hands. Though they feel burnt, and there's smoke coming up from them, the pain is fading fast and they don't look damaged. No blisters, no burns. They're not even red.

"Where would they be? Could they have gotten out?"

Light from the crystals around us fills this end of the tomb, fading off into darkness the further in it goes.

"I don't see how," I say. "Not unless somebody opened the door and let them out." That's not something I want to think about. Bad enough they almost got loose in the living world, I can't imagine what kind of mayhem they might get up to over here.

"How are you feeling?" she says.

"You mean am I a garden gnome?" I feel fine. Which, come to think of it may not be a good sign. When I was first changing it was agony every time I tapped into the power. It left me shaking and weak afterward. Mictlan-tecuhtli told me that when it stopped hurting was the time to worry. I haven't hurt in a long time from it, but opening the door was agony. The only difference now is that the feeling passed quickly.

"I think I'm okay," I say. I pull my left sleeve up and see that I am so not okay.

Shoots of thin, green lines follow the veins into my hand. Dark green stone extends up my forearm and into my wrist. There's a slight numbness where the stone is. Nothing too noticeable, just an absence of heat or cold.

And it's spreading.

The green stone swallows up my flesh, spreading like a wildfire. Within seconds my left hand is engulfed in stone.

"Oh, Jesus, Eric," Tabitha says. She looks me in the eyes and her own go wide in shock, horror plain on her face. She steps back.

"What? I'm not gone yet. Shit. It's not just my hand, is it?"

"No, it's not."

The vision in my left eye is suddenly tinged a light green. I tap at my face with one of my newly jade fingers and hear the cold tapping of stone on stone.

"Is it still spreading?"

"You can't feel it?" she says.

"Not really. I mean it doesn't hurt. Feels a little numb, but not everywhere."

"It looks like it's stopped. It's covering the entire left side of your face, though."

I wave my hand in front of my eyes and see it go green as it passes into my left field of view. "Kinda figured that part out, yeah. I'm still moving, so there's that at least."

Dammit. I hope I don't tap Mictlantecuhtli's power for anything else. This spreads anymore and I'm done. I draw the obsidian blade. Nothing like running out of time to keep you focused.

I'm so close and suddenly I'm not sure what to do. I think back to my conversation with Darius. From my meeting with him I know there's something I'm forgetting. I almost have it, but that's the magic. If I try to remember it I can feel it just out of reach.

I step into the tomb, a long, wide chamber that's more a vault than anything you'd call a tomb. There are no decorations, just rough stone hollowed out hundreds of years ago. The soft light from the glowing crystals outside barely penetrates the gloom.

The floor is still littered with the bones of Conquistadores who'd died when they went up against Mictlantecuhtli. Discarded pieces of armor, broken weapons. Now that I know what really happened here I can see the pattern of chaos. It's clear some of the men died fighting, swords still clutched in their hands. But the way so many of the skeletons are facing, and how close they are to the door tells me that most of them died running.

"You coming?" I say.

"I'll hang back," she says. "I'm not sure Mictlantecuhtli would be thrilled to see me."

She's probably right.

I shuffle through the piles of bones littering the floor. Tabitha stands in the doorway behind me. I stop when I reach an unusual pile. Long, blackened leg bones. Cracked and burnt skulls like twisted hyenas. Elongated snouts, long, curved fangs.

"Found the demons," I say.

Before they ended up down here they'd been twisted into a thing called an ebony cage, a structure made of their still-living bones which continually released an elixir of liquid magic. It's like the magic in the local pools, only in a drinkable form. Distilled and concentrated. Useful when you need some extra muscle in your spells but don't have the ability to pull very much.

"You're not screaming. That mean we're safe?" Tabitha calls from the entrance.

Alex had the cage under his bar in Koreatown and was using the sorts of late night dramas bars are known for to feed emotional power into it and tapped the juice coming out to sell for a tidy profit.

After he died Vivian stuck the cage into storage where it broke, releasing dozens of these things. If they'd gotten out into the general population they'd have killed a lot of people and possessed their corpses, and L.A. would have been in the shit.

They almost killed me but I was able to open a passage into the tomb and toss them in. I figured Mictlantecuhtli would be pissed off at having his living room invaded by a bunch of unwanted guests.

Didn't realize how pissed off.

"From them, yeah," I say. But from Mictlantecuhtli? When I was here last he'd been an unmovable statue, inert and lifeless. That was mere hours before I sent the demons here. And just after I did is when I really started my transformation to jade.

Did that little bit wake him up enough that he could destroy all these demons? He is a god, after all, so I suppose it fits. But if that's the case how has my continued transformation affected him? I was hoping to find him as a statue at the end of the tomb, not powerful enough to destroy demons. Suddenly I'm not sure how well this whole walk-up-and-stab-him plan is going to go.

The farther into the tomb I get, the less light from the outside reaches it. Soon the gloom gets too strong. I can't see the end of the chamber. I start to cast a light spell and think better of it. I can still feel Mictlantecuhtli's power thrumming through my body. It's like that tense twitchiness you get in your muscles when you've just taken some meth but it hasn't cranked up to full blown grind your teeth levels. If I cast a spell, even a small one, will it tip me over the edge?

"Hey," I say. "You mind shining a light in here?"

I feel a spark of magic as she casts a spell, and a glowing sphere appears near the ceiling casting light through the entire chamber. I can't believe what I'm seeing. Or more to the point, what I'm not.

"You have got to be fucking kidding me," I say.

"What is it? What's wrong?"

"Mictlantecuhtli," I say. "He's not here."

"What? No, that's not possible." Tabitha comes into the tomb, stepping hurriedly over bones and weapons. "How could he get out? He's locked in jade."

"I'm gonna go with: Not anymore."

I should have guessed something like this would happen. I was banking on the idea that he wouldn't be able to move around until he was completely free of the jade. And even if he was that he'd still be stuck in here. Wrong on both counts.

"Is there another entrance?" Tabitha says.

"He wouldn't need one."

"So now what?" Tabitha says.

"I'm not sure." Where would he go? "Where's Santa Muerte now?"

"Probably in Chicunamictlan. She travels through Mictlan all the time, but now that the mists are open and souls can get through they're going to be flooding the place. I can't imagine she won't want to be there to greet them as Mictecacihuatl."

I look at my left hand, the light reflecting off the polished jade. I'm glad I don't have a mirror. I run my hand through my hair. It moves, but it feels stiff, brittle.

I'm running out of time. Whether I use Mictlantecuhtli's power or not, it's still spreading. Soon, today, tomorrow, an hour from now, it's going to be all over.

"Then that's where he is. Can we get there through the Crystal Road?"

"Mostly. But there's no guarantee *she's* there. I could find her, though. She'll either know where Mictlante-cuhtli is, or she'll be able to find him."

"No." The only way Tabitha could do that is if I take off the cuff and reconnect her to Santa Muerte. I'm not prepared to do that.

"Eric, you're not going to last much longer. What happens if we get there and she's not? What if she is and we can't find him in time?"

"I said no." But what if she's right? It's a good possibility. Mictlan's a big place. They could be anywhere. And I'm sure they know by now that I'm here and looking for them, even if they can't find me. All things considered I don't see how I have any other choice.

"All right, then. Let's get going."

———

"End of the line," Tabitha says. Bright light shines through a cave opening and the road slopes up to meet it. We come out into another copse of madrones, more of the Cihuateteo. I can hear a quiet shift in the wood as branches bend toward us.

"Is that normal?" I say.

"Yes. They're tasting the air," Tabitha says. "Wondering if we're a threat." A moment later the branches shift back.

"Guess they like us."

"More that they like me. I've been here before. They never really got along with Mictlantecuhtli." I follow her through the grove.

"So what *is* Chicunamictlan, exactly?"

"It's a city. Looks a lot like Tenochtitlan or Teotihua-can, but bigger. Stone carvings, jaguar sculptures. Homes,

markets, ball courts for ōllamaliztli games. Lots of tzompantli. Skull racks never really go out of style. Then
there's the Bone Palace."

"That doesn't sound at all ominous."

"It's just a building, Eric. It's not even made of bone.
It's where Santa Muerte holds court. She and Mictlantecuhtli used to use it for rituals, but that hasn't happened
in half a millennium. If she's anywhere in the city she'll
be there."

We push our way through the trees. Unlike when we
were heading toward the Crystal Road entrance outside
the mists, the trees aren't hampering our way. They bend
aside to open a path for us.

When we get out of the copse onto a boulder-strewn
desert landscape, I can see what she means. Chicunamictlan glitters on the desert horizon with a skyline to rival
New York. A sprawling metropolis of Mesoamerican architecture that never existed on Earth. Stone buildings
the size of skyscrapers, carved from limestone and red,
volcanic rock. Everything brightly painted in reds, greens
and blues, a stark contrast to the dead, colorless ruins in
the land of the living.

In the center of the city stands an immense pyramid
that reaches toward the sky. When I met Santa Muerte
in a slice of Mictlan that extended to L.A., she had the
same thing sitting where Dodger Stadium should have
been, only on a much smaller scale.

I whistle. "Big place."

"And then some. There's more underneath. Hard to
pin down its size. It shares space with Xibalba."

"The Mayan land of the dead?" Interesting. I always
assumed that all these places were sequestered from
each other, but with so much overlap in religions that

kind of makes sense. "If the Spanish had gotten through to here—"

"They could have taken a hell of a lot more than Mexico."

What would have happened if they had? If Mictlantecuhtli hadn't gotten rid of Darius? If Quetzalcoatl hadn't been kicked out? Belief's a powerful weapon. Gods have rules, constraints. Humans, not so much. What could a bunch of zealots do in a place like this? Create a new Spanish pantheon? Elevate themselves to godhood? Would the Aztecs have even been remembered?

The more I learn, the more I think we shouldn't be fucking with these things. Gods are bad, people are worse. "Does Santa Muerte always stay in the palace?"

"Not all the time, no. Sometimes she wanders the streets, but eventually she'll be back. Once she hears you're in the city she'll come looking for—"

Tabitha falls face first into the ground. At first I think she's tripped, but then she gets yanked back toward a boulder behind us, her hands scrabbling in the dirt. That's when I see the hand grabbing her ankle and the long, ropy tail it's attached to.

I jump after her, but the Ahuizotl is fast. Faster than me by a long shot. Shooting it with the Browning is out of the question. Even if I could get the gun out in time I honestly don't think I'd hit it. Same with the pocket watch. Its time bending isn't exactly precise. It'd be just as likely to kill Tabitha.

The only other thing I can think of is a spell. But ever since I opened the door to Mictlantecuhtli's tomb his power's been sitting there inside me itching to get out. And if I let it, I'm fucked.

The trick is to cast without touching that power. It's so tightly tied up with my own at this point I don't know if that's possible. But if I don't, who knows what the Ahuizotl will do to Tabitha.

I throw out a minor levitation spell that I hope is strong enough to help, but not so strong that it will tip me over the edge. I don't have to use magic to stop the Ahuizotl, I just need to slow it down.

The tail pulls taut as my spell takes hold, grabbing it and yanking it toward me. I haven't stopped running and the pause before it breaks free is just enough for me to get close in with the obsidian blade.

I slash at the tail, opening it along its length, hot blood spraying from the wound. The Ahuizotl lets loose a shriek, dropping Tabitha and jerking back its tail, the hand at its end spasming.

Tabitha scrambles to her feet as the Ahuizotl leaps to the top of the boulder it had been hiding behind. It lets loose a roar, showing fangs dripping with green pus. It looks a lot more dangerous up close than when I saw it at the entrance to the Crystal Road.

It occurs to me, as I'm standing there holding Mictlantecuhtli's blade, that maybe I should have pulled out the Browning, instead. Blowing holes into it from a distance just seems like a better idea than trying to take it on with a glorified steak knife.

A ball of blue fire flies over my shoulder and slams into the Ahuizotl's chest, throwing it off the boulder and setting it ablaze. Of course. Just because I can't cast spells, doesn't mean Tabitha can't.

"Come on," she says, grabbing my hand and pulling me along with her. We run as fast as we can.

"You don't think that killed it?" I say.

"I know it didn't. I've tried that before. Makes it nice and pissed off, though."

"That's a plus how?"

"It isn't."

The Ahuizotl roars behind us. I can hear it running. I'm afraid to look back, but I know that if I don't do something it's just going to keep coming.

I pull the Browning and turn around to face it, knife in one hand, gun in the other. I get off two shots that hit center mass and do fuck-all to slow it down. Twenty feet away from me it leaps. I lift Mictlantecuhtli's blade high as it comes down on top of me. A part of my mind is trying to figure out how big it is. Too big for a jaguar. Too small for a tiger. Though once you get past really fucking big, it's pretty much a moot point.

The rest of me only knows that it's really fucking heavy and fast and it feels like being hit with a truck. Its weight bears down on me, and I slam into the ground.

Its roar turns into a scream as the blade punches through its abdomen. Hot blood sprays me from its opened gut. I push the blade down, ripping through more of its flesh. It rolls away, slashing its claws against my side, shredding my jacket and striking sparks when they hit the stone.

I try to get up but the wind's been knocked out of me. I can't move. It's then that I realize I don't have the knife or the Browning anymore. The blade stuck in the Ahuizotl's belly when it rolled off me, flinging it into the dirt a good ten feet away. I don't see the gun anywhere.

I use the same levitation spell to grab the knife, but I twist the magic a bit to pull it to me. It zips toward me, but before I can get hold of it the grasping hand at the end of the Ahuizotl's tail wraps around my neck and jerks me up off the ground. It brings me close, looks at me with bright, green eyes, its face twisted into a scowl of pure hatred.

"Liar," it screams. "Welcher, cheater, grifter. What do you have to say?" It loosens its grip enough that I can take a breath.

"I'd say somebody bought you some of that word-a-day toilet paper." My voice comes out in a strained croak.

"Quetzalcoatl is waiting. Why have you not fulfilled your bargain? Why does Mictlan not burn?"

It takes a second for me to realize it's not speaking English but I can understand it just fine. Nahuatl? Good bet. I had something similar with Mictlantecuhtli last year, but I couldn't tell because all I heard was English. The Ahuizotl looks like a badly dubbed Kung Fu flick.

"You do get that you're gonna go up like everything else here, right?"

It tightens its grip around my neck. "As was promised me, yes. Mictlan burns, and I am released."

"So he did send you. I told him I had things to do first."

"I have been waiting for five hundred years to be free of this hole." It loops its tail around my neck a couple of times and squeezes tighter. I can feel trapped blood pounding inside my skull. The edges of my vision fade to gray. You'd think with all this turning to stone crap I'd be immune to strangulation. But no. I claw at its tail, try to loosen its grip. It's no use.

"If you will not free me with the release of death then I will free you and feast on your carcass. I will crunch your bones between my teeth and lap up your blood.

You are no good to me if you will not fulfill your end of the bargain."

I would really like to tell it that I'd be happy to keep up my end of the bargain, but that I'll have to be alive to do it. But its grip is too tight and I can't get a whisper out, much less a full sentence.

"You want to be free?" Tabitha says behind it. "I'll free you." It whips its head around to face her as she steps in close, slashing Mictlantecuhtli's blade hard through its throat. The knife tears a massive gash that opens up all the way to its spine.

Arterial blood fountains out of its neck like a busted hydrant. It tries to slash at her, but its already dying and she easily blocks each strike with the knife, slicing into the hands, lopping off fingers.

It recoils from the pain, but Tabitha keeps up her attack. She steps in close, reaching up into the massive gash in its throat and yanking its tongue out through the hole. On one hand, Jesus fucking Christ. On the other, she just pulled off a pretty flawless Colombian Necktie.

The Ahuizotl knocks her aside, scrabbles at its throat with its lacerated hands. The tail loosens around my neck and I fall to the ground. The Ahuizotl tips over, a thick, wet sound coming from its ravaged throat. Tabitha rushes it again, slashing with the knife. It tries in vain to ward off Tabitha's attack. When it finally stops moving Tabitha doesn't seem to notice. She keeps slashing at it with the knife like a crazed butcher. I pull myself free of the tail, wait until her strikes slow and finally stop.

She stands next to the Ahuizotl's corpse, her breath coming in hitching gasps. She wipes blood out of her eyes. We're both drenched in it.

I come up to her and before I realize what's happening, she has the Browning pointed at my head.

"Tabitha—"

"You are going to tell me about Quetzalcoatl and this burning down Mictlan bullshit right the fuck now," she says. "Or I will goddamn shoot you."

"You think I didn't put a spell in that cuff you're wearing to keep you from killing me?"

She calls my bluff and pulls the trigger.

Chapter 22

The round hits the left side of my face, snapping my head back and making the inside of my skull ring like a bell. Half an inch to the right and it would have hit flesh and not stone.

I stagger more from shock than any actual pain or damage. The bullet flattened when it hit the stone and bounced into the dirt at my feet. I wonder, if it had hit flesh would it have blown out the back, or just bounced around the inside of my stone skull?

"Jesus fuck, Tabitha."

"You were saying?"

"Fine, I lied about that part." I touch the spot where the bullet hit me, but all my hand comes away with is Ahuizotl blood. I start to wipe my hand on my pants leg but that's covered in blood, too.

"You want to know what's going on? I'll tell you. But I'd really like to do it when I'm not covered in blood." She's in just as bad shape as I am. Her blue flannel shirt is soaked through with blood and her jeans are so thick with it they're almost black.

"You're going to fucking tell me now or next time I won't miss."

"Can we at least go somewhere we can get cleaned up? Or do dead Aztecs not bathe?"

She lowers the gun, but keeps her finger on the trigger. "There are homes just outside the city. We can stop at one of those. Just so you know Santa Muerte will know we're here no matter what cloaking spells you've got. She knows whenever anybody sets foot near Chicunamictlan. She'll come looking."

It's a gamble, but I'm betting that she's going to wait for me to come to her. She's proud. She likes to hold her power over people. She comes to me and she might as well admit that I've got her scared. That's just how she's wired.

Or I could be wrong and she could show up at any moment and stomp me flat.

Tabitha turns on her heel and starts to walk toward the city. I get into step behind her, the coppery stink of blood thick in my nose. My coat's a loss. Covered in gore, slashed to hell. The shirt's just as bad. I can probably get away with hanging onto the pants for the moment. They're black and, besides making the fabric stiff and sticking to my legs, it's not too bad. And the messenger bag, well, to be honest it's been through worse.

Even if she hadn't shot me, from her body language I can tell Tabitha's furious. I can't blame her. She clearly cares about this place and about these people.

I'm not sure I don't. They haven't done anything, and I'm not really up for mass murder. Hell, it's beyond murder. Kill somebody in the living world and their souls go on. Kill them here? That's it. End of the line.

I won't do that unless I absolutely have to. "So what do you want to know?" I say.

"Isla de las Muñecas," Tabitha says.

"Creepy place. What about it?"

"What you did to the portal. Is that where it started? The only way to close it was to free the spirits trapped in the dolls," she says. "When you came through you stank of smoke, covered in soot. I know you set fire to the place, but it had to have spread fast. So it was a magical fire. Quetzalcoatl did that?"

I clench my left hand over and over as we walk. It doesn't hurt, but it doesn't feel normal, either, especially when I tap my fingers together and heard the clicking of stone on stone. My vision isn't doing much better. Having one eye tinted green kind of screws things up a little. I keep tripping over shit.

"Would you believe a magic Zippo?"

"This is you we're talking about," she says. "So yes, actually, I would. But it doesn't answer the question."

"No. It's not where it started and he didn't do it. He just gave me the lighter. You know why I did it. Those spirits were stuck and they were in agony. They were going to be stuck there screaming until someone destroyed the place. I made that call."

I bring out Quetzalcoatl's lighter to show it to her. She puts her hand out to take it but I slide it back into my pocket.

"Quetzalcoatl and Mictlantecuhtli haven't gotten along since he stole the bones of the dead to reboot humanity," Tabitha says.

"I've heard this," I say. "Quetzalcoatl supposedly came down here during the Aztec's . . . Fourth Era? To steal bones of that era's humans to kick off the Fifth.

They died out or something? I was never very clear on that. Every religion's got an origin story. They know that's not how life actually happened, right?"

"If they do they don't care. Truth is different from fact and truth is flexible when you're dealing with gods. It's true to them, and here that's all that matters. Anyway, they've been holding a grudge against each other ever since."

"Man, gods don't fuck around with their grudges," I say.

"Which is why Quetzalcoatl doubled down and sided with the Conquistadores," she says.

"And that's why he wants to burn down Mictlan?" I say. That's a hell of a grudge. How pissed off do you have to be to help wipe out all your followers?

"Probably, though it's hard to tell with him. What I'm wondering is why you want to do it," she says. "Is your hate for Santa Muerte so strong that you'll destroy everything around you?"

"No. It's not like that." But it was like that. When I started all this, all I was thinking of was killing Santa Muerte, Mictlantecuhtli, and even Tabitha. Burn the place down after? Sure, sign me the fuck up. Salt the earth, never look back.

But now? I don't think I can do it. "I didn't even realize what I was signing up for," I say. "Last year, when I left your place to talk to the Santa Ana Winds? Turns out he's got a connection to them. He's a wind god, they're wind spirits. I got what I needed and in return I promised to burn my home down."

We stop at a rise, and I can see Chicunamictlan more clearly. It really is fucking huge. Nearby are a handful of buildings. Too small for villages, too big for compounds. Fields of corn, groves of lime and avocado trees.

I don't see any livestock, but of course they wouldn't have any. The Spanish introduced cattle, and why would they need them, anyway? They're all dead. But then why the hell would they need corn? Or anything else for that matter?

"Turns out the wind knew about my connection to Mictlantecuhtli before I did," I say. "I didn't know it would lead to this."

"So of course you said yes."

"I needed information. They had it."

"Do you ever think about consequences?" Tabitha says.

"I did what I had to do. I ran into Quetzalcoatl in Zacatecas and he gave me the Zippo. Said it'd burn anything. Figured I'd give it a try on the island."

"I understand why you want to kill Santa Muerte and Mictlantecuhtli," she says. "I even understand why you want to kill me, but you can't do this. You know that, right?"

I don't know exactly when I decided I wasn't going to let Mictlan burn, but I know I won't. I take this place down what happens to all those souls? Do they burn along with it? Do they get ejected into the ether?

When it comes to death I'm used to being the smartest guy in the room, or at least the guy who knows what the hell is going on. Someone kicks, I know they're dead, but not, you know, *dead* dead. Their soul goes somewhere or it sticks around. They don't get destroyed unless something actively makes it happen. But I've only dealt with ghosts, spirits in transition. Souls who've moved on? Above my pay grade.

The souls in Mictlan are just people. I might not like some of them, but people are people wherever you go. Some of them are good. Some of them aren't.

None of them deserve to be on the receiving end of a genocide.

"Yes. And I don't want to. I think Quetzalcoatl knows that, too, which is why he sent the Ahuizotl to keep tabs on me. But if I survive this trip and I don't burn down Mictlan, Quetzalcoatl hunts me down. I'm already trying to get out of a jam with a pair of psycho gods. I don't really want to get into another one."

"So you'll let thousands of souls burn for your convenience. Nice."

"Oh, screw you. You think I haven't thought about this? Do I want to do it? No. Do I want Quetzalcoatl coming after me? Also no. You know how I get out of this without lighting all this shit on fire? The answer is, I don't. I suck it up and do the right thing and keep this fucking lighter in my pocket. I'm a lot of things, Tabitha, but I'm not a mass murderer."

"Just the regular, everyday, one at a time kind, right?"

She's not wrong. I've killed a lot of things that could easily be called people, whether they were human or not. But it's rich coming from her.

"Stones and glass houses," I say. "Every one of Santa Muerte's murders is on you, too. Now that we've firmly established that we're both horrible people, are we done? Or would you like to shoot me in the face again?"

She wants to say something, I can tell. Her face twists into an ugly sneer. "I can see why Vivian hates you," she says, and heads down the hill toward Chicunamictlan.

"Yeah? Well, you are . . . too. Shit."

"I'm sure you'll hit me with a stunning riposte, eventually, Eric," she calls over her shoulder. "Staircase wit. You should look it up."

Somewhere, deep inside, I can feel Mictlantecuhtli's power stirring. I think it's laughing at me.

———

When Tabitha knocks on the door of a house on the outskirts of Chicunamictlan and the occupants see two people covered in dried gore they freak out for about thirty seconds before they realize they're talking to their queen's avatar. Then they freak out for entirely different reasons.

Their entire demeanor is subservient, respectful, afraid. She's polite, pleasant. They don't seem to know what to do with that.

Their names are Tenoch and Mahuizoh, a man and a woman. They're dressed simply, like many of the Aztecs I've met on the other side of the mists. They offer us food, water. But more importantly they offer us baths.

Turns out dead Aztecs don't have indoor plumbing. Who knew? Instead they have a stone tub with a firebox beneath it and a rooftop cistern.

"Does it rain in Mictlan?" I ask Tabitha.

"About six months of the year," she says. My surprise must show on my face because she says, "What, you think it doesn't have weather because it's the land of the dead? The souls who come here are what give it shape. They want weather, they get weather. Who knows what it will be like when the new ones finally get here."

"Probably a lot of Norteño music," I say.

"Oh, joy."

Tabitha calls dibs on the bath. She takes my Browning and the knife with her in case I get any ideas. I'm going to have to get them back at some point, but I'd rather do it in a way that doesn't end with one or both of us dead.

While she's getting a hot soak I'm outside scrubbing as much of the blood off me as I can. I've stripped down to the waist, making the jade's progress even more apparent. My entire left side and most of my right is stone. It covers half my head, goes down my throat and completely engulfs my chest and stomach. From what I can see from my reflection in the water the only thing left of me that's flesh is most of my right arm and the right side of my face.

On the plus side, stone is easier to rinse off than flesh, though the Ahuizotl's blood makes even that difficult. It's thick. Almost pasty in consistency. It coats my remaining skin in a thick sheen like layers of latex paint I can't quite peel off.

I wonder what rain of shit's going to come down on me for killing Quetzalcoatl's pet. Sure, I'm not the one who sliced its throat open and yanked out its tongue, but he's not gonna care. One more thing to toss onto the pile, I guess.

If I get out of this, Quetzalcoatl's going to come gunning for me. If he can't destroy Mictlan, maybe he'll content himself with turning me into a smear. Lucky me.

It takes almost half an hour to get the worst of the blood off. My hosts come out and nervously give me a change of clothes and a rough towel to dry off with. The clothes are simple, a cloak, a short sleeved shirt and a loincloth.

There is no way in hell I'm wearing a loincloth.

The pair say nothing when they come out. They're clearly terrified, whether from all the blood or because they can see that I'm almost entirely made of jade, I'm not sure. Hell, maybe it's the eyes. Or maybe it's just me.

I change into the shirt, can't figure out how the hell

the cloak's supposed to be worn, so I don't bother. I wad up my shredded jacket and shirt, transferring anything I still have in the pockets into my messenger bag. I should find a place to dump these. It feels weird to leave them out here. Like I'm committing some sort of sacrilege. Like that's anything new.

It's quiet here. Peaceful. I clearly don't belong. Even so, the calm of the place is infectious. For the first time in weeks I don't feel completely on edge. I know it's an illusion and it's not going to last. But for a few minutes it feels nice to just lie here and listen to the water lapping at the banks of the stream.

I can see how this could be somebody's idea of paradise. At least on the surface. Tabitha said the people shape the place, and in my experience people don't do peaceful well. The Aztecs were big on blood sacrifice. Do they still do it here? How? They're already dead.

"Oh, yeah. They still do it. What do you think that big palace over there is for, anyway?" Alex. Sitting on the banks of the stream next to me. Every time I see this fucker wearing my dead friend's face it's a kick in the teeth.

"So now I don't have to be asleep or concussed to see you anymore. Awesome."

"For me, sure. I get to make fun of you for a little while longer. But for you it just means you're changing faster." I show him my jade middle finger. "Oh, I see you noticed."

"What do you want?"

"Just a little chat. Pick up from before we were so rudely interrupted by our mutual friend."

"I'm surprised you remember that."

Annoyance on his face. "I don't. I remember you remembering it."

"So the fact that I don't remember all of it must drive you batshit."

"Two minutes. That's all that's missing," Alex says. "And it's not even missing. Just stuck behind a wall. I can't believe you let Darius of all people dick around with your memories."

"I trust him more than I trust you."

"Really?" Alex says. "Do you have any idea how many deaths he's responsible for? Do you realize how many people are here, or were stuck behind the mists because of him? He killed the other gods. He murdered my friends. My family."

"Yeah, I don't know anybody who's murdered my friends and family."

"That wasn't me, Eric. That was your wife. And though I don't like that she did it, I understand why she did it. She wants to make this place whole. She wants to undo all the crap that fucking Djinn did half a millennium ago."

"I like how when you're trying to make something feel like my fault you call her my wife, and when you're just annoyed at her she's your ex."

"What did Darius tell you, Eric?"

"You know as much as I do."

And that isn't much. I remember Darius telling me he needed to give me information and that at some point I'd remember. Though when and how I have no idea. I have a vague feeling that I didn't like what I heard, but besides that, I don't know what the message was.

"Why do you think he did it? To hide it from me? Who am I gonna tell? I'm just a little chunk of Mictlantecuhtli cut off from the rest of me."

"He hasn't lied to me so far," I say. "Unlike some people."

"Oh no, he doesn't lie. He just doesn't tell you all the truth. He feeds bits and pieces to build a narrative where he's the good guy, the victim. He's just an old, trapped Djinn who wants nothing more than to be left alone and make the world a better place. I know him, Eric. I've seen what he can do. He's playing you."

"Why would he? What does he gain from helping me here?"

"I don't know," Alex admits. "Let's hope for all our sakes you don't find out."

"Are you talking to someone?"

I turn to see Tabitha coming down to the banks of the stream. When I look back, Alex is gone.

"Nobody important," I say. "You look nice."

She's wearing a bright red, cotton skirt and a sleeveless, pullover shirt adorned with black and gold calaveras on the edging. A blue and red cloak adorned with black feathers woven into it drapes over her shoulder and she's traded her shoes for sandals. She's holding a package wrapped in rough cloth in one hand.

"Thanks." She chews her lip, doesn't look at me. "Here." She hands me the package. The minute I take it I know what's inside, the Browning and the knife.

"I thought—"

"She's coming," Tabitha says. She shows me the cuff on her wrist. It's glowing and the skin under it is turning red from the heat. "She's trying to find me and she's trying to break this. If she does . . ."

She doesn't have to finish the sentence. If she breaks the spell then they re-establish their connection with each other. If I understand it right, Tabitha stops being Tabitha. I tell myself I don't care. That I shouldn't care. I'm going to kill them both, anyway.

Only I know I'm lying to myself.

In the distance I can see rising dust and it doesn't take long to make out the men marching toward us. I don't see any sign of Santa Muerte with them, but if Tabitha can feel her then she'll be along eventually.

I think for a fleeting moment that Tabitha can run. I have to be here, she doesn't. But she wouldn't get far with that cuff on and where would she run to? And why? What would be the point? Eventually, no matter where she is in Mictlan, Santa Muerte will find her.

I had hoped to kill Mictlantecuhtli first. My gut tells me that's a better bet for fixing me, but I'll take what I can get. That's assuming I get a shot.

The only way out is through. I unwrap the bundle, check the Browning and slide it into the holster clipped to my waistband. I hang onto the obsidian knife, grip it tight in my hand, and wait.

Chapter 23

The warriors arrive first. Twelve of them, heavy jaguar skins draped over their shoulders, macuahuitls, obsidian-edged swords tight in their hands, grim faces. There's no point in fighting them, there's no point in running. If I take one down there are eleven more. If I could risk a spell, maybe.

Tabitha's not in any shape to do anything, either, not that I'm sure she would. These are as much her people as they are Santa Muerte's now. The cuff around her wrist turns an ugly, bright orange, the heat blistering her skin. She doesn't wince, or cry out. There's nothing but defiance on her face.

And then Santa Muerte comes.

She appears as Mictecacihuatl, fading into view with a scent of smoke and roses. Flesh on her bones, face shifting between skin and a grinning skull until it finally settles on a calaveras in bone-white face paint with turquoise circles around her eyes, lips marked with black lines to simulate teeth. Artistic swirls and small jewels fixed to her skin give the appearance of carvings in bone. Her long, black hair flows down her back, shimmering in the light.

She's shed her wedding dress and scythe, swapping them for a long, red dress of rough cloth embroidered with skulls along the hem, a red, feathered cloak over her shoulders. From her neck hangs a heavy necklace of small, golden skulls interspaced with squares of green jade. A thin, matching circlet sits over her brow and jade and gold plugs hang in her earlobes.

She is beautiful and terrible and I have never been more afraid of her in my life.

I feel a tightening in my chest. It takes me a second to realize that it's the tattoo of the ravens. The flesh they're drawn on is jade now, but I can still feel a pulling, as if the skin were trying to tear itself free. I don't know what that means, probably nothing good, but I can't see that there's anything I can do about it now, so I ignore it the best I can.

"Husband," she says, her voice different in this form. Younger, musical. She's looking at where I'm standing but I don't get the feeling that she's looking at me.

"You're looking good," I say. "I like what you've done with, you know, everything."

She bows her head slightly. "As are you," she says.

I can't help but laugh. "You still can't see me, can you?" I say. The spells in my tattoos make me invisible to her, but they don't mask sound. I haven't figured out how to fix that. Pretty soon, one way or another, it won't matter.

"I don't have to," she says. "You leave a distinctive hole in the fabric of Mictlan. I have known you were here since you entered through Isla de las Muñecas. I just had to look for an empty space shaped like you."

She turns to Tabitha. "And you. I am surprised, Avatar, that you would not break the bond my husband holds over you with a thought."

Tabitha catches the question on my face and says, "I could have snapped out of the cuff any time I wanted. I just didn't want to."

"Why?" Santa Muerte says. I'm wondering the same thing.

"It was nice having my own thoughts for a while."

"You can be forgiven for that," Santa Muerte says. "This once. Now break the bond and come back to me."

"No," Tabitha says. "I don't think I will." She winces as the cuff glows brighter.

"Stop it," I say, stepping in close to Santa Muerte and pressing the obsidian blade against her chest. Her warriors step forward, raising their weapons, but she stops them with a wave of her hand.

"As you wish," she says. The cuff cools and Tabitha lets out a long held breath. "I see you still aren't sure whether it is I or Mictlantecuhtli who is the true threat."

"Oh, I'm pretty sure it's both of you," I say. "I just haven't found him, yet. He's not in his tomb." Santa Muerte looks over at Tabitha, surprise on her face.

"It's true," Tabitha says. "The tomb is empty. We were hoping he might have come here, to Chicunamictlan."

"I have not sensed him." She looks over at her warriors as if sizing them up for loyalty. I wonder how many are more devoted to Mictlantecuhtli than to her. She seems to come to some sort of decision.

"You are too dangerous here on your own, husband," she says. "Men, take the blade."

"You don't want to do that." I press the knife hard against her chest until I feel the solidity of her sternum beneath it.

"You forget where you are," she says, "and who rules

here." In the blink of an eye the obsidian blade is in her hand and her men surround Tabitha and I, their weapons at our throats. "I control the very fabric of this place, husband, and until you destroy Mictlantecuhtli you only have a thin sliver of his power."

"I can't very well kill him without the knife."

"Nor can you kill me. When he is found you will get it back." She turns it in her hands inspecting it closely. "I have not seen this blade this close in a very long time."

"Want to see it closer?"

She smiles and I suddenly have a very hard time reconciling this woman with Santa Muerte, whose skeletal grin made reading her face impossible. If she had appeared to me like this, things might have turned out very differently.

"I was there when it was made," she says. "I've seen it close enough. I'll have my men escort you to the Bone Palace. We can search for Mictlantecuhtli together."

I don't like this but I don't see what I can do about it. Will the warriors attack me if I resist? Could they even hurt me? Most of me is jade at this point. But then what can I do against them? Any spells I cast could tip me over the edge. The Browning won't slow them down and the pocket watch would be pointless. What good will a time bending watch do to souls that last an eternity?

And even if I did have something that could hurt them, Santa Muerte can just blink at me and it would all be pointless. She's in charge here, not me.

"Sounds like a plan," I say. Maybe I can figure something out on our way to the palace. "Tabitha's been helping me track him down. Between the three of us—"

"My Avatar and I have things we must discuss," she says. "She will not be joining you."

The warriors crowd around me, pushing their way between Tabitha and I. Tabitha scowls at Santa Muerte but says nothing. If we get separated, I have no doubt that one way or another that cuff is coming off and then, what? What's going to happen that wasn't already going to happen? Did I think I wasn't going to have to kill her? That I could save her from being Santa Muerte's puppet? That she was even telling me the truth and wasn't just an extension of her this whole time?

Yes. The answer comes to me faster than I expect it to. Somewhere along the way I started to believe that Tabitha was telling me the truth and started to think we might get out of this alive together.

"That's not happening," I say. I call up my magic, doing my best to keep the taint of Mictlantecuhtli's power out of it, and blue fire springs up around my hands. Whether Santa Muerte can see me or not she's got to be able to feel the magic.

The warriors look to Santa Muerte for guidance. I know this isn't much of a Mexican stand-off and I can't keep this up forever. With every second I can feel Mictlantecuhtli's power creeping into my own. Pretty soon this little display is going to cost me, and it's not going to gain me a goddamn thing.

"Eric," Tabitha says, stepping between the warriors and putting her hand on my shoulder. "It's okay. It's going to be fine. I'll see you at the palace. Please."

"When I see her again," I say, staring into Santa Muerte's eyes, "she better be her."

Santa Muerte takes Tabitha's hand. That overpowering scent of smoke and roses fills the air and the two of them begin to fade away. "I would not harm my Avatar, husband," she says just before they disappear. "She is far too important to me. Just as you are."

That's what worries me.

———

The warriors box me in as we walk through Chicunam-ictlan. Three in front, three behind, three on either side. The hike to the city is deceptively short. What looks two miles off is in front of us in minutes. Spaces seem different here, distances shorter. I didn't notice that happening anywhere else. Is that part of the breakdown of the rest of Mictlan?

The city is immense. Towering pyramid structures, massive buildings of alternating limestone, onyx and jade bricks rival New York's skyscrapers. Everything is bright, primary colors, complex designs of eagles, snakes and above all else, skulls. Trees and flowering plants line the streets making it feel bizarrely more alive than any place I've ever been.

The people of Chicunamictlan reflect their city. Un-like the couple on the outskirts, the residents here wear bright clothing, sport intricate facial tattoos, cover themselves with gold and jade jewelry.

And with all that, things must be pretty boring here. People are lining up on balconies and the side of the street to openly stare at me as we parade through. I'm probably the newest thing they've seen in five hundred years. When all those Mad Max cars finally show up at their gates they're gonna shit bricks.

As we get closer to the Bone Palace the crowds thin, the novelty of Mictecacihuatl's jade consort wearing off. Exhaustion pulls at me. I haven't had a good night's sleep in weeks and beyond the white sapote I had on the Crystal Road I haven't eaten anything. I'm starting to stagger a little.

I dig an Adderall out of the bottle in my messenger bag and dry swallow it. A couple of the warriors give me side-eye but they don't do anything about it. The pills can't replace sleep. When I finally crash it might just kill me, but something tells me I don't need to last very long, anyway.

"Hey, you guys aren't the ones who chew on coca leaves, are you?" Blank stares. "No, that was the Incas, wasn't it? Damn. I could really use some of that right about now."

I'm not sure they understand me. Whatever quirk had me understanding Nahuatl doesn't seem to go the other direction. Or they're just not talkers.

I spend my time walking to the palace sizing them up, looking for something I can exploit. Jade's harder than obsidian, so if I keep my left side open I should be fine. The blades should just skid along the surface. But there are twelve of them. No matter what, part of me will be exposed.

The Adderall is starting to kick in, pushing my exhaustion into the background. My pace is picking up and I'm getting that tense, antsy feeling in my skin. I start to think I can really take these guys and have to remind myself that it's the drug talking. Still, the energy is good. I'm going to need it.

The Bone Palace looms ahead of us, the tallest structure I've ever seen. A giant, bone-white Aztec pyramid with tracings of dark red mortar between the bricks, a single, wide staircase heading to the top toward a squat, stone structure. It's hard to make out so high above me, but I think I can see part of an altar sitting at the edge.

"How does this whole sacrifice thing work?" I say. "I mean, do you guys get gutted and your hearts grow back, or something? Because otherwise, after a while, wouldn't you run out of people?"

"Yes," Alex says, appearing alongside me. "They 'die,' which here is more like sleeping. Eventually they wake up and everything's normal again. It's a great honor to be chosen. Only the most devoted are taken."

Interesting. So they can die, if only temporarily. Maybe I can get out of this after all. But I'm going to need some kind of distraction.

"Like an Employee of the Month," I say. "Maybe they should hold out for a prime parking space, instead."

"You just have to make everything crass, don't you?"

"It's my superpower," I say. The guards are looking at me wondering who I'm talking to. I'm walking through the streets of Mictlan with green, stone skin. I'm not really worried about a handful of Dead thinking I'm nuts.

"Why are you here?"

"Oh, gloating mostly," he says. "That and to help."

"You're a voice in my head," I say. "I don't see how you can do anything."

"I know this city. Its streets, its alleys. And I can guide you to where you need to be."

"That's awfully kind of you," I say, wondering where he thinks I need to be. Wherever it is it's not here, so that's a point in its favor. "But you have seen these up-standing, steely-eyed gentlemen with no sense of humor, haven't you? I don't think I can take them." I glance around searching for comprehension on their faces. If they understand what I'm saying they're doing a great job of ignoring me.

"You don't need to kill them," Alex says. "Just run away from them."

"That'd be a neat trick," I say. "Got any suggestions how?"

"You're all going to turn left in a moment. There's a building you'll come to with an open doorway. You can run through it, go upstairs and escape across the rooftops. When I give the word, make a run for it."

"Easy for you to say. They can't stab you."

"You big baby. You'll be fine." Mictlantecuhtli's power wells up inside me, pushing at the edges as if it wants to tear its way out of me.

"Are you doing that?"

"That's all you, Hoss," he says. "But if I could, I would. I want you to get out of this as much as you want to get out of this."

Great. The last thing I need is to let what little control I have over this thing slip. "If I turn into a rock before we get out of here you're going to be stuck with me for eternity."

"Point taken."

True to his word we make a sharp left onto another avenue and sure enough there's an open door in a boxy, five story building on the left hand side.

"Now would be a good time," he says.

I start to duck to my left, hoping I can push through the three warriors there when searing pain rips through my chest. Instead of breaking through them, I stumble into them. Their surprise is focused on me for only a moment. And then the screaming starts.

The warriors run past me, macuahuitls raised high. I risk a glance behind me as I stagger through the door. The street has reared up in giant tentacles, paving stones rippling along the surface like snakeskin, to grab at the warriors. It twists, constricting tight around one of them. After a loud, wet crunch, the man goes limp and is tossed away like a piece of trash.

I don't bother to see what else it's going to do and run inside. From all the yelling the warriors have more pressing things to worry about than me. The tightness in my chest begins to subside. I take a set of stone stairs up.

The nearby buildings are shorter than this one, so unless Alex's information is out of date I should be able to cut across the tops of the other buildings. I saw the palace not too far off. I still need to get there. I just don't want to do it with an honor guard.

I figure out that this is an apartment building when I hit the second floor and see people poking their heads out of rough-hewn, wooden doors. Like people everywhere they want nothing to do with all the noise and hubbub and quickly run back inside.

Downstairs I can hear some of the warriors breaking off from the fight with the street and heading inside. I take the steps to the third floor two at a time, drawing the Browning once I clear the next landing.

I see one of the warriors poke his head around the corner and I take a shot, not expecting it to actually do anything to him. But the round catches him just under his left eye, blowing out the back of his skull, spraying bone and brain, but surprisingly very little blood, across the wall behind him. The others don't seem quite so eager to follow.

The roof is through a locked wooden door, "locked" in this case meaning a hemp twine wrapped around a couple of pegs to hold the door in place. It snaps with a little force and I'm on a wide terrace overlooking the block around me.

And it's then that I realize I've made a huge mistake. Sure, this building's higher than the others but the space between them is too wide. I'll never make that jump.

The remaining warriors, three now, pour through the doorway. I take one down with the Browning, blowing out a chunk of his skull that skitters across the roof while the other two try to flank me.

One of them steps in fast, swinging his macuahuitl. The blow glances off my left shoulder, shredding my sleeve and skidding harmlessly down the jade.

He feints, bringing his weapon up and over, catching me on my right forearm, slicing the skin down to the bone and knocking the Browning from my hand.

I grit my teeth against the pain, duck low under his backswing. I hook his legs with my left arm, tackling him to the ground. I do a graceless roll that gets me near the Browning as he pulls himself off the ground. I grab the gun, swing around and put a bullet through his guts. It makes him pause, so he doesn't cleave my skull open, but he's still moving. I fix that with a bullet through his head.

That leaves one more. I find out where he is when he gets his arm around my throat from behind and drags me across the roof toward the edge. I fire blindly, hoping to catch him over my shoulder, but the angle's off. All it does is leave me deaf with hot brass bouncing off my face.

I need to end this fast. I bring my legs up and bend forward, flipping him over. It breaks his hold, but now he's on top of me and I've lost the Browning. The gun skitters across the roof like a frightened spider.

This is not much of an improvement. The warrior tries to get his hold back, but we've rolled into a tangle of flailing limbs. I ram my knee hard into his nuts and he howls, doubling over to clutch at his crotch. You'd think the dead wouldn't feel any pain. I slam my head into his nose and there's a crunch of bone and more screaming.

I roll off of him and get to my feet. Blood is pouring from the gash on my right arm, dripping off my fingers. He's not sure if he needs to hold on to his face or his crotch, so I complicate the decision and kick him in the teeth.

He screams some more so I kick him until he stops moving and his face is a pulpy mess of bloody meat. Then I get down with him and punch his face with my jade left hand until there's nothing recognizable left.

"You have anger management issues," says a voice behind me that I don't recognize. I swing around, ready for another fight and freeze.

The man in front of me is tall, gaunt. Skin so tight I can see bones and organs pressing from the inside as if they're struggling to break through. The flesh on his skull is almost superfluous, paper thin and shot through with veins of green. I can see the hinge of his jaw, teeth pressing against emaciated lips. The dozen eyeballs strung around his neck look crazily in all directions before finally focusing on me.

"Mictlantecuhtli."

"Nice to finally meet you in the flesh, Eric," he says. "Such as it is."

Chapter 24

"You're looking better than the last time I saw you," I say. Considering he was a rock at the time that's not really surprising. As I become more like him he's becoming more like me.

"You're looking worse," he says. "Might want to do something about that arm."

"Huh? Oh, right." My right forearm is a bloody mess with a short, deep gash in it. I can still move my hand and I have feeling in my fingers. The bleeding is bad, but it's not going to kill me anytime soon.

I check my messenger bag for some bandages and come up with a roll of duct tape, instead. One of these days I'll remember to stock a first aid kit in this thing. I wrap the tape tight around the wound. The pressure should stop the bleeding. And if it doesn't, well, I'm probably not going to live much longer, anyway.

"I'm no expert," Mictlantecuhtli says, "but I don't think that's hygienic."

I'm so used to hearing and seeing him as Alex that it's just as disconcerting as Santa Muerte appearing as a flesh and blood woman and not a pile of bones in a wedding dress. The voice is wrong, but he's still as big a smart ass as the chunk of himself still in my head.

"Yeah, well. Needs must and all that," I say. I might not have a first aid kit, but I think I saw some dental floss in the messenger bag. If I get some time I can always stitch it up with that later. Of course, that depends on what happens between now and later. "Thanks for the assist, by the way."

"Just because I have a vested interest, doesn't mean I'm getting in the way of a fight. Come on. We won't have much time until they wake up. And then there's going to be a lot of noise."

"Even this guy?" I say nudging the warrior with the pulped skull with my foot.

"Even him. Might take a him a little while, though. And the guys you shot. And the others who you crushed with the street. Come on." He steps to the edge of the building and raises his arms. Loose stones, dirt and sticks from the street down below rise up and interconnect, mashing themselves together until there's a bridge of debris going from one building to the next. He walks across it to the other roof.

"Wish I'd known that trick," I say, eyeing the structure and pushing my foot against it. It looks like it's going to disintegrate in a stiff breeze, but it feels solid enough.

"You do know that trick," he says. "It'd just be a real bad idea for you to try it. Just like it was a bad idea for you to use that trick with the street."

"I didn't do that. It just happened."

"Sure. That's up there with, 'I just fell on it, doc'. It's a miracle you didn't turn into a statue right then and there. Now come on. I can't hold this thing forever." I hurry across and the moment I step onto the other roof the bridge collapses behind me.

"All right, now what?" Mictlantecuhtli does his trick again and we walk quickly to another roof. He's visibly straining each time he does it.

"Now we get you into the palace so you can get my knife back. Then you go stab my ex-wife. Speaking of which, how come you didn't when you had the chance? I was watching you when she showed up. You had a perfect shot."

"With a dozen armed warriors surrounding me? Seriously?"

"Still think it was a missed opportunity."

"Whatever. Probably should have stuck with the warriors. I was on my way there, already."

"You were on your way to a cell," he says. "She was going to lock you up and then find me. I'm too weak to fight her right now, since most of my power is sitting inside you. Then she sticks me in there with you so you can stab me. You finish turning into a rock, I get reborn into a meatbag. Nobody's happy except her."

"So what's your plan?" I notice that though we've cut across several buildings and are taking a more indirect route, we're getting steadily closer to the Bone Palace. "I take it we don't just show up at the steps to the pyramid and walk on up."

"My plan?" he says. "I don't have a plan. What's yours?"

He pulls together more debris, but this time it's a ramp leading down to an alley. He's visibly straining to keep it in one piece, and it disintegrates as soon as we're on the ground.

"I figured I'd just show up at the steps to the pyramid and walk on up."

"That explains so much. No, we're not taking the

stairs. Don't be an idiot. Mictecacihuatl and I kept this area around the Palace clear of souls. Added privacy. There's nobody in these buildings from here until we reach it. Just follow me and don't do anything stupid like turn into a rock before we get there."

"Thanks for the vote of confidence."

"You could have had this sewn up months ago," he says, anger in his eyes. "You could have gotten here in the blink of an eye. And if you didn't want to, you could have come in through Mitla. So why didn't you?"

"I needed a back door," I say. "I needed to get as close as possible to Santa Muerte. I wasn't going to rush in here and start stabbing people. What do you think would have happened if I'd just shown up at the front gate? I wouldn't even be here by now."

"Oooh, that's a fib," Alex says appearing next to me. "Go on. Tell him the truth. I know he'd love to hear it. You wanted to save your new girlfriend and kill everybody else. Go ahead and keep lying to yourself, but we both know that's why."

"She's not my girlfriend," I say under my breath.

"What?" Mictlantecuhtli says.

"Nothing. Go on, please. You were berating me for not doing things the way you would."

He gives me the kind of glare you can only get from a death god. "If you hadn't wrapped yourself in spells to keep me out I could have helped you," Mictlantecuhtli says. "You still don't trust me."

"Look, I've got a chunk of you still with me, so believe me I've been getting plenty of commentary."

"That's because I'm tired of only having you to talk to," Alex says. "It's really frustrating that you won't let me out to talk to him. You've got lots of charms to keep him out, but nothing to shut me up. If you'd open things up a little—"

"Let's just go and get this over with," I say, cutting them both off before they can say anything else. I follow close behind Mictecacihuatl through the twisting alleys toward the Bone Palace.

Something is bugging me about what Alex just said and it takes a little while before I figure it out. With the spells in my ink, Santa Muerte couldn't see me. But Mictlantecuhtli can. Why?

"That's a really good question," Alex says.

"Will you just shut up?"

"I didn't say anything," Mictlantecuhtli says, annoyance in his voice.

"Not you. The other you."

"Oh. You're talking to him?" Mictlantecuhtli looks around me trying to see the sliver of himself in the air.

"It's really more at him."

"Ah. So exactly how you talk to me, then. Nice to see some things never change. You sound annoyed."

"You don't say?"

Are the spells in my ink just not working? Or is it because of this unwanted connection I have with him? There's part of him still inside me, so even if he can't get into my head, it doesn't mean I can hide from him. Dammit. I thought I'd fixed that.

We make a turn and straight ahead of us is the palace. It's immense. Hundreds of feet wide, thousands high. We come to the side of it and I don't see how we can possibly get in.

We get in close to the limestone bricks and Mictlantecuhtli peers at them, looking for something. "All right," he says, brightening. "Now we're talkin'."

There's a section of wall that looks just a little darker than the surrounding brickwork. Mictlantecuhtli presses his hand against it and it disappears. As it does I can feel the pull of his power inside me wanting to get out, rejoin him. It doesn't hurt so much as it's just uncomfortable.

"Secret passages in Mictlan? Who the hell are you hiding from that you need secret passages?"

"Oh, you'd be surprised. Other gods, my wife, the occasional fling gone bad."

"There was one time when we had to hide from all three," Alex says.

The passage is wide and made of bone white bricks. A soft glow emanates from the walls illuminating our path. Behind us the gap in the wall seals back up as if it had never been there, cutting off the noise from the city as if somebody had thrown a switch. The only sound is my own breathing.

"I feel like I'm skulking through some medieval castle," I say. Between this and the Crystal Road it's a wonder I'm not claustrophobic by now.

"Yes, it's all very Macbeth."

"How—"

"I was in your head for months," Mictlantecuhtli says. "I even know what *Star Wars* is."

A cracking sound like calving ice echoes through the passage. "Do I want to know what that was?" I say.

"That was you," he says. He nods toward my right arm. I pull up my sleeve. The green stone inches its way toward my hand. In here where there's no ambient noise the sound of the jade crawling down my right arm might as well be a gunshot.

"That stunt you pulled out on the street has cut your

time even further. You don't have much left," Mictlantecuhtli says, as if it's something I don't already know.
"Pretty soon it'll be too late."

"I told you I didn't— Ya know, never mind. Let's just
keep moving."

There's only one way to go: up. So up we go. We walk
through the passage, footsteps echoing back to us. We
make some sharp turns, but mostly it just curves a little
with a gentle upward slope. I really hope that the weird
time and distance thing where everything felt further
than it was that I experienced outside the city is working
here, too. Otherwise, if we need to get to the top of this
thing we'll be at it for days.

After what feels like an hour the hallway dead ends
in a blank wall. Mictlantecuhtli stares at it for a long
time.

"Problem?"

"I haven't been here in five hundred years," he says.
"Cut me some slack. Oh, there we go." He presses a por-
tion of the wall that looks like everything else in here
and the wall fades away like smoke. The doorway opens
onto a wide room with lit pine torches and tzompantli
lining the walls, the impaled skulls grinning at us.

"How high up are we?"

"Couple floors," he says.

"That long for a couple of floors?"

"From the top."

"Oh," it hadn't felt like we'd gone that far in that
amount of time. "Would she have brought Tabitha here?"

"Her avatar? Possibly. Why?" We walk through the
room into an adjoining hallway. Everything looks pretty
much the same as everything else. How the hell does he
know where we're going?

I tell him about the handcuff, about blocking the connection between Tabitha and Santa Muerte. How Tabitha refused to take it off. And that last bit is something I don't even know what to do with.

"She didn't seem happy when they left," I say.

"I don't doubt it," he says. "Avatars aren't meant to be individuals. They're extensions of gods. They're our eyes and ears outside. Most gods can't actually leave their domains. Mictecacihuatl and I can't. We can project our consciousness, but physically move among mortals? We need an avatar for that."

Something about that twigs something in my memory but I can't place it. It's just out of reach, and the harder I grasp at it the further away it gets. I let it go. If it's what I think it is it'll come to me when I need it.

"So what do you do when an avatar stops being just an extension?"

"Simple. Get rid of it. Find another one."

"Get rid of how?" I say, knowing I won't like the answer.

"Kill it. How else?"

That is so not going to happen.

"Where would she be keeping her? You mentioned cells before. Would she be locked up? On this floor? Or another one?"

"How the hell would I know what she's doing with it?" he says. "The cells are in the basement, but I doubt she'd put it there. If her avatar is broken, and it sounds like it is, the sooner she gets rid of it the better."

"So she's got her with her. Okay. I can work with that." I find Santa Muerte, I find Tabitha, I find the knife. I kill everybody who gets in my way.

"Hey. Stay focused," Mictlantecuhtli says. "You don't

have time for this bullshit. That means I don't have time, either. We find Mictecacihuatl, get the blade, and you finish the job."

"Excuse me?" I say. "You're acting like I give a flying fuck about you. You want this to end well? Then you fucking help me find her."

"We are in this together, you little shit," he says. "So when I say—" He stops when footsteps round a corner. We both turn to look.

Warriors in jaguar skins. At least twenty pour into the other end of the hall with macuahuitls and spears and sneers showing too many teeth.

I think one of them is the guy whose head I pulped on the roof. It's partly his look but really more that he's the first one who screams and rushes us.

"Run," Mictlantecuhtli says, and bolts down the hall.

Chapter 25

"Run?" I yell as I catch up to him. "You're Mictlante-cuhtli. You're the king of Mictlan. Aren't they supposed to listen to you?"

"I'm not exactly at my most imposing at the moment." All of the halls and rooms look the same. Bare floors, pine torches, tzompantli on fucking everything. You'd think after a few hundred years they'd come up with something a little more interesting than skulls. "I'll draw them off. You find Mictecacihuatl and get that knife back."

He shoves me and I stumble through a doorway, catching myself on the edge before I can fall over. I press myself up against the wall. The warriors sandals slap on the hard stone as they pass by.

At least one of them has stayed behind. I can hear him in the other room. He's trying to move slowly but his sandals are scuffing the stone floor. I'm sure he can hear me just fine. Between the two of us I'm the only one breathing.

I don't want to use the Browning. The noise will just bring everybody running. I don't have the knife anymore, but now that I know I can at least inconvenience these guys for a little while I dig around in my messenger bag until I find my straight razor, unfolding it and holding the blade in a pinch grip. Useful things, straight razors. Good for getting a little blood for rituals. Even better for getting a lot of blood in a fight.

I take a deep breath, loud enough he has to be able to hear it, then hold it and duck down low, pivoting into the doorway. He's taken the bait and his macuahuitl swings high above my head, leaving him wide open. I step forward, coming up and blocking his backswing. I run the razor through his throat. The wound's largely bloodless, but it must hurt because he drops his weapon and grabs at his open throat.

I follow it up with a left hook that knocks him back a little, but he's not going down. He rushes me, hitting me hard and knocking me to the floor. The wound in his throat is a deep gash that keeps tearing the more he moves his head. Pretty soon he'll be able to pass a baseball through it. It isn't slowing him down much.

Because why would it? The ones I took out on the roof I either put holes in their heads or crushed their skulls into oblivion. He's already dead. The hell does he need a throat for?

I block his swing with my left arm and his hand cracks on the stone. It's the swing you don't see that always gets you. His left hook hits the flesh and bone part of my face and I go down.

He bends down to grab me for some more beating, the back of his throat visible through the gash in it. But I manage to grab hold of the discarded macuahuitl and swing it up. The blades bite into his neck, ripping through muscle and tendon, sticking on bone. I yank it down and the blades tear free, shredding their way through until his head is hanging on by scraps of flesh and stringy meat.

He looks at me, more annoyed than anything else, and falls motionless to the floor.

I'm wheezing from the fight and the slash on my arm is oozing blood out from under the duct tape. Mictlantecuhtli must have gotten them far enough away that I can't hear the other warriors. He'll be a good distraction. He knows this place.

And I'm not completely buying that those warriors wouldn't listen to him if he turned around and told them to stop. Either I've got more confidence in his abilities than he does, or he's lying to me. Guess which one my money's on.

Okay, so he's lying. The question is why? Something's tugging at the back of my brain, trying to get out, but it's not quite there. The memory from my conversation with Darius? Fuck, this is maddening. I know why he did it, but so far my tattoos have kept the piece of Mictlantecuhtli in my head from getting out.

I think. But how do I know for sure? He can see me where Santa Muerte can't. There's no way I can be certain that the piece of Mictlantecuhtli in my head isn't talking to him.

I know I'm being played. I've known for a long time. I know they don't just want me to kill the other. I just don't know why or what the endgame is here. I've been so focused on just getting here and staying alive during the journey, I haven't had a chance to give much thought to what I'm going to do now.

Sure, stab them. But I need to get close enough. I need to be fast enough. And let's not forget, I kinda need the blade. All of which is pointing me in one direction. Up. So how do I get up there?

"I could tell you," Alex says, appearing next to me. "It's hidden. Secret passage."

"Why the hell would it be a secret passage?"

"To keep the riff-raff out, of course. Only Mictlante-cuhtli and Mictecacihuatl are allowed up there. Along with whoever they're sacrificing. And I know where it is."

"I'm sure you do. What'll it cost me?"

"Tell me what Darius said."

"You'll know what Darius said as soon as I do. I can't hide it from you."

He glares at me. "It's in there in that fucking melon of yours, and I want to see it."

"I don't know what he said. I don't know how to break that lock he put on it. And, in case you haven't been pay-ing attention, it's there specifically to keep you out."

"Tell me and I'll show you the secret passage. You're running out of time."

"Yeah, that means you're running out of time, too. So how about you stop trying to screw me and just tell me where it is."

"Show me," he says. An edge of desperation is creep-ing into his voice.

"I've made one hell of a lot of bad choices when it comes to you fucking gods. I'm gonna make a hell of a lot more. But this isn't one of them. So tell me what you know, or shut up."

He opts for the latter and disappears. At least I don't have to listen to him whining at me anymore. But it doesn't solve my problem. And then it hits me. I've got the perfect thing to get me out of here. I just have to ask it.

I close my eyes and open myself up to Mictlantecuhtli's power. I'm really not sure this is a good idea, but if it's a secret passage not only do I need to find it, I need to open it. I'm betting I'll need the door to think I'm him.

The power floods through me, a great wash that pours through my limbs, into my mind. Throttling it back is like trying to tie a knot in a running firehose.

I wrestle with the power until I can get enough of a handle on it that only a little is available to me. The rest of it is hammering on the walls of my psyche, trying to break through. I grab that power and channel it into a location spell.

"All right," I say, gritting my teeth from the massive pressure in my mind. It feels like it's going to split me open any second now. "Show me where the passage is and let's get this show on the road."

The pressure focuses on one side of my head, a sharp migraine that bursts inside my skull, driving me blind for a fraction of a second before receding. When my vision clears I see a wide, glowing line running along the floor, out through the doorway, and down the hall.

"Much obliged." I follow the line through a dozen rooms, the maze-like route leaving me lost in a matter of minutes. Every room looks the same. Every grinning skull grins in the exact same way.

Until they don't. The line stops at a tzompantli larger than the others. The rack takes an entire wall, the skulls twice the size of normal. The rack lights up and I feel a tugging in my hand.

I remind myself that I need this. That I asked for it. That there's no way to get from here to there without doing this. Then I press my hand against one of the skulls and Mictlantecuhtli's power pulses through it. The rack and wall behind it disappear into smoke, revealing a wide staircase heading up.

That's when the pain kicks in, my vision goes green and I pass out.

———

When I wake up I take a few seconds to marvel at the fact that I can wake up at all. Everything has a green tint to it. The jade's engulfed the rest of my head and progressed all the way down my right arm. The only piece of me that's still me are the last two fingers on my right hand.

But on the plus side I got the door open. So, yay me?

I pull myself up from the floor and stagger through the doorway to a staircase. The wall seals up behind me. I take the stairs two at a time.

"Kinda dicked yourself there, didn't ya?" Alex says, appearing in front of me. I walk through him, ignoring him. He appears a few steps higher, an annoyed look on his face.

"I could have saved you all that trouble," he says. "Now look at you. You're—" He cuts off as I walk through him again. "Oh, come on."

Funny, I've never really ignored him. Even when he was actually Mictlantecuhtli and not this seed of his personality in my mind. I kinda like it.

"Will you just stop for a second and fucking listen to me?" I give him my answer by walking through him again. I hear an exasperated sigh behind me. He doesn't reappear again.

Dim, gray light shines through a doorway ahead of

me. I can hear raised voices. Santa Muerte and Mictlantecuhtli. They don't sound happy. I suppose that's to be
expected. From what they've both told me they can't
stand each other.

I stop a few feet from the entrance, something else
from Darius's message leaking into my mind. Not memories, not even words or concepts, really. Just this strange
feeling that I've said something wrong. I listen, straining
to hear. There's a background noise of wind whistling
through the doorway making it hard to catch what
they're saying. I give up after a few minutes and keep
going, pausing only for a moment at the doorway before
stepping out onto the roof of the Bone Palace.

The sky has opened up. Rain comes down in sheets,
the wind buffeting me, tearing at my clothes. A heavy,
stone altar, red from all the blood, sits in the middle of
the roof, a prone form lying on top of it, soaked through
from the rain.

Santa Muerte and Mictlantecuhtli stand on the other
side of it, arguing loudly, though over what I can't tell.
Santa Muerte holds the obsidian blade in an overhand
grip. A shitty way to hold a knife if the person you want
to cut can see you coming. It's a stabbing grip.

Fuck. I run to the altar, neither god paying attention
to me. They're too caught up in whatever they're fighting
about. It's Tabitha on the altar, unconscious but still
breathing. The cuff is still around her wrist. She's wearing
a simple, red robe open to expose her sternum. It couldn't
be more obvious what's happening if she had a big, red
X painted on her chest.

She's held to the altar at her upper arms and calves by
thick, metal straps. I pull at them, but they don't budge.

I've got nothing to pry them open with, either, not that I think anything would work. At that thought Mictlantecuhtli's power perks up. It could do it. It could cleave through these straps like they're paper.

"I know what you're thinking," Mictlantecuhtli says. They've stopped their bickering and they're both looking at me. "But it's a bad idea. You do that and you're not coming back from it."

He's right. It would be the end of me. I have two fingers left, and even those are starting to feel a little numb. I'm surprised just thinking about the power doesn't tip me over the edge.

Mictlantecuhtli looks more human than he did downstairs. Long, black hair falls over his shoulders. His face is more fleshed out, but not enough to hide the skull beneath. His cheekbones are a little too sharp, his lips a little too thin.

"Why don't you just stab him?" I yell. The wind has picked up and I'm having trouble hearing myself over it. "You've got the knife. You'll get what you want. You'll get what you want for me. He dies, I go back to normal, and we rule here together. That is what you want, isn't it? You've told me that plenty of times."

Before she can say anything I turn to Mictlantecuhtli. "Or you? Are you saying you're so weak you can't get the blade away from her? You can't wrestle it away? Hell, you don't even have to do that. Just get her wrist bent the right way and shove. Inertia does the rest. What are you two waiting for?"

"You," Santa Muerte says. "We're waiting for you."

"We can't kill each other," Mictlantecuhtli says. "Isn't that obvious? Otherwise don't you think we'd have done that a long time ago?"

"You need to choose, Eric," Santa Muerte says. "This is as much your destiny as it is ours. You need to be the one to choose which god dies."

"Am I executioner?" I say. I nod toward the blood red altar where who knows how many hearts have been torn from ecstatic breasts. "Or priest?"

"You can call it whatever you like," Mictlantecuhtli says. "But the fact remains that you need to kill one of us."

"How about both of you?" I say. "I like that plan better."

Mictlantecuhtli looks at Santa Muerte and sneers. "I told you," he says.

"Told you what?" I say.

"He believes that if I gave you the knife that you would try to kill us both," Santa Muerte says. "He thinks that I chose my consort, his replacement, poorly."

"She doesn't realize just how pissed off you are," Mictlantecuhtli says. "But I've seen it up close and personal."

"So I am reconsidering," Santa Muerte says. "As I am reconsidering my avatar. I will kill her and sever my connection. And then I will decide if I'm going to kill you or simply let Mictlantecuhtli's fate be yours."

"For the record," Mictlantecuhtli says, "I am not a big fan of this plan."

"You're not killing her," I say. "You're going to give me the knife, and you're going to cut Tabitha loose. And then we'll talk."

Santa Muerte turns the knife over in her hands. "And what will you do if I don't?"

I can't use my magic, I can't cast any spells. Bullets will do fuck-all and a straight razor isn't going to be any better. At this point I can safely say harsh language isn't going to make any difference.

But I do have something. Quetzalcoatl's Zippo is in my hand. I flip it open and thumb the wheel. It casts an intense, white light, throwing long shadows across the roof.

"I'll burn this place to the fucking ground and all of us along with it."

Chapter 26

"I told you he was angry," Mictlantecuhtli says.

"What is that?" Santa Muerte says. She peers at it, recognition and panic slowly dawning on her face. "Where did you get that?"

"The important question is who did I get it from. And I think you already know the answer."

"The fire of Xiuhtecuhtli. I haven't seen that in a long time," Mictlantecuhtli says. "Not since Quetzalcoatl stole it from him. And back then it was just a pine torch. How is the old boy these days?"

"About the same as both of you. Old, used up, not worth a good goddamn. But he does hold a grudge like nobody I've ever met. I agreed to burn Mictlan down for him. I'm starting to think it's not a bad idea."

"Do not dare," Santa Muerte says. She steps forward and I bend down to hold the flame inches from the roof, rain spattering on it, but never touching the flame. She freezes.

"He told me this would burn anything. And Mictlan in its entirety. I already tried it out on an island on the living side of things and boy howdy did that place go up like a Molotov cocktail. So I got no reason to doubt that this'll do the trick."

"Oh, it will," Mictlantecuhtli says. "We all have our shticks and that was one of his after he stole it from Xiuhtecuhtli. Before the Conquistadores came we had ourselves a little war. Quetzalcoatl and a handful of others were on the other side of it. He tried to burn the thirteen heavens and only managed Omeyocan, the highest. Killed Ometeotl, the two faced god who made everything. Stars, earth, the other gods.

"So, yes," he continues, eyeing the flame closely, a scowl creasing his face, "it'll do the trick."

Santa Muerte screams. It's a sound of fury, anguish, pure, unfiltered rage. "You dare bring that thing here? Into my home?" Her body shifts, grows taller. Skin bubbles, splits, pours off her bones like boiling wax. The rain spatters off her skeleton, makes it slick and gleaming in the light. Her finger bones stretch, grow sharp and hooked with barbs on the end. The blade looks tiny in her hand.

Mictlantecuhtli watches this display like he's already bored with it. "She does this," he says. "Give it a second."

Santa Muerte turns her rage toward him. "How did he get this into my domain?"

"I'm assuming he had it in his pocket," he says.

"Why did you not—"

He puts up a finger in warning. "Don't."

She pauses, hand outstretched, bits of liquefied flesh still dripping into the puddle of meat at her feet. She shrinks, skin and pouring back up her frame, torn cloth mending until she's standing there as before.

"Good choice. The knife, please," I say, holding out my hand. "And don't try to stab me with it. You don't want me to drop this." Reluctantly, she hands the blade over.

"And Tabitha?" The metal straps holding Tabitha's arms and legs pop off. Her eyes snap open and she sits up.

"Eric? What's going on?" She looks down at her open robe, clutches it closed. Her hands are shaking. I wonder if she knew what was going to happen.

"We're just having a friendly chat."

"Why do you have the lighter out?" She slides to the floor on my side of the altar. Two humans separated from the gods by a single slab of bloody stone.

"To keep the chat friendly." I can see her out of the corner of my eye, staring at me.

"The jade —"

"He's not going to last much longer," Santa Muerte says. "He has to kill Mictlantecuhtli or be consumed. Tell him, Avatar. Tell him the truth."

"I —" Tabitha says. "I don't know what the truth is." She turns a glare onto Santa Muerte. "You've kept it from me. Gaps in the memories you've given me. Why? Why were you keeping things from me?"

Something clicks. "Because you're a part of this, too," I say. "They're playing us both."

"Oh, come on," Mictlantecuhtli says. "What the hell am I going to get out of this?" He pulls at the skin on his face, the flesh covering his features like a badly fitted sheet. "Why would I even want this?" He steps slowly around the altar, hands up.

"Slow your roll there, chief." I bring up the knife, get ready to drop the lighter and set everything ablaze. He slows, but doesn't stop.

"You don't have any time, Eric," Mictlantecuhtli says.

"I don't have time. The last bits of you are already starting to change. I know you can feel it. Save yourself. Save me. Kill Mictecacihuatl and this all goes away. You know you have to."

"I don't care what happens to you, vermin," Santa Muerte says. "But if you don't murder him right now I will make your eternity in stone a nightmare you can't possibly imagine."

"She killed your sister," Mictlantecuhtli says, continuing to get close. "Everything that's happened is because of what she's done. I've seen your pain. I've seen what you've been through. Lucy and Alex dead. Vivian hates you. She used Tabitha to move it all along. I know how much you want revenge. Killing her will fix all of this."

His eyes never waver from mine. He steps in close, the blade inches from his chest. He's either really confident or really stupid. Possibly both.

"I like his pitch better," I say to Santa Muerte. "But he's closer." I lunge, the knife snaking out to his chest. The blade will cut anything, will kill anything. It should slice through him like a perfectly cooked steak. If I can take him out, hopefully I'll have enough time to do the same to Santa Muerte before I turn into an ornament for a Zen garden.

That's when Darius's spell holding my memories at bay unravels and I remember it all.

———

"The thing you gotta know," Darius said, "is that Mictlantecuhtli and Mictecacihuatl can't leave Mictlan. They're stuck there."

"Then how did they even talk to me?"

"Son, you think I'm actually sitting here having this

conversation with you? I'm stuck in a goddamn bottle buried someplace in L.A."

"Point taken," I said.

"It's actually pretty goddamn impressive that Mictecacihuatl has been able to rebrand herself as Santa Muerte. Had to start small once everything went to shit, but she's done good for herself. She's been invading dreams, moving shit around, getting people all worked up over her for the last few hundred years. And now look at her. She's a savior, she's a devil. Nobody can shut up about her."

"Okay, so she can't get out," I said. "She gets herself an avatar. Now she can move around."

"Not quite. She can influence her avatar. She's connected to her the way a transmitter's connected to a receiver. But she can't completely rule her. She's still her own person. What she needs is to swap places with her avatar."

"Swap places," I said. "You mean the way Mictlantecuhtli and I are swapping places."

"Exactly. It looks more obvious on you because what I did to him with the jade is transferring over to you, too."

"Tabitha's becoming Santa Muerte the way I'm becoming Mictlantecuhtli?"

"Right now, it's swapping. You're turning into a rock, Mictlantecuhtli's turning to flesh. But the point isn't to be a swap. It's to be a replacing. But that part doesn't happen until there's also a sacrifice."

"The obsidian blade," I said. "It's a sacrificial knife. But . . . wait a minute. They're not trying to get Tabitha and I killed. They've been trying to get me to kill the other and . . . Oh, goddammit."

"I know that look," Darius said.

"*They* are the ones who need to be sacrificed," I said.

"You and that girl are vessels. They've been grooming you. Seeding you. When you kill them, they will become you. They'll kick out your souls, or eat them, or whatever, but you'll just be shells with new occupants. They'll leave Mictlan, travel to the living world. Once they do that, they can do whatever the hell they want. Probably try to pick up where they left off five hundred years ago. I can tell you there'll be a lot of blood, a lot of torn out hearts.

"Your sister? She's dead because they knew it would piss you off and make you come running. All that distrust they've been sowing in you? That's to get you so mad you want to kill them both. They been feeding you this bullshit and you've been eatin' it up."

"And Tabitha? Did Santa Muerte just promise her life?"

"I doubt it. That girl's got her head out of her ass more than you ever did. Probably promised she'd be more, do more. Make a difference. Probably showed her what was wrong with Mictlan, told her she could help change it. I figure she went along with it even though it got her hands dirty. Necromancers don't seem to have problems getting their hands dirty.

"You lot, necromancers, y'all go in one of three different directions. Seeing all that death changes a person. There are the batshit crazy ones, the cynics, and the idealists. I'm not sure if you're the first or the second, but she's definitely the third."

"And why the fuck didn't you tell me?" I said. "You could have said something when I came to you to ask about Santa Muerte the first time, over a fucking year ago. I came to you when I thought I had to take her deal to get Alex back from Boudreau. Why didn't you tell me then?"

He put up his hands, trying to calm me. "I couldn't. I wanted to. I wanted to tell you all about it. I—"

"Bullshit," I said. "You didn't tell me because you wanted me to do your fucking dirty work. You didn't tell me because you knew at some point I'd be here looking to take them out. You couldn't do it. But you figured I could. Jesus, you're just as bad as they are."

"Some folks would say I'm worse." His eyes took on a dusky, red hue and any thought that he and I were ever friends was gone. He's not human and it showed. "Point is, it doesn't change what's going on one goddamn bit, does it?"

"I can't kill them, can I?" I refused to agree with him. It was true, but I wasn't about to give him the satisfaction. "So what do I do?"

"Oh, you can kill 'em. Just not the way you're thinkin'. But sadly, this is where the narrative stops," he said. "I can't tell you what to do. I can nod my head or grunt a negative, but I can't come out and say it. And no, this isn't me trying to play you or anything. This is Mictlantecuhtli's magic. It's weaker than it was five hundred years ago, or I wouldn't have been able to tell you this much, but a straight answer? Can't do it, Chief."

"Since when have you ever given me a straight answer to begin with?"

"Fair point," he said. "So let me give you one now. You're gonna have to guess. I can't help that. Sorry. And then I'm gonna have to make you forget it. Because here and now I've got things blocked off for you. But if I don't twist your memories a bit, the second you wake up they'll know what I told you. They'll know what you've guessed. They're gonna suspect no matter what. But if they don't know for sure they'll keep playing the game, waiting to see if you really figured it out or not."

"I don't see how. I've got them blocked off."

"Yeah, no you don't. Those spells you got inked to hide you from them? That handcuff you got on your lady friend? They don't work. Everything that chunk of Mictlantecuhtli in your head knows, he knows. They can see you, find you, talk to you. You can't hide from them."

"Oh, you are fucking kidding me. Those tats cost a fucking fortune." This entire time I thought I was safe, but they were just letting me think that. A slow pounding started going through my skull at that point. How the hell do you get a migraine inside a dream? "Fine. Let's get this over with. Is it bigger than a breadbox?"

"No," he said.

It took me a little less than twenty questions to get my answers and I didn't like them one bit.

———

I pull back, yanking my hand away from Mictlantecuhtli's chest and almost tripping over my own feet. I only barely manage to hang onto the knife. Mictlantecuhtli grins at me.

"So you did figure it out," he says.

Would I have, if Darius hadn't clued me in? Maybe but probably not. I started to. Little things that didn't add up, but I couldn't get them to connect. Like why the king of Mictlan ran from his own people. Why they both wanted me so desperately to kill the other. Why they kept goading me on until I knew I was going to kill them both.

And why they were going to let me do it. I knew I was being played, but I had no idea how.

Mictlantecuhtli's hands shoot out and grab mine. I can't move them. I can't even drop Quetzalcoatl's lighter. He closes the lid with his thumb. "Let's not do anything rash, shall we?" he says. He pulls the blade back to his chest, leans in until the point presses in. "I fall forward or you shove that knife in, either way, it counts."

"Eric, what the hell is he talking about?" Tabitha says.

"Quiet," Santa Muerte says. "It'll be your turn next."

"My turn for what?"

My mind is racing. I try to pull back but his grip is like iron. He squeezes so hard cracks are forming in the jade. I try calling on his power inside me, not caring that it will tip me over the edge. I just need a second.

But it doesn't want to listen to me, anymore. I can't think of any spell of my own that would do a thing to him. My own magic is useless.

I hear Tabitha and Santa Muerte arguing behind me but I'm not quite sure about what. There's a rushing in my ears and my vision is starting to go dark around the edges.

Jade is slowly crawling up the last two fingers that are still flesh. I feel a tightening in my chest. So this is how it ends. My soul torn apart by an Aztec death god, or an eternity encased in jade. Goddammit.

All I need is one fucking second.

My raven tattoo gives it to me.

The birds tear free from their place on my chest, ripping through cloth, taking pieces of jade along with them. They've been feeling different for weeks and now that they've gotten loose I can see that they are different, and not just because they took the initiative and went out on their own.

It's their coloring, their texture. When they've been released before they were inky black, but now they've taken on the qualities of the jade. Green, stone feathers, jeweled eyes.

But it's also how they feel. Angrier. Bigger. Meaner. Much more dangerous. And they popped out all on their own.

Mictlantecuhtli figures this out the hard way. He shrieks as they tear into him, pecking out pieces of him with their beaks, gouging out chunks with their talons. They multiply in the air around him. Suddenly there are a dozen, two dozen. He swats at them, the ones he hits bursting into flame only to be replaced with five more.

He loosens his grip and I pull my hands free, falling onto my back. I don't have much time. Seconds, maybe. I hesitate for a fraction of it, hoping what I learned from Darius is right.

Killing Mictlantecuhtli with the knife isn't an option. That will just be a sacrifice as far as the magic is concerned, completing the ritual and kicking me out of my own body as his dies and he moves in. Same with Santa Muerte. That will just do the same to Tabitha.

I can't sacrifice him. I can't sacrifice her. That only leaves me with one other option.

I shove the obsidian blade deep into my own chest. It parts the jade flesh, punches through the stony bone of my sternum and tears into my heart. I twist to make sure I've really got it.

The pain is indescribable. Bone is cracked, my heart is a shredded mess. Green blood floods through the gash, pouring onto the floor. I twist some more, my vision going black, and yank, tearing out a green, fleshy chunk of my own heart hanging onto the end of the blade.

Distantly I can hear Mictlantecuhtli's screams. Tabitha's

and Santa Muerte's, too. Pain, panic and rage respectively. It lasts forever. It lasts no time at all.

A burst of green light tears out of the hole, enveloping Mictlantecuhtli. I can feel the jade, his magic, every piece of his personality wrapped up in my soul leaving my body. And in return I feel myself coming back from him.

I had lost more than I knew. Sensations I hadn't realized I was missing, senses dulled that I hadn't noticed. Everything is a burst of light and color and sound.

Sound comes back first. Tabitha's panicked yelling, her screaming into my face, asking me what the hell I'm doing. Santa Muerte's furious shrieks and accusations. How I've destroyed everything, how I'll pay for it.

I had thought, hoped at least, that I could do this and just turn around and take care of Tabitha, too. But she doesn't know what I know. All she sees is this idiot on the ground who's just stabbed himself in the chest and pulled out a chunk of green meat. If I turn around and stab her, I don't think she's going to be very receptive to it.

But it's a moot point, because I can barely move anyway.

"What the hell did you do?" she says, trying to pick me up, see if I'm still breathing. I'm not sure if I am. I must be, right? Because I'm still alive? I think I'm still alive.

I manage to twitch my head up as my vision comes back, seeing Tabitha's face swimming in front of me, blurred and indistinct.

I look for Mictlantecuhtli, finding him next to me. Turned back to jade, but with one crucial difference. He's nothing but a pile of green rocks and dust.

Santa Muerte looms over us. Seven feet tall, a demonic skeleton with razor claws at the ends of her fingers, her skin in a puddle around her ankles.

"I will murder you," she shrieks and her hands shoot out toward us.

I'm actually okay with that. I've had a good run. And honestly I really wasn't expecting to survive this. I'm only sorry I wasn't able to do the same for Tabitha. Would have been nice if I could have gotten her out of this, too. But the dying bit? I'm okay with that.

So I'm really surprised when a scream bursts from Santa Muerte's mouth. I turn my head to see that Tabitha has grabbed the knife and punched its obsidian blade through the goddess' sternum.

No. Oh, no. Tabitha doesn't know what she's done. Maybe it won't happen. Maybe their plan won't work. But I know that it will. They were putting it together for five hundred years before I came along and fucked it all up.

A red light bursts out of the wound in Santa Muerte's chest and envelopes Tabitha before she can move out of the way. I watch her burning in the light. Skin and hair going up in flames. With each passing second Santa Muerte is getting smaller while Tabitha burns ever brighter.

I will my legs to move, my arms to push myself up. I stagger over to them, expecting to burn, but to me there's no heat. It's a fire that only Tabitha can feel.

She turns her head toward me, panic and confusion in her eyes, her arms and hands shaking, unable to tear herself free.

I reach between them, pull the obsidian blade from Santa Muerte's chest, and in the same motion plunge it deep into Tabitha's. The flames sputter for a moment, and I twist, tearing into her heart, making sure I destroy as much of it as I can. This might not work. This might not save her. It might be too late. But maybe I can keep her from becoming Santa Muerte's new home.

The light twists between them, Santa Muerte catching the flame. Only Tabitha hasn't stopped burning. They are both being consumed by the light pouring from each other. The snake eating its own tail.

The light grows brighter and I have a sinking feeling I know what happens next. I don't bother to move. Where the hell would I go? Instead I close my eyes and wait for it.

The world explodes.

Chapter 27

I'd just drive the Caddy out to Venice Beach, but after months of dirt and dust and general abuse, it's not doing so hot. Just as well. I need people. Live people. Normal people. People who aren't trying to twist the universe into knots. So I hop onto a bus of the L.A. Metro that I keep wanting to call the RTD. Funny how some habits never quite shake loose.

The bus stinks of sweat and food and cheap booze nipped from years of flasks and paper-bagged forties. I sit in the back across from a guy in ratty jeans and sores around his lips. He keeps looking at me. Pensive. Finally says fuck it and pulls out his works to shoot up.

Doesn't get much more normal than that.

A few not so upstanding gentlemen seem to think this makes him an easy target. I disabuse them of that notion with a little magic and a lot of terror. They get off at the next stop, shaking. One of them has pissed his pants.

An hour later, I leave my sleeping bus companion and step off the bus on Washington Boulevard in Venice Beach. It's bright, the sun shining through a crystal blue sky. The Santa Ana winds have blown all the crap in the air out over the ocean and a ring of shining, white clouds surrounds Los Angeles.

I don't know what happened after the explosion. Everything's a blank. I woke up alone in the middle of the desert, my clothes torn and stained with blood. The jade was gone, though it wasn't until I found a town on the edge of the Arizona/Mexico border where I could find a mirror that I discovered my eyes were back to normal.

But I still had the wedding ring. It used to change from jade to gold with tiny Calaveras carved into it, but now it's just the gold. It comes off my finger, which it didn't before, but I don't understand why I still have it at all. I'm not sure what it means.

I take a short walk from the bus stop and turn in toward the canals. The canals are a holdover from when some guy named Abbott Kinney tried to turn the beach into a tourist trap and make it look like Venice, Italy. Hence the name. It didn't work out so well, but the canals and the tourists are still there.

The canals are quiet, the sounds of traffic on nearby Venice Boulevard muted. It's around noon on a December Tuesday and most people are at work. The Venice canals are a strange neighborhood. Houses on narrow plots with little boats tied up in the canals right outside. It's hidden away, and hard to find if you don't already know it's there.

It's an upscale neighborhood, and a disturbing number of the residents have gone all Martha Stewart on their Christmas decorations. The decorations feel out of place. The demographic's a little too old, a little too gentrified, but it's candy cane fucking central all along the canals.

I pass a handful of ghosts on my way over. After

seeing what some people's idea of the afterlife looks like, seeing the usual Wanderers and Haunts is a comfort. I understand them. They make sense to me.

But Mictlan? That there's some twisted shit. Tabitha said that the people shaped the place. I wonder if the other afterlives are as fucked up. The fact that human beings can even come up with a concept like Hell speaks volumes about us.

It took me over a month to get out of Mexico. Five days finding a town, three weeks recuperating in a shitty little hotel where all I did was sleep, eat tacos and drink tequila. I needed to recuperate, sort through everything that happened, figure out what to do next.

The obsidian blade and Quetzalcoatl's lighter are gone. Destroyed? I don't know. I don't even know if Mictlan is still in one piece, or if either Tabitha or Santa Muerte survived. I saw Mictlantecuhtli's shattered remains, but that doesn't mean he's gone. If I've learned anything it's that I know fuck-all about gods.

Once I'd gotten enough sleep and drank enough tequila I caught a train down to Mexico City and found the Cadillac parked in Xochimilco. It hadn't been touched. The wards carved and painted into its frame saw to that. Anybody who tried to break in, damage it, or even leave a ticket, would have had themselves a very bad day. Waking nightmares, shitting themselves, temporary paralysis. Nothing life threatening, just really, really unpleasant.

I took a drive along the river's edge to see Isla de las Muñecas. The entire place was burned to the ground. The fires had spread about a quarter mile in either direction, blackening the shore and turning the trees to ash. Nothing stood. More importantly, the souls of all those dead children had moved on to wherever it was they needed to move onto.

I hope it's better than being trapped inside a doll.

Lucy's house in Venice is a boxy, two-story affair of stucco and glass with large windows looking out onto the canal and a balcony high enough to see a sliver of the nearby Pacific Ocean. It must have cost a fortune when she bought it, and is certainly worth a much bigger fortune now. Lucy didn't lack for money. When both your parents are mages, money isn't a problem. She was left a hell of a trust fund when our parents died.

When I was here last a window facing the alley had been boarded up. Her murderer had jumped through it and proceeded to turn her into hamburger. It's repaired now, and through it I can see that the rest of the room has been painted over, carpet torn up and replaced. Walls cleaned of any trace of a murder.

Too bad cleaning crews can't clean a place of ghosts.

After I got the Caddy back I drove into Tepito. To look at Santa Muerte's shrines you'd think nothing had changed. And really, has anything changed? Whether Santa Muerte is alive or dead is irrelevant to her followers. It's not like they ever talked to her outside of dreams, anyway.

The storefront that Tabitha worked out of had already been repurposed into a place selling cheap clothes, crappy luggage and bootleg electronics. There was no sign of Tabitha, not even a feeling of her. As far as this place was concerned she might as well have never existed.

The drive up from Mexico City was easier than the drive down. I knew where I was going this time, not bouncing around from town to town looking for traces of Tabitha, beating up Narcotraficantes, looking for a door into Mictlan. Even crossing the border into San Diego was easy. It helped that I used Sharpie magic to make the border guys think I was an FBI agent.

Sometimes magic is pretty cool.

I can feel Lucy's Echo still lingering in the house waiting to come out and replay her death. I know it's not really her. There's no consciousness there. This is just the imprint left behind from her passing. Nothing but a constant howling pain. Her ghost is defined by nothing more than her final moments alive.

Over time she'll fade, grow gray and staticky like an overused videotape. But that will take too long. For a long time I couldn't come back here. But I have something I have to do, and I've finally pushed aside the cowardice that kept me from doing it.

"Glad you made it," Vivian says, opening the door for me, a thick manila folder in her hand. Her red hair is cut into a bob and she's wearing a gray sweater dress with long, black boots. "I was half expecting you'd chickenshit out and not show up."

"Almost did," I say, stepping into the foyer. Lucy's ghost is just outside my consciousness. A building pressure behind my eyes.

"That's uncharacteristically honest of you," she says. She closes the door and leads me into the kitchen. The house has been furnished. To sell it, she told me over the phone. If I'd been much longer chances are I'd have had to break my way in.

The image of her in Canter's Deli the night my parents died flashes in front of my eyes.

"I'm a changed man."

"I can tell. You're not looking so green. So it went well?"

"I wouldn't go that far, but I'm . . . cured I guess is the word."

"And Tabitha?"

"I don't know." I've been thinking about telling her what happened—she was Tabitha's friend, after all. At least until she learned she was involved with Santa Muerte. But I decided that would be a bad idea. After today I don't expect we'll see each other again.

That's how it should be.

"You still have the ring," she says. "Does that mean this isn't over?"

"I don't know that, either."

She looks out the window into the alley, avoiding my eyes. "Where's the Cadillac?" Lots of questions. I can't tell if it's small talk or delaying tactic, and I don't suppose it matters.

"Broke down pretty much the minute I got back into town. I've got it in the shop. Going to cost a fortune to get some of the wards redone. I took a bus."

"A bus? You know they have this thing called Uber, right? Or taxicabs?"

The last time I was in a cab I found out the driver was a serial killer whose last victim's ghost was haunting the back seat. I killed the driver in the Santa Monica mountains and hid his car in a ditch.

"I don't really like cabs. Is that it?" She's holding the manila folder with a grip tight enough to leave dents.

"Yeah." She looks at it, then up at me. "Are you sure you want to do this?"

"Yes. Are you sure you want me to? It is mine to deal with."

She hesitates. Finally hands me the folder. I get the reluctance. It's Vivian's final tie to my sister. Once she passes this on there's nothing left but her memories and grief.

The folder is surprisingly heavy, and when I open it I can see why. Aside from being stuffed full of paperwork there are several sheets of paper with keys taped to them and addresses neatly typed next to each. House keys, safe deposit keys, padlock keys. A couple of them don't just have addresses, but sigils next to them.

"Some of these are warded?" I ask.

"Couple storage units. A safe deposit box," she says. "Lucy could never get in. They responded to her but she didn't have the power to unlock them. Alex and I both tried, but they wouldn't budge. Maybe you can."

It sounds like something our parents would do. Lock some secrets up that only family can crack. Probably did it before Lucy was born, or they would have made it so she could get in, too. Must have driven her crazy.

I'm not surprised my parents never told me about these. A secretive bunch, us Carters.

"How many properties are in here?" There's a lot of paperwork. I actually own a house in upstate New York under a fake name. Haven't seen it in about six years, but I don't remember there being this much paperwork. I see my signature forged across everything in Vivian's neat, tight script. Not sure how I feel about having my real name on official documents.

"Lucy's house. Your parents' property in the hills. A couple others scattered around L.A. I haven't seen all of them, but Lucy had someone check a couple years ago. They were all empty."

It's a lot to take in and I'm not going to get through it all standing here. I close the folder.

"Do I need to sign anything?"

"It's handled. Keys, paperwork. Property taxes are paid up through next year out of your trust fund."

"My what?"

"Your trust fund. The money your parents left you? It was merged with Lucy's. Paid the taxes out of it. You did know you inherited money from them, right?"

"I do now." I had no idea. She doesn't look surprised.

"Well, details are all in there. I know money isn't something we worry about, but it's there if you get sick of magicking ATM machines."

"Thanks for this. And for everything you did for Lucy. I'm sorry things went the way they did."

I know that's not enough, but it's all I've got.

"I'm thinking of leaving L.A.," she says, not looking at me.

I thought as much. With Alex gone and this last piece of business to complete, there's not much reason for her to stay. "Good. This is a shitty town. I hope things go better for you wherever you end up." I don't ask her where she's planning to go. I shouldn't know.

"Thanks," she says, surprise clear on her face. "I'm not sure when. Might be a while. I'm still trying to figure some things out. But I thought you should know." Translation: "I figured I shouldn't be as big a prick as you were and just up and disappear." Fair enough.

"That's it, I guess," she says. "You have the paperwork, you have the keys. Oh, there's a lawyer's card in there, too. You're going to want to talk to him if you have any questions."

"Cool. Lawyer. Got it."

She steps forward uncertainly, arms out, steps back. I

do the same. It's the Hug Don't Hug dance. We settle on shaking hands and I walk her to the door. I stand there until she gets into her car and pulls into the alley.

It's a weird feeling watching her drive away. The last time it was me who was leaving. I left in the middle of the night without saying goodbye. She's classy enough to tell me, though god knows I don't deserve it.

I really am sorry things went the way they did between us. But it was over a long time ago. It's just taken me this long to let it go. I take a deep breath and close the door. It's time I let go of something else, too.

I head into the living room, sit cross-legged on the floor, open my messenger bag. I start to pull out the things I'll need, salt, a bundle of sage, a jar of red pepper flakes, sulfur. I stop when I find the Lotería cards.

I've been through this bag a hundred times since I left Mictlan. I know for a fact that these cards weren't in there. LA MUERTE, LA CORONA, EL VALIENTE, EL ALACRÁN, and finally EL CORAZÓN. The five cards Tabitha drew for me from her deck in Tepito.

I can think of a connection to each one of those cards. Some more literally than others. I look at EL CORAZÓN, the Heart. "No me extrañes corazón, que regreso en el camión," is printed beneath the image of a heart surrounded by the same wedding band I'm wearing, calaveras carved along the side and everything. It's not an image I've seen before, and it's very clearly specific to me. But I don't know what it means.

"Do not miss me, sweetheart, I'll be back by bus," I say, translating the phrase. "Well, goddamn." She even predicted the Caddy breaking down.

I stack the cards neatly into a pile and slide them into

my coat pocket. I'll puzzle these out later. I have more important things to do right now.

I pour the salt and red pepper flakes into a wide circle, light the sage and put it out to let the pungent smoke fill the room. I can feel Lucy's Echo become sharper in the background. I have its attention, or as near to that as you can get with a mindless projection of someone's final moments.

I sit in the middle of the circle, and pull out my straight razor and a small, silver dish. I cut myself on my left forearm, blood dripping into the dish. I focus my magic on the blood like I've done a thousand times before. Shape the magic with my will, tie it into knots, let it flow out of me like water.

And say goodbye to my sister.

Joe Sunday's dead...

...he just hasn't stopped moving yet.

Sunday's a thug, an enforcer, a leg-breaker for hire.
When his boss sends him to kill a mysterious new business partner, his target strikes back in ways Sunday
could never have imagined. Murdered, brought back to
a twisted half-life, Sunday finds himself stuck in the
middle of a race to find an ancient stone with the power
to grant immortality. With it, he might live forever.
Without it, he's just another rotting extra in a George
Romero flick.

Everyone's got a stake: a psycho Nazi wizard, a
nympho-demon bartender, a too-powerful witch who
just wants to help her homeless vampires, and the one
woman who might have all the answers — if only
Sunday can figure out what her angle is.

Before the week is out he's going to find out just what
lengths people will go to for immortality. And just how
long somebody can hold a grudge.

City of the Lost
by Stephen Blackmoore
978-0-7564-702-5
